THE GIRL WHO TALKS TO GHOSTS
Book 2 of the GhostWriters series
Published by DEATHZONE BOOKS

DeathZone Books, Ltd.
www.deathzonebooks.com

The Girl Who Talks To Ghosts
Copyright © 2017 by J.H. Moncrieff
Print ISBN: 978-0-9877129-5-0
Digital ISBN: 978-0-9877129-6-7

Editing by Chris Brogden, EnglishGeek Editing
Cover design by Kelly Martin

Interior Format

The Girl Who Talks to Ghosts

J.H. Moncrieff

DZB

ALSO BY J.H. MONCRIEFF

GhostWriters Series
CITY OF GHOSTS

—

THE BEAR WHO WOULDN'T LEAVE

MONSTERS IN OUR WAKE

LOST

DEDICATION

For Russell R. James, who insisted
Kate needed her own book.

~ CHAPTER ONE ~

THE WOMAN WAS HYSTERICAL, SOBBING so much I couldn't understand her. As I pressed my cell harder against my ear, the wind sprouted claws and slashed at my meager sweater until I shivered. Phone calls used to be rare, but I'd been getting more and more since Jackson and I had gone public with what had happened to us in China. Now everyone in Vermont seemed to know my name, and they all needed help.

"Hello? This is Kate, please talk to me."

The crying increased in volume, blistering my ears. I would have hung up if not for the wind. Its power intensified, churning the dead leaves and other debris from the sidewalk around my feet. There was something strange about its sudden force, which drove me against the brick facing of Hildy's Fine China & Sundries. (Hildy'd had an ampersand before it was trendy.)

"Hello?" The single word contained the edge of my fear. Both my voice and hands were shaking. Something did not want me to talk to this woman. Something did not want me to help her. I'd taken hundreds of similar calls over the past few years, but had never felt anything like this. "Please say something. I'm afraid we're going to lose our connection."

Clutching at my sweater to keep it from being blown away, I ducked my head, shielding my face as my hair whipped around in a furious tangle. I huddled against Hildy's shop, wondering if I should go in, but the older woman wouldn't be impressed to see me on my phone. Her establishment was a temple, a library. The loyal customers who kept her in business spoke in whispers and walked on tiptoes. By bursting in like this and continuing my shouted, one-sided conversation, I'd have become the proverbial bull. Not good.

"Miss Carlsson? Kate Carlsson?" The woman had regained her composure enough to gasp my name. The grip around my heart tightened, even though I'd known all along the call was meant for me.

"Yes, speaking. What's wrong?" There was no point wasting time with idle chitchat. Obviously something was wrong—very wrong. Another gust of wind knocked my skull against the side of the building and pain jolted through my brain.

The caller was silent for so long I ordinarily would have assumed she'd hung up, lost her nerve. It happened. It wasn't easy for people to admit they needed my help. It was a leap of faith, a willingness to open their minds to the possibility that something they'd spent their entire lives denying could be real after all.

But the wind told me otherwise. I waited for her to speak again, raising one arm between my face and the building to protect my head. The chill had seeped into my bones, and what I wanted more than anything was to run home and immerse myself in a steaming hot bath while I drank a cup of the pumpkin spice tea I'd just purchased. I didn't want to talk to this woman. I didn't want to hear about what terrible things were happening at her home, for surely terrible things *were* happening. But I'd learned long ago that my gift was bigger than me, and if this woman needed it, I wasn't going to turn away from her.

Finally she spoke. I could barely hear her over the gale, which shrieked like a tortured soul. "My mother is attacking my child." Her voice trembled with fresh tears. "I can't believe it, haven't wanted to believe it, but it's true. I've seen it."

"Is your mother dead, Mrs…"

"Walkins. My name is Walkins. Yes, she died last year. But she was such a good woman. She loved Lily. I can't believe she would do these things. *Why* would she do these things?"

I could feel curious eyes burning into me, watching me struggle to stay on my feet. Pushing my hair away from my face, I risked a glimpse and was immediately sorry I had. The leaves around my feet had arranged themselves in the form of a girl, a girl not much shorter than me. As I stared, my pulse throbbing behind my temples, the terrifying apparition raised a rustling arm toward me before collapsing onto the sidewalk.

"Whatever is hurting Lily isn't your mother, Mrs. Walkins. What's your address? I'll be right there."

☾

Mrs. Walkins resembled my other clients in every way but one. She had the gaunt, drawn face of someone whose last decent meal had been consumed days before. Dark circles rimmed eyes that were bloodshot and caked with dried tears. Her entire body shook as if she were unbearably cold.

These things were to be expected.

The angry scratches running up and down her arms were not.

"Did your mother do that to you?" I turned one of her arms toward the light to get a better look. Her skin felt as fragile as dead leaves under my fingers. One of the scratches was new, the unshed blood glittering in the afternoon sun that poured through her living room window.

"No, it's Lily." Her sallow cheeks colored. "I can't understand it, Miss Carlsson. She's always been such a good child. She's never done anything like this before, but in the past few weeks, she's become quite violent."

"Call me Kate, please. Is Lily home?" I knew she was. As soon as I'd stepped into Mrs. Walkins's tidy bungalow, I'd felt the dark malevolence radiating from the end of the hallway.

"And I'm Vittoria. Yes, she is. She seemed fine this morning, but when I called you, she went…well, she went crazy. She's hurt me before, but not like this." The woman bent her head, her bony shoulders shaking as she cried. I was no psychic, but it was easy enough to read her tortured thoughts, her fears that this was her fault—that despite her best efforts, she'd been a horrible mother and somehow managed to raise a monster.

A monster that had sprouted fangs overnight.

I put my arms around her, shocked at the number of spirits who were desperate to speak to this woman. It was a regular mob, screaming and crying in outrage. Everyone had an opinion. Everyone wanted to speak their piece. At the edge of the gathering, cloaked in shadow, was a sad-faced woman with gray hair. I was willing to bet she was the grandmother in question.

It took a considerable amount of strength to force them aside. Once this situation was resolved, Vittoria Walkins was going to get a lesson in letting people go. With that many souls hanging around, I was surprised she hadn't had trouble long before now.

The spirits clinging to her weren't the problem, though. It was the one shadowing her daughter.

I walked Vittoria to her kitchen, its cleanliness showing me she was like my own mother. Both women cleaned in times of stress, subconsciously believing that if their homes were in perfect order, their lives would be too.

If only it were that easy.

"Can you make us both a cup of tea? And set out some cookies, if you have any. Cookies would be nice." The cookies were more for her, but I had a feeling my strength was going to be depleted by the end of my meeting with Lily. Mostly I needed to give this woman something to do that would keep her busy and out of my way. Northern hospitality wouldn't allow her to refuse me, and I was counting on that. "I'm going to talk to Lily for a bit."

Although it wouldn't be Lily I spoke to, and we both knew it.

Vittoria hesitated, glancing toward the hall. It was clear from her body language that her daughter's room had become a dreaded place. Hell had invaded her home, and she had no idea what to do with it. "I should introduce you. I never told Lily you were coming over. She's shy— she always did have a problem with strangers."

It almost made me laugh. Lily was definitely having a problem with strangers now. But sadly, nothing was funny about this situation.

"It's okay. She already knows I'm here. It would really be best if you weren't there when I met her. Can you make the tea for us? Please? I shouldn't be too long." *I hope.* "I just need to determine what the problem is."

Vittoria's shoulders sagged with relief, but her expression was still doubtful. "If you're sure…"

"I'm sure. I need you to stay here, no matter what. Even if you hear someone cry out. I promise Lily will be fine. I'm not going to hurt her. If you hear her crying for you, it's a trick."

At my words, tears streamed down her face. "I hear her crying all the time, like she's in pain. It's terrible."

Seeing the poor woman's torment reminded me why I could never turn my back on The Gift—a "gift" which was often an awful, dark thing I would never have asked for and didn't want. But without it, Vittoria Walkins would be lost and so would her daughter.

"I know. It'll be over soon." I tried my best to sound more confident than I felt. Faking confidence came with the territory. "What about Lily's father? Is he in the picture?" The last thing I needed was some man charging into the room at a sensitive moment.

"He's at work. He won't be home until five."

I could see us both doing mental calculations. It was a few minutes past two. I hoped it would be enough time.

"He didn't want me to call you. He doesn't believe in any of this stuff. He blames everything on the 'terrible teens.' Lily's barely twelve, but he says everything happens earlier these days." Her words caught on a sob. "I didn't want to believe it either, but what else was I supposed to do? These horrible things keep happening, and Lily goes on and on about my mother. This *isn't* puberty, I don't care what he says."

But she did care, clearly. Otherwise he'd know I was here. All the more reason to make sure I was finished before five. This work was exhausting enough. I wouldn't have the energy to convince a bullheaded man that Lily's problems had nothing to do with her impending adolescence.

"You're right. It's not normal, but it's not that unusual, either. You're not alone, Vittoria. Plenty of people in Nightridge have called me."

I'd often considered forming a support group for my clients, so they could safely discuss their experiences, assured that not a single person in the room would accuse them of being insane or in it for the publicity. It was a good idea; I just hadn't found the time yet. My clients tended to be protective of their privacy, for obvious reasons. It would take some convincing.

Tomorrow. There was always tomorrow.

The darkness seeping from Lily's room like an oil spill both beckoned and repulsed me. I'd wasted too much time already.

"I'll be back in a bit. It would be lovely to have a cup of tea afterward. And cookies—don't forget the cookies."

I left before Vittoria could say anything else.

The walls leading to Lily's room were pristine, painted white (although I'm sure it wasn't called *white* but some bullshit name like Moonbeam or Manifest Destiny) until I got close to her door. Here the drywall was cracked, the ugly crevices radiating out from the frame. There were dents and pockmarks in the heavy wooden door, marred by splinters.

Before I could raise my hand to knock, the door staggered open, hanging off its hinges like a dangling tongue.

A young woman was in the room, sitting cross-legged on a bed. Thick, dark hair hung to her waist. I could see she had been lovely once, before whatever had a grip on her had sunk its teeth in. When she saw me, her lips curled into a sneer. There was a flicker of something red in her dark eyes, there and gone so quickly many would have missed it, but I didn't. Thankfully her parents hadn't seen it, or they'd be in the cardiac wing of Nightridge Memorial.

"What the fuck do you want? Get the fuck out of here."

I'm guessing Vittoria's elderly mother had never used such language.

"Nice to meet you too. I'd like to talk to Lily Walkins, please." *Crap—was her last name Walkins?* I'd forgotten to ask. This case must really have been throwing me to make such a rookie mistake. At thirty-five, I was far from a rookie.

"I *am* Lily," the thing on the bed growled.

"Nice try, asshole. I know you're not Lily." I could see it wasn't the maligned grandmother, either. Whatever was tormenting Lily was much bigger and more powerful than the sad-faced woman I'd glimpsed earlier.

The girl's cheeks reddened until they were nearly purple, and I feared for her health. At least she was young, so she had a better shot of surviving this relatively unscathed. But I couldn't worry about her right now. I had to deal with the asshole first.

It released a string of invective at me, spittle flying everywhere, making me glad I'd kept my distance. I only caught a word now and then, but it was enough.

"Well done, Lily. When did you learn to speak fluent Italian? Your parents will be so pleased."

Another snarl from the bed. More nasty Italian hurled my way. Apparently this spirit wasn't aware of the whole sticks-and-stones thing. Now that I was here, facing the jerk, my fear and dread were gone. A calmness had settled over me. The spirit wasn't *that* strong—if it were, it would have tried to attack me physically, and it hadn't even used Lily to do that yet. Which was a relief, because manhandling children hadn't gotten easier over the years.

Best of all, Lily was still there. I could feel her own spirit reaching out, melding her energy with mine. Together we would break this monster's hold and send it back under whatever rock it had crawled out from.

"We can't have a proper conversation if I don't know your name. I'm Kate Carlsson—who are you? And don't give me that 'I'm Lily' crap, because I can see your dick from here. Not that it's anything to see."

Thankfully, I couldn't, but I wanted to let him know the jig was up. This spirit was definitely male, and dude did *not* look like a lady, even with his Lily mask on.

I'd guessed pride was his sin of choice, and I was right. He curled Lily's nose in disdain and spoke to me in perfect, Italian-accented English. "Why should I demean myself by speaking to you? You have no idea whom you are addressing, peasant."

Peasant? Showed you what he knew. This sweater was 100 percent cashmere. "So enlighten me. Because as of right now, I don't see a special snowflake. I see an average, run-of-the-mill, obnoxious, bullying ghost. You jerks are a dime a dozen, as my grandma liked to say. If you're going to impress me, you'll have to try harder."

Lily's spine creaked as her body stiffened. Her chin tilted upward, and her face took on a smug expression I was willing to bet she'd never worn in her life. "I am *not* a ghost, you impertinent, misguided peasant."

Uh-oh. The ones with delusions of grandeur were always the hardest to crack. So damned stubborn. For now it was easier to play along. "Sorry, I must have mistaken you for some other dead guy. Who are you?"

"I am Dr. Abbandonato. If you have not heard of me, you soon will. The research I am doing is revolutionary. It will change the world. *Everyone* will know my name."

Jesus, what a megalomaniac. "Sure, buddy. I'm sure they will. So you're Italian?"

The sneer took on even more ugliness. "I am *Venetian*."

My mind raced. It had been a long time since I'd studied Italian history; Mediterranean ghosts weren't common in Vermont. How far back were we going if Venice was considered a place apart from Italy? I suspected quite a bit.

As I spoke to the spirit, he came more and more into view, almost completely obscuring Lily's features, but it didn't help me nail the time period. He wore a white lab coat, which indicated he was most likely telling the truth, at least about being a physician. Doctors' uniforms hadn't changed much over the centuries.

I shuddered at the idea of this man caring for patients. Even though death, especially violent death, could warp a soul beyond recognition, I could tell he had been a bad dude in life. Shadows clung to him like mold. He reeked of rot, and as he came more into focus, the tang of blood filled my nose until my stomach churned.

Now that he was closer, I could see he held something on his lap. Something strange and birdlike. It was still too hazy to make out, but it gave me the creeps. "So you're from Venice. Why don't you go back there? I'm sure people are missing you, especially if you're as important as you say."

"They can wait. I must treat this child. She has a disturbing malady of the brain. It must be attended to, and I am the only one with the expertise to cure her."

The only malady in her brain is you, asshole. I'd seen this before. When spirits believe people need them here on earth, they're nearly impossible to shake. "She's fine. Lily will be fine. I'll take care of her. Your patients in Venice, they need you more."

The doctor widened Lily's brown eyes. "My patients are not in Venice, dullard! They must remain separate from the common population. My work is done on Poveglia."

Poveglia. The name rang a bell, but I wasn't sure why. "They're calling for you in Poveglia, Doctor. Your patients are calling. They need you. Can't you hear them?"

"This girl called for me. I will not abandon her in her hour of greatest need."

Shit, Lily. What did you do?

"Her physician does not approve of your treatment, Doctor. You must leave her to his care. Go back to your other patients. Lily will be just fine."

Hoping to catch him off guard, I reached for Lily's spirit, trying to get a grip on her so I could yank her out of this guy's grasp. He pulled away, inserting himself between us so I could no longer detect the sweet nature of Vittoria's child. This guy was stronger than I'd initially thought, too strong for being this old and this far away from his own turf, and Lily, through her own ignorance, was to blame. I cursed the kid under my breath.

"No other doctor is capable of treating her. She will come with me. I must take her to Poveglia."

"No…" I leapt for her, but it was too late. I'd been too aggressive, scared him too much. "Shit!"

Lily's body flopped back on the bed, her eyes glazed.

Her skin lost its pallor and the sores on her face and arms healed as if they'd been absorbed. The man was gone, but so was Lily's spirit. How was I going to tell Vittoria that her daughter was catatonic?

"Okay, Lily. Let's find it."

I yanked open the preteen's closet and rifled through her clothes. I peered in her dresser drawers and looked behind her drapes.

It was under the bed.

A battered spirit board that looked like it was at least a hundred years old.

Crap.

I knew it.

~ CHAPTER TWO ~

VITTORIA STOOD WHEN I ENTERED the kitchen, wringing her hands like some clichéd 1950s housewife. I used to think nobody actually wrung their hands, but I know better now.

"Is Lily okay?"

"I'm afraid not." Before Vittoria could start sobbing again, I added, "but she will be."

She slumped in a chair, and I noticed a tray of assorted cookies on the table. I couldn't imagine eating now. "I—I don't understand. What happened?"

Ordinarily I believe in getting straight to the point, but given Vittoria's fragile emotional state, blurting out that her daughter appeared to be in a coma was not the best idea. Instead I set the spirit board on the table, careful to touch it only by the edges. Even then, it made my skin crawl. Loathsome thing.

"Do you recognize this?" My tone was casual, but inside I was screaming, *"Please don't tell me you gave this to your daughter."*

Wiping her eyes, she squinted at it, leaning forward for a better look. "Yes, I think it was my great-grandmother's. Or perhaps her mother's. It's been in our family for generations."

I sat down to keep myself from launching across the room and smashing something. Taking a deep breath, I reminded myself that it wasn't Vittoria's fault. The evil that radiated from this board was obvious to me because of The Gift, which she didn't have. It wasn't that she was stupid, or foolhardy. She just didn't know better. "Do you have any idea how it came to be in Lily's room? I found it under her bed."

Vittoria's brow furrowed. Her confusion doused a lot of the rage that had been broiling in my gut, since it was obvious she hadn't offered her daughter up to that *thing*. Finally the woman's expression cleared. "I remember now. She found it in the attic a few weeks ago." If she thought it was odd I'd been digging around under her daughter's bed, she didn't say. I guess at this point odd was relative.

A few weeks ago? No wonder the doctor had such a tight grip on Lily's soul. If only Vittoria had called me earlier. "Did anything strange happen around that time?"

"Now that you mention it, yes. Lily began talking to herself, a lot. I would hear her murmuring at night after she was supposed to be asleep. At first I thought she was on her smartphone, which is off-limits after a certain time, and I tried to catch her in the act." Vittoria frowned, remembering. "She was always alone. Her father and I discussed it, and he said not to worry about it, that it was an imaginary friend and every kid had one."

It took all my self-control to keep from groaning. Not only was Lily too old for an imaginary friend, but there was no such thing. Before adulthood roughens them like a callus, kids are emotionally raw and open enough to see spirits without dismissing them out of hand. But now was not the time to share this with Vittoria. She was upset enough.

"Please, can I see her? Is she okay? Please tell me what happened. I'm going crazy, just sitting here like this."

She reached for my hand and I took hers in mine, even though it required an immense effort to keep the spirits surrounding her at bay. They started to shriek their demands as soon as she touched me. Closing my eyes, I centered myself, focusing on the woman in front of me.

"Do you have faith, Vittoria?"

Silence fell over the room. Even Vittoria's ghosts waited for her response. Opening my eyes, I saw the woman was staring at the table, a troubled expression on her face. Finally she answered. "I was raised Italian Catholic, but I left the Church some time ago. I haven't been in years."

"It's okay. I'm not asking to judge you. It doesn't matter to me if you go to church every day or haven't gone since grade school, or if you're religious at all." I squeezed her hand. "What matters to me is that you are capable of faith, because in order to save your daughter, you're going to have to have faith in me."

Her large, brown eyes, so like her daughter's, pinned me to my chair. "What do you mean?"

"There's no easy way to tell you this, but Lily has made contact with a very dark spirit through this board. I have no doubt he seemed friendly at first in order to win her trust. From what you've said, he pretended to be your mother, and the more Lily talked to him through the board, the greater the hold he acquired over her. And now he's in complete control."

"Are you saying Lily is *possessed*?" Her words caught in her throat. This was the toughest part of the job. I wanted to weep with her, but I couldn't. Crying wouldn't bring Lily back.

"Not possessed, no. This type of spirit doesn't possess someone as much as shove them out. They're bullies. Look at what he did to you." I gently turned Vittoria's arm over to display the ugly scratches. "The good news is, Lily had nothing to do with this. She's the same girl she's always been."

Vittoria sagged in her chair. "So she's all right?"

"She'll be fine. I promise. Her physical body is sound, and her spirit is as well. They're just—well, they're not exactly united at this moment. But they will be."

"What are you talking about? What's happened to my daughter?" Ripping her hand from mine, Vittoria pushed back from the table. I stood to block her. I had to explain before she burst into Lily's room and saw her daughter lying on the bed like a porcelain doll. The shock could break her. "Get away from me! I want to see her. I want to see what you've done."

She was taller than me, and in better days was probably quite strong, but her ordeal had weakened her. I easily resisted her attempts to get around me. "Of course you can see her, but calm down. There are some things you need to understand before you go in. Otherwise you'll only make it worse for her."

That stopped her, like I'd suspected it would. I hated having to manipulate her like that, but as they say, desperate times called for desperate measures. "I tried my best to get the spirit to leave your daughter, but he was too powerful. He took Lily's soul with him to someplace called Poveglia. It's near Venice."

Vittoria shook her head. "This is crazy. I don't understand

any of this. How could a ghost take Lily's soul?"

"Because she let him. By using that board, she inadvertently showed him the way in. Once I have Lily back, I'm going to get you to destroy it. It has to be you, since you're the closest living relative of the owner. But until then, I'll need to use it to communicate with your daughter." *And her newly self-appointed physician.*

"What are you saying? That Lily is *dead*?" Her voice rose an octave.

"She's not dead, not at all. Her soul has split from her body, but I promise you I will get her back. It'll just take a little time, and I'll need your help."

She latched on to those words like a drowning woman, as I'd hoped she would. "What can I do?"

"I need to go to Poveglia to save your daughter. I realize this sounds bizarre, and I wouldn't blame you for not believing me. But this is where your faith comes in. You have to trust me completely. Can you do this?"

It's a cliché that eyes are windows to the soul, but it's also true. When I looked directly into Vittoria's, I knew she would see my honesty and integrity, my pure intent. At least, it had worked before. She nodded, her mouth slack with shock.

"I won't charge you my regular fee. I can't bear to charge you at all, but I will need you to cover my expenses getting to and from Poveglia, and I might require someone else to come along and help me. Are you able to afford this?" Even asking made me cringe inside. I'd be putting my own life on the line to rescue Lily, but I still felt slimy asking for money. Sadly, there was no alternative. An impromptu trip to Italy was not in my budget.

"I—I have a little money of my own. An account my

husband doesn't know about. It will be enough for your expenses." Her hands flew up to her mouth. "Oh my God. What am I going to tell my husband?"

"Don't worry; we'll take care of that. But before I explain the rest, why don't we visit Lily? Try your best to stay calm. I understand this is extremely upsetting for you, but I promise it's better than it looks."

Instead of charging down the hall, as she'd intended to do a few minutes ago, she cowered behind me. While it was awful to see her in such distress, her caution was a good thing. It meant she believed me.

When we got to Lily's room, she rushed past me. "Lily! Lily, can you hear me?" She shook her daughter's shoulders and cradled the girl's head, weeping. "Baby doll, please speak to me."

But Lily couldn't speak, as I well knew. In many ways, that was a blessing, because if Vittoria had heard that horrible man's voice issuing from her daughter's lips, she would have lost it. I was grateful I'd been the only one treated to that lovely performance. *Ugh, what an asshole.*

"What's wrong with her?" Vittoria held her daughter as if Lily were an oversized doll. "Why can't she talk?" Lily's eyes stared sightlessly at the wall. It was more than a little creepy.

"Because that isn't really your daughter. It's just her shell, the vessel for her soul. Do you understand now why I have to go to Poveglia and bring her back?"

Vittoria reached out her hand to me again. "Please help her, Kate. Please save my little girl."

"I will. But in the meantime, you have to keep her body safe. That's critical to her survival."

"How? How do I do that?" Vittoria pulled her daughter

even closer, in the kind of embrace Lily probably hadn't allowed since she was nine.

"In most cases, I'd tell you to keep her here, making sure she stays warm and comfortable, but since I have to go overseas, this could take a while. My advice is to bring her to the emergency room."

Any color remaining in her face vanished. "The hospital? I can't bring her there. They won't understand."

"They won't need to. They'll think she's in a coma of undetermined origin. Yes, they will do tests, which won't be pleasant, but Lily won't experience any discomfort or pain." I didn't mention how much discomfort and pain I suspected her *soul* was currently experiencing. No need to torture Vittoria further. "The hospital will make sure she stays hydrated and fed, and will keep her clean. You can't feed her yourself while she's in this state, and we don't want her to wither away."

The preteen didn't have much in the way of meat on her bones to begin with. The last thing I wanted was to risk my own life returning Lily's soul to a corpse.

"How long is this going to take?"

Considering I had no idea where Poveglia was—or what it was—that was a tough question to answer. "It could take a few weeks or longer. I'll try to return her to you as soon as I can."

"A few *weeks*?" Vittoria collapsed into sobs again, rocking her daughter back and forth.

And that was *if* I could reach her. With this, as with so much in the spirit world, there were no guarantees. Only one thing was certain.

I was going to need some help.

~ CHAPTER THREE ~

THE GIRL'S EYES FLEW OPEN, her heart leaping into her mouth when she found she couldn't move.

Using every ounce of strength, she fought to bring her hands up, but could only raise them a few inches. She turned her head to the side and saw thick canvas cuffs on her wrists—cuffs that were chained to a metal bed she'd never seen before. It was much smaller than her bed at home, barely wide enough to hold her.

She bit her tongue in her panic. Whimpering, she longed to cry out for help, but some instinct advised her to stay quiet.

"You're wise to listen to your instincts, Lily."

Whipping her head to the left, Lily flinched when she saw the woman standing there, watching her. She'd thought she was alone. As she continued to stare, she saw something wasn't right about this woman. Lily could see the wall behind her, *through* her. One second the woman was as solid as she, and the next she wasn't. She flickered in and out like a bad satellite signal.

Lily dug her heels into the hard mattress and struggled to scoot her body away from the apparition, but the same kind of cuffs that bound her wrists also held her ankles.

The most she could do was shift her body slightly to the right. The woman frowned, and any impulse Lily had to scream died in her throat. *She's going to kill me. I'm going to die.*

"I'm not going to hurt you."

The woman appeared more real now, less transparent. Lily could see her long, red hair and her T-shirt, which said something about Salem. "Are you a witch?"

The second the words were out of her mouth, she wished she could take them back, but the woman didn't seem offended. She smiled. "No, but I'm sure a few people have thought so."

"Are you—are you a ghost?"

Lily used to be scared of ghosts. She'd had nightmares about them coming in her room, invading her closet, waiting under her bed to steal her covers and grab her by the feet. But she was older now; she knew better. And since Nonna and the others had been coming to visit her, she understood ghosts were nothing to be afraid of.

They were still spooky, though.

"No, I'm not a ghost. I'm your friend."

Lily studied the woman, who certainly didn't look like any friend she remembered meeting. She didn't even move her mouth when she spoke. Instead, her words appeared in Lily's mind as if this stranger had whispered them in her ear. "Have I met you before?"

"Not until now. I'm a friend of your mother's, and that means I'm a friend of yours too."

Lily pictured her mother, whose idea of dressing down was not wearing her diamond earrings. She couldn't imagine what she'd have in common with this woman in her T-shirt and jeans.

"Can you tell me what you've seen? Who strapped you down?"

At least the bizarre conversation had temporarily distracted her. Panic caught in her throat again as she admitted the truth. "I don't know. I woke up like this. Can you free me?"

The sadness on the stranger's face told Lily all she needed to know. "I'm sorry; I can't. But you might be able to free yourself. Close your eyes."

In spite of the strangeness of her situation, there was something about the woman she trusted. Her instincts told her the redhead wouldn't hurt her. She lay back on the mattress, her neck already stiff from keeping her head up, and let her eyelids drift closed.

"Can you feel your hands?" The woman's voice was softer than before, soothing.

Lily flexed her fingers. She nodded.

"This will be hard for you to believe, but your body is different here. You can move it in ways you'd never be able to at home. Imagine your arms are like water, running through the restraints. Can you do that? Concentrate."

Arms are water; arms are water. It sounded like a meditation exercise. She'd done a lot of meditation with her mother and she'd gotten quite good at it. Confidence eased some of the fear in her heart. *Arms are water; arms are water.*

Rather than the sensation of floating she'd become accustomed to while meditating, Lily's left arm grew heavy. It sank down, down, down, until it encountered the part of the cuff that rested against the mattress. To her surprise, her wrist drifted right through it. Her eyes opened, gaping at her left hand, which she could now wave in front of her face. The empty cuff lay useless on the mattress.

She grinned when she saw how excited the woman looked. "That's amazing. You're an extraordinarily quick study. Can you do the other one? Same thing: close your eyes and imagine your arm is water."

Lily flopped back down on the mattress, more eager this time, so it took a bit longer to quiet her mind. *Arm is water; arm is water.*

A loud noise made her flinch. It was like a gunshot.

"Cosa fai? Non sei il benvenuto qui."

A man in a white coat shook his fist at the woman. His nostrils flared, his face flushing bright red. Thanks to her nonna's lessons, Lily could understand him, but she could see the woman didn't.

"He says you're not welcome here." This time she spoke to the woman with *her* mind, hoping it would work.

Tell him I have come for you, and I'm not leaving without you.

"Lascerà senza di me!" Lily shouted out loud, not wanting this scary man anywhere near her mind.

He didn't spare her a glance, but advanced on the woman as if he intended to hurt her. They circled each other.

"Lei è malata. Ha bisogno del mio aiuto."

"He says, 'She is sick. She needs my help.'" Lily shivered as the man's meaning dawned on her. "Does he mean me? I'm not sick…am I?" She'd been fighting with her mom a lot more lately, ever since Nonna died. Had her parents gotten tired of her crap and thrown her in a mental hospital? She'd heard stuff like that could happen. Lily's stomach twisted with dread. Suddenly she really had to pee, but damned if she was going to ask this man for help. She'd piss the bed if she had to.

Of course you're not sick. He's insane; don't listen to him. Tell him he has the wrong person.

"*Hai la persona sbagliata. Io non sono malata!*"

The man's lips curled into a sneer, and Lily saw they were wasting their breath. Some adults thought they knew everything, just because they were older. She was pretty sure he was one of them.

"*Si presume di dirmi la mia attività? Io sono un medico e tu non lo sei.*"

"He says he is the doctor and you are not."

Tell him to go screw himself in the nastiest way you can.

Even though she was scared of the man, Lily felt brave as she yelled, "*Vai a farti fottere!*"

He lunged at the redhead with a growl, but she sidestepped him. At first Lily thought she was imagining the blue light surrounding the woman's body. But every time the man swiped at her, the light grew deeper and brighter. Soon it was difficult to look at her. The blue was so intense it hurt Lily's eyes. But she kept staring anyway, because it was the most beautiful thing she'd ever seen. She wondered how the woman did it. Was she a superhero?

I'm not a superhero. You're seeing my aura because I'm not on a physical plane.

It didn't make much sense to Lily, but she was happy the aura seemed to hurt the man. The last time he'd tried to grab the woman, he'd cried out, snatching his hand back as if he had been burned.

The brighter the light around her, the more exhausted the woman looked. She managed to stay one step ahead of the man as he chased her around the room, but her eyes were half-closed and she was starting to stumble. *Lily, I have to go for a bit. He's too strong for me.*

Terror wrapped itself around Lily's chest and squeezed. "Don't go. You can't leave me here."

You're going to be fine. Use your words. Keep telling him you are the wrong person, you are not his patient, you're not sick.

"But what's he going to do to me?" She could see colors swirling around the man now too, alternating between a dirty gray and a dusty black. Rather than emit light, they absorbed it, creating more darkness in the shabby room. Every time he regarded her, she felt like a specimen under a microscope. This man wouldn't care about her feelings, her pain. He had his own agenda. An agenda that horrified her.

He can't hurt you. Your body is safe with your mom and dad. I know it's scary, but the rules are different here. Remember, your arm is water. Your arm is water, so he can't hurt you.

The woman's aura flickered. "You're lying," Lily said. "He *can* hurt me, and you know it. Please, get me out of here."

I'm sorry. I would if I could, but I'm not strong enough yet. Soon, though. I'll come back for you, I promise. Until then, keep him away from you as much as you can, and remember everything you see. Every detail, no matter how small, will help me find you.

She was transparent again. Lily could see the angry man through the woman. "Wait—what's your name?"

My name is Kate. Stay strong, Lily. Never forget your arm is water.

The room shook when the woman vanished, as if her leaving had caused a seismic wave. Lily had no idea what this place was, but the rules *were* different. There was a sifting sound as flecks of paint drifted from the walls onto the floor.

When the man turned to her, she shifted on the bed so he wouldn't notice she'd freed one of her wrists. He was panting and haggard, as if the confrontation with the woman had drained him. Lily was relieved she didn't have any trouble understanding him—or vice versa. She'd often struggled with Nonna's lessons, but now she was glad she hadn't given up.

"Who was that woman?"

"I don't know. I've never seen her before," Lily said, grateful she didn't have to lie. She prayed the woman would return, and soon. This place gave her a bad feeling. More than anything, she wanted to give her mom the biggest hug and tell her she was sorry for causing so much trouble lately. And after that, she would eat spaghetti and go to sleep in her own bed. Things she'd taken for granted seemed like luxuries now.

The man's thick black brows met in the middle of his forehead as he glared at her. "Visitors are not allowed. We cannot have anyone interfering with your treatment."

Treatment. The word made everything inside her clench and retreat, as if trying to find a corner to hide in. Then she remembered Kate's advice. She would use her words. "I am not sick. I am not your patient."

"Ridiculous lies. Certainly you are sick. Why are you here, if you are not ill?" Without warning, his hand snaked out and seized her chin, turning her face toward his. She gasped, wrinkling her nose at his breath, which carried the stench of rotten meat. He pried her lips open and shone a light within, *tsk-tsking* to himself. "The wild fluctuations of mood, hearing and communing with voices that are not there: your illness is very serious indeed. Do not let that woman deceive you. Are you still troubled by headaches?"

Wait. She had been moody lately. And she had been speaking to a voice that wasn't there. She'd thought it was Nonna, but now she had her doubts. She'd always gotten headaches. Could this man be right? Was there something wrong with her? Was she going crazy?

No. NO. He was trying to trick her.

"I am not sick; I am not your patient."

The man released her jaw. "Your delusions are extraordinarily persistent. There is no guarantee I can cure you, but I must try. You are too young to be condemned to this hell." He placed a spindly hand upon her forehead, tracing her eyebrows with the other. She tried to squirm away from his grip, but he was too strong. "Here is where the injection must go," he said, tapping the bone ridge above her eye.

Injection? No way in hell was this lunatic sticking a needle in her face. "What injection? I don't understand."

The man straightened, a chilling smirk playing across his lips. "For the leukotomy, of which I am master. Within days, you will be an entirely new person. Everything that currently troubles you will vanish once I am done with your brain." He grinned at her, displaying large teeth. "The girl you are now will cease to exist."

As the man caressed her skull, Lily's bladder let go.

~ CHAPTER FOUR ~

IT TOOK ME SEVERAL TRIES to find what I was searching for, since I had no idea how to spell "Poveglia." Not being Italian, the possibility of a silent *g* hadn't occurred to me.

But once I'd found it, I was really sorry I had.

If anyone had attempted to write a horror movie about the so-called "Plague Island," it would have been thrown out of Hollywood for being too over the top. Its history was so unbelievably dark that Lily couldn't have found an uglier place if she'd gone searching for Hitler. I looked askance at the battered spirit board on my desk, its planchette resting on *Good Bye,* not at all sure I wanted it in my house. Had it originated with the people of Poveglia? It certainly appeared old enough, but I wasn't an antiquarian. There was no way to tell. Even now, in my exhausted state, I could see a circle of beautiful, dark-eyed women standing around it: Lily's ancestors, I had no doubt. But how did the doctor factor in?

My hunch had been right. I was going to need help, and there was only one person who would be willing to assist me. Scrolling through the contacts on my phone, I selected his name and then hesitated. After we'd worked together to break the story of what had happened to the women of Hensu, we'd kept in touch—for a while. But that contact had dwindled over the past year, to the point where we hadn't spoken in weeks. Last I'd heard, a publisher had given him a big enough advance to quit his job and focus on writing. Who was I to blunder back into his life and mess things up? Ghosts weren't his favorite thing, especially the angry ones. And this doctor was definitely angry. He made Yuèhai look like a kitten in comparison.

My finger hovered over the power button. I imagined the confusion in his voice as he said, "I'm sorry, who did you say you were? Kate *who?*"

Then I remembered Lily's eyes as the doctor loomed over her, Vittoria's sobs as she cradled her catatonic daughter.

I made the call.

Before I could second-guess myself again, he was saying, "Kate! Damn, girl, where you been hiding?"

His greeting was an embrace after such a terrible day. "Jackson, how are you?"

"I'm good, really good. Hey, it's great to hear your voice. It's been too long. How are you?"

"Not too good, and that's why I'm calling. I need your hel—" I stopped when I heard the unmistakable sound of a female giggle in the background, followed by Jackson's shushing. I froze, barely resisting the urge to throw my phone across the room.

"What's that, girl? You know what, hang on. Let me go in the other room. I'm at a party, and things are a bit chaotic right now."

Oh Jackson, don't lie to me. I know you're not at a party. We'd always been honest with each other. I hoped that hadn't changed.

After a moment, I heard a door close in Minneapolis and Jackson's voice came back to me clearer, louder, as if he were in the room with me. "Sorry about that. What did you say? I didn't catch it."

"What's her name?" I strived to sound cheerful, happy for him, as any true friend would.

"Who? Oh, I guess you heard that, hey?"

"Of *course* I heard it. It wasn't exactly subtle. So what's her name?"

"Destiny. We're just friends. For now, you know. Hanging out, testing the waters, so to speak. Having some fun. Life is short—take the roller coaster."

I couldn't figure out why I was so upset. Sure, we'd had a moment in China, but with the geographical distance between us, we'd both agreed it was for the best if we remained friends.

And what had I expected? Jackson was a gorgeous, intelligent, funny man. Did I think he'd sit around at home, pining for me? I was being ridiculous.

"She's not you, though. Not even close."

Heat crept into my cheeks, setting them aflame. "You don't have to say that."

"I know I don't. It's true, though. You ever decide you're tired of living in the boonies, let me know."

I couldn't imagine relinquishing the beauty of Nightridge to live in Minneapolis, even for a man like Jackson. Different day, same ol' impasse. Clearing my throat, I attempted to bring the conversation back on track. "I'm guessing Destiny wouldn't be too happy if you went to Italy with another woman."

"*Italy*? Screw Destiny; I hardly know the girl. What's going on, Kate?"

Trying not to stumble over my words too much, I filled him in on my visit with Vittoria and what was happening to Lily.

"Let me get this straight. This evil dude took the girl's soul over to some godforsaken Italian island?"

"That pretty much sums it up, yes."

"But how is that possible? This Lily chick—she's alive, right? I didn't think ghosts could do stuff like that."

Trust Jackson to pinpoint exactly what had been bothering me so much about this case. "Normally, they can't. Or at least I haven't had something like this happen before, especially a spirit able to maintain that level of strength from so far away. It must have something to do with the family history. Or with Lily herself. From what I saw today, she's not an ordinary girl. I suspect she has mediumistic abilities."

After I'd told him about the ancient spirit board, how the mad doctor had pretended to be Lily's grandmother, and about the women who were now hovering over my desk, he whistled. "Wait, what's a spirit board? Is it like a committee of ghosts sitting around having boring meetings?"

"I forgot how funny you're not. Ever heard of a Ouija board? It's basically the same thing. Misguided people use them to communicate with spirits."

"Those things actually work? I thought that was only in horror movies."

I glanced at the board. One female spirit had edged her way to the center of the circle. She was the same elderly woman I'd seen before at the Walkinses' house. Wringing her hands, she stared at me with sad eyes. "Oh, they work all right. Not every time, but enough to be dangerous.

And they can be *extremely* dangerous." I sighed, feeling the exertions of the day in my sore muscles and aching neck. "Spirit boards are the bane of my existence."

"I'll keep that in mind. So, how can I help? What do you need?"

"Are you sure you have time for this? What about the book?" Crossing my fingers under my desk, I held my breath while I waited for his response. I couldn't imagine going to Poveglia with anyone else.

"I always have time for you, darling."

"Cut the crap, Jackson. I'm serious."

"Sorry, force of habit. The truth is, it's going okay, but I've been putting it off more than I should. I've actually been meaning to call you, 'cause the details have gotten a little fuzzy. So this would help me too. I can interview you about some of the stuff that happened in China along the way."

"Sure. I'm always happy to help; you know that." I'd never forget Yuèhai. Of all the stalker spirits I'd encountered, she'd easily been the most obsessed. She'd ensured Jackson wouldn't feel right with himself until he told her story properly. "I'm glad to hear you're available, because I really need your help with this one. Remember what happened to me in Hensu?"

"Of course. I thought you were going to die. That was some scary shit."

And I might have. Communicating with spirits meant taking on their pain. Once that link was forged between us, I could feel everything they'd gone through when they were alive, and there had been many instances when my own mortality was closer than kissing distance. "Well, Poveglia makes Hensu look like a playground."

"What are we talking about, Kate? Was it a concentration camp?" The gravity in his voice told me I had his full attention. The playfulness was gone.

"Pretty damn close, yeah." I thought about everything I'd read and the best way to give Jackson the highlights without overwhelming him. Poveglia would overwhelm almost anyone. "In the 1800s, victims of the plague were burned there, and they weren't always dead before they were used as kindling, either. And that's not the worst of it. Some of the accounts I found suggested that healthy people might have been taken to the island and abandoned there to become infected and die, just because someone had a grudge against them."

Another low whistle from Jackson. "That's twisted."

"And that's just the beginning. In the '30s, it was a repository for the mentally ill. Of course, not everyone imprisoned there had a mental illness. Some had a physical malformation, like a missing limb or a harelip."

"Sounds like a lovely place for a vacation. Count me in."

"There's something else you need to know." I took a deep breath. "There was a doctor working there during that time. I can't find any mention of his name, but this guy definitely had a God complex. He performed barbaric experiments on the patients, often without using any anesthesia. Most of them died in his care, and those who survived were living zombies. The Italians called him *Medico della Morte*—the Doctor of Death."

The lamp on my desk flickered as the bulb made a sizzling sound. There was a squeaking noise from the spirit board, and the elderly woman retreated to the edges of the circle again. The rest of the women huddled together, muttering in Italian. One shook her head at me.

"So it wasn't a concentration camp, but we have ourselves a Nazi."

Picturing the man I'd encountered that afternoon, I shuddered. As altruistic and noble as his motives might have been in the beginning, I could see he enjoyed hurting people—a lot. I had to get Lily's soul away from him before he did irrevocable damage. "Yeah, pretty much."

"And let me guess. This Dr. Doom is the spirit who's kidnapped your client."

"I think so, yes. It certainly looks that way. The man I encountered this afternoon told me his name is Abbandonato, but I couldn't verify that he's the same doctor I've been reading about. I've been able to find out tons about what the mad doctor did to his patients in Poveglia, but not a single mention of his name."

"How'd he die?"

"No one really knows for sure. CliffsNotes version: he fell from a bell tower. But was he pushed or did he jump? That's the question."

"Can't you ask him?"

I smiled, biting back a sarcastic response. Even after our time together, Jackson still didn't understand how this worked. "We're not that close. I like to know a person a little better before I ask him whether he killed himself or not."

The light bulb went out with a loud *pop*, making me flinch. Another distraught squeal from the spirit board.

"What the hell was *that*?"

"Nothing. My light just burned out. No big deal." But it was more than that. For one thing, the temperature in the room had dropped at least ten degrees. Taking the afghan from my office chair, I wrapped it around my shoulders. It didn't help. This was a cold you felt in your bones.

"Are you sure you're okay?"

"Yeah, I'm fine. I'm still in Vermont, not Poveglia."

That spirit board was the problem. I'd kept it to communicate with Lily, but that meant someone else could use it to communicate with me.

"How many people died on that island?"

That was Jackson for you, always cutting to the heart of the matter. "Conservative estimates say at least a hundred thousand."

"*A hundred thousand?* Jesus Christ, Kate! You're not going to be able to get anywhere near it."

"I will, but not for very long. I'm hoping we won't need that much time. But now you understand why I need your help."

"Do you have to be on the island to help her? Taking on that much suffering could kill you. Remember Hensu."

"I'm well aware of the risks, Jackson." I instantly wished I could take back my response, along with my condescending tone. He was worried about me, and with good reason. I was worried too. I'd never willingly put myself in the midst of that much death before. "Sorry. I shouldn't snap at you. I know you're trying to help. My first wrestling match with the doc took a lot out of me. I have less patience than usual."

He laughed. "Less than usual? God help us all."

"Fuck off." But I was smiling as I said it.

"Love to, but I wouldn't want to mess with our business relationship. And it sounds like this is going to be all business—do I have that right?"

"Always." Unless some girl named Destiny—or, more likely, *Destini*—put the kibosh on the whole thing.

"How about I catch a flight to Burlington tomorrow, and we go to Venice together? You can tell me the rest on the way."

I'd never been afraid to be in my own home before, but there was something about this darkness. It felt heavier than usual. Thankfully, light poured out of Jackson like he was a human manifestation of the sun. As long as he kept talking to me, I felt safe, and knowing he would be with me tomorrow, that we would face this thing together, was a huge relief. "I'll transfer the money to you."

"Are you kidding? Hell no, you won't. I'd pay double for an excuse to get out of Minneapolis."

"There's no need for you to do that, seriously. The client is paying for it."

"I'm sure she's paying enough, having her daughter's soul in the hands of some deranged death doctor—am I right? Besides, I can't think of a better way to spend my advance. I'll see you tomorrow. I'm going to text you my flight as soon as it's booked."

"Are you sure? It's really unnecessary for you to pay for this." *But also kind of sweet.* Factoring in the Walkinses' hospital bills, this little adventure would cost them dearly by the time it was over.

"Have you ever known me to do something I wasn't sure about? I should go, babe, but I'll see you tomorrow." He paused. "Are you *sure* you're okay?"

"Of course. Why wouldn't I be? I'm thrilled you're able to come with me. We make a great team."

"The best. But what about tonight?"

"What about tonight?" Part of me couldn't understand why I was acting coy. I knew exactly what Jackson was getting at, and it wasn't like me to play games, especially with him. We'd been through too much. But I couldn't help myself.

"That Dr. Doom guy—he can't hurt you, can he?"

"That 'Dr. Doom' guy is dead, Jack—"

The phone whipped out of my hand before I could finish my sentence. I heard it crash against the wall.

IO NON SONO MORTO!

A blast of icy wind blew my hair back. I could feel the doctor's warm, foul-smelling spittle hit my face.

Ugh.

I can't stand ghosts who don't have the decency to accept they're dead.

~ CHAPTER FIVE ~

IT TOOK FOREVER, BUT AT last Lily's left leg slipped free from its restraints. Easing herself into a sitting position, she stretched, keeping a close eye on the doorway. It was dark outside the room and mostly dark inside too, except for the moon peering through the only window.

The tingling pain that normally resulted from her blood returning to numb fingers and toes never arrived, heightening her fear. *Am I dead?* She didn't remember dying, but then again, she wasn't sure if anyone did.

If she wasn't dead, how on earth did she end up here? Wherever here was, presumably somewhere in Italy. People couldn't teleport across a continent and an ocean within seconds.

Two years ago, Lily had believed in the possibility of magic. She refused to turn her back on Santa Claus, the Easter Bunny, and the potential for benevolent lions in the wardrobe. Whenever she lost a tooth, she was convinced it was the Tooth Fairy who left a pack of sugar-free bubblegum under her pillow, not her parents. But eventually the jeers and laughter of her peers had done their damage, and she didn't believe any more.

It figured that the proof she'd searched for would appear

once she stopped looking. But if this was magic, Lily was pretty sure it was the bad kind.

"Nonna?" she whispered into the darkness, hoping for a reply but not expecting one. It was her grandma's spirit who'd told her she was ill, who'd told her stories about this amazing doctor who could cure her. Lily had been horrified to hear that some disease was destroying her brain. She'd felt nothing but relieved that there was a doctor who could help.

Until she met him.

The first time the man had appeared in response to her efforts with the Ouija board, she'd been scared until he explained he was the doctor Nonna had talked about. Even with her grandmother's ringing endorsement, Lily was skeptical. There were a lot of things about this man that troubled her.

For one, he liked to wear this mask that made him resemble some kind of monstrous bird. He seemed to delight in frightening her, throwing back his head and laughing when she cried out.

Whenever he touched her with his thin fingers, she shuddered. It was as if worms were oozing under her skin—not exactly pleasant. Before long, the doctor was *always* the one who responded when she used the spirit board. Her grandmother was nowhere to be found, even when Lily asked for her. The more she talked to the man, the more questions she had, but either he wouldn't answer, or he fired back his responses in such rapid Italian she couldn't understand him.

How did he know something was wrong with her brain without CAT scans or MRIs? Without a thorough examination of any kind? She wasn't stupid.

Something was rotten in Italy.

Flexing her feet, Lily lowered them to the floor. No point hanging around waiting for the red-haired woman to return and rescue her, assuming that was even her intent. The tiles were cold under her skin, and almost immediately she stubbed her toe. Broken ceramic made a loud clinking sound. Lily froze. Kneeling, she was able to see that the floor was covered in rubble—destroyed tiles and other nastiness, from the look of it.

This isn't a hospital, then. No hospital would ever be this dirty.

She stiffened as she waited for the doctor to arrive. He'd no doubt be furious when he saw she was free. She'd have to use all her strength to keep him from putting those restraints on again, and she was only twelve. He was so much bigger. If the redheaded woman couldn't defeat him, what chance did she have?

A whimper from the gloom outside her door decided it. She couldn't waste time standing there like an idiot, waiting for a man who had proven to be cruel and whom she now suspected was insane as well. Lily hopped from tile to tile, avoiding the debris as much as she could. When she reached the doorway, the depth of nothingness beyond intimidated her, making her hesitate.

"Hello?"

Whimper.

The sound was more animal than human, as if an abandoned puppy, scared and starving, cowered outside the room. *What would a puppy be doing here?* It could be a trick. It probably *was* a trick. But Lily had never been able to ignore a plea for help, and she wasn't about to start now.

With scenes from every scary movie she'd ever watched running through her head, she crept forward into the abyss.

Judging by the absence of light in this room, there were no windows. Still, it felt big, as if the hospital or whatever it was had opened itself up to her. That was more frightening than her blindness, this sense that she would plunge through empty space at any moment. The only illumination came from the room she'd left, the moonlight trailing weakly behind her. She sucked in her breath when she realized she cast no shadow.

Dead, then. I must have died.

She didn't fully believe it, though. Couldn't believe it. She felt too alive to be a ghost.

Waving her arms in front of her, pawing at open air, she tiptoed into the new space.

Step…pause.

Step…pause.

Step…pause.

It was not her fingers but her feet that encountered something blocking her path.

Something soft.

Whimper.

Clutching at the darkness as if she could grab hold of it, Lily knelt before what she'd thought was a puppy. She touched cloth tattered by age—a hospital gown. "Hello?"

Another whimper, this time directly in front of her, close enough to make her breath catch in her throat.

"*Come ti chiami?*" (What is your name?)

No answer. Lily's fingers followed the cloth to a bony leg, which twitched away from her.

"*Mi dispiace. Non riesco a vedere.*" (I'm sorry. I can't see.)

She had so many questions. Was she dead? Was this hell? It couldn't be heaven, certainly never any version she'd read about. How many people were here? She'd heard what sounded like hundreds of people scurrying around that afternoon, but of course the acoustics of the building could have played tricks on her.

Are we damned?

The darkness was impenetrable. She'd gone too far to see the moonlight trickling in from her own room anymore. How would she ever find her way back? If only there were a light. She was afraid of what the man would do if he discovered she was free, but she was willing to risk it. The horrible feeling that something was sneaking up on her was worse.

"*Dove è la luce?*" (Where is the light?)

The thing in front of her grunted and seized her hand. Lily's impulse was to pull away, but she had a feeling whatever it was wanted to help her.

The hand holding hers was small and very warm—oddly so, since the place was quite cool. Lily heard the person's slow, shuffling progress, and it made her think of the zombie movie she'd watched before any of this happened, before she'd come across the Ouija board.

Stupid thing. I wish I'd never found it.

A whitish glow appeared in their path, growing stronger and stronger. Once she was closer, Lily saw it was the room she'd just left. Either the stranger had misunderstood her, or this was the only light available.

"*Mi chiamo Lily,*" she said, touching her chest. "My name is Lily. What's yours?"

She needn't have bothered. The stranger never looked up. With the help of the light coming in the room's window, Lily could see she was a young girl. Tangled, dark hair reached the girl's waist, and as the stranger hid her face, she reminded Lily of a daisy unable to keep its head up. The shoulders of the girl's dressing gown were stiff with starch, but as the child moved closer to the light, Lily noticed the hem was in filthy tatters.

Heart pounding in her ears, she felt a desperate need to connect with this girl, to communicate. Everything was easier with a friend. If they worked together, perhaps they could escape. Or fight the doctor off. Maybe there were more kids here who would join them.

"*Ciao? Puoi capirmi? Perché non parli?*" (Hello? Can you understand me? Why don't you speak?)

This time the girl didn't muster a whimper. Lily wondered if the sound she'd heard earlier had actually come from the child, or something else, something that still waited in the nothingness beyond her room.

We don't have much time. I've got to get out of here before the doctor wakes up. She didn't know why she thought he was asleep—*do ghosts need sleep?*—but, whatever he was doing, he wasn't nearby. There was a suffocating heaviness pressing down on her chest when he was around, a convenient warning.

I don't like this.

The longer the girl stayed silent, the more anxious Lily became. *Something's wrong with her. What if she works for the doctor? What if she's on his side? What if she's summoning him somehow?*

In her old life, Lily would have mocked the idea of "summoning" another person without a cell phone or a computer, but everything was different now. The lion was in the wardrobe, along with the witch. Santa Claus was real, and so was his evil counterpart, Krampus.

With a shaking hand, she dared to touch the girl on the shoulder, hoping to awaken her from whatever trance she was in. The girl's head shot up as if a bolt of electricity had arced through her, a gasp rattling in a throat rusty from lack of use. As the moonlight illuminated the child's features, Lily saw the reason for her silence.

The girl's tongue was gone.

So were her eyes.

Lily screamed.

~ CHAPTER SIX ~

JACKSON'S FLIGHT WAS LATE, GIVING me an extra hour to wonder if calling him had been the right thing to do. The muffin I'd purchased from the airport's overpriced coffee shop sank to the bottom of my stomach and sat there like a stone. I tried to read the latest Marian Keyes, desperate to escape into a world of witty British banter, but I couldn't focus. After reading the same sentence five times, I gave up and tucked the book into the inside pocket of my jacket.

I ambled over to the information desk to ask if there had been any updates, more to stretch my legs than anything else. A delayed flight is like a watched pot. I swear the planes slow down according to the number of people waiting. And if you're a passenger with a super-tight connection? Good luck.

The Filipino man sitting behind the desk widened his eyes when he saw me coming. "I'm surprised you're still here. Your flight came in twenty minutes ago."

"It did?" *How had I missed it?* But it was true—the word ARRIVED was flashing beside Jackson's flight number in the same place DELAYED had been only moments before. "What carousel?"

He pointed to the left. "Five. I hope your friend is there."

"Me too. Thanks."

Pushing through the crowd, I attempted my first sprint since high school. It wasn't a pleasant experience. I screeched to a halt at carousel five with my lungs on fire and sweat turning my forehead shiny. Exactly how I wanted to look when I greeted Jackson.

My spirits plummeted into my ill-fitting boots when I saw the carousel was deserted. Only an elderly woman with what looked like twenty suitcases piled on a teetering cart remained.

Great. What now?

When the woman shuffled past, cart wheels creaking in agony, I saw that I'd missed someone. A beautiful black man in a navy pea coat, with a scarf in vibrant shades of orange and purple casually draped around his neck, sat in one of the chairs against the wall. The second I noticed him, he looked up at me and smiled.

Pushing my damp hair out of my eyes, I was overcome with a feeling so foreign I didn't recognize it initially. Then it hit me. *I'm actually shy.* I hoped my cheeks weren't as red as they felt.

For a second I thought he was feeling the same, that at least we'd be able to laugh about how awkward this was and what dorks we were. But before I could say a word, he snatched me up and was spinning me around in a circle so fast my legs flew straight out behind me. So much for shyness. I had to hold on to him for dear life to keep from being catapulted into the ceiling.

By the time he put me down, we were both laughing.

I love this man, I thought but could never say. Just being near him made me feel better than I had in a long while.

Everyone needs an ally, and Jackson was mine—for the time being at least.

"I'm so sorry I'm late. For some reason there was a delay on the screen and I didn't know your flight had come in and I—"

"Kate," Jackson said over my rush of words. When I didn't stop, he laid his hands on my shoulders. "It's fine. I knew you'd come. I'm just happy you're here now."

There was something about the affection in his voice that made my eyes sting with tears. To say the last twenty-four hours had been draining would be the understatement of the century.

"Hey, what's this?" He brushed a tear from my cheek with his thumb. "Do I look that bad?"

I slapped him on the arm, pulling away. "Of course not. You look amazing, as you well know. You always do."

"Well, right back atcha, girl." His brow furrowed, belying his jovial tone. "Although you do look exhausted. Did you sleep at all after we talked?"

"Couldn't. I spent half the night trying to reach Lily." Which had been a waste of time, but not necessarily a cause for concern—*yet*. My prolonged struggle with the death doctor had depleted my energy to the point where I could barely pour milk over the cereal I'd eaten for dinner. Once I'd had some rest, I'd try again. Now that Jackson was here, I'd be able to close my eyes without worrying about what might sneak up on me.

"Let's get you home so you can rest. She needs your strength." He wrapped his arm around me. "When's our flight tomorrow?"

"We have to be here at four a.m."

He winced. "The things I do for adventure."

"I tried to get us on a plane this evening, but there was nothing available." Which was a good thing, since I hadn't had time to pack. Then I noticed the small leather duffel Jackson had slung over his shoulder. "Is that all you brought?"

"I pack light. You know that."

We walked out of the airport arm in arm, and I smiled, remembering his backpack during the China trip. It had weighed at least twenty pounds less than mine. Sometimes he'd carried mine too if I wasn't stubborn enough to fight him over it. "I don't get how you do it."

"Hey, you need this from me." He tapped his temple. "And this," he said, laying a hand over his heart. "Not a fashion show."

"This is true. Although you're looking pretty slick today."

"Well, we *are* going to Italy. I figured a T-shirt and khakis wasn't gonna cut it."

When he saw my car, he whistled. "This is yours? Nice. Good color."

The Mini Cooper in British racing green had been my only significant adult purchase aside from my home, so I was thrilled whenever someone complimented it. I'd agonized over buying that car. *What make? What model? What color?* But the effort had been worth it; it fit me like a pair of broken-in Levis. "Thanks."

The glow of Jackson's praise didn't last long. I paused with my hand on the door handle, wrestling with my conscience.

He gave me a funny look. "Something wrong?"

"Yeah. Yeah, there is." I inhaled deeply, filling my lungs and letting the brisk fall air clear some of the fog from my head. "I haven't been completely honest with you, and I don't want to start out like that. You came all the way over here to help; you deserve to know exactly what you're getting into."

"Kate, I've had a ghost grab my *dick*. You don't have to sugarcoat things for me."

"I'm sorry. It's been a while since we've talked about this stuff and I have a long history of hiding this part of my life. I'm not used to having people around who can handle it."

"Well, I can handle it. So spill."

"Okay. When I told you I hadn't slept, I *was* trying to reach Lily. That much was true."

His brown eyes searched mine. "But it's not the only thing that kept you awake."

"No, it's not." I told him about the death doctor's visit, along with the damage that had been done to my home—and to me. As I spoke, Jackson's features became more and more pinched until he dropped his duffel and walked around to my side of the car.

"Show me." He held out his hand, waiting.

"It's not a big deal. I've had worse, as you know—"

"*Show* me, Kate."

I extended my arm and he took it by the wrist, easing up the sleeve of my jacket. When he sucked in his breath, I glanced down. The doctor's fingerprints were more visible the morning after, blazing against my pale skin. They looked like burns.

"I'll kill him." Jackson clenched his teeth as he let me go.

"The man's already been dead for almost a hundred years, Jackson."

"Then I'll kill him again. I am going to kick his transparent ass. *"

We were off to a great start.

❦

For obvious reasons, I wasn't in a hurry to get home. Once we arrived at my place, shit was going to get real, and I wasn't ready for that yet. I owed it to Vittoria and her family to rescue Lily as soon as possible, but it had been over a year since I'd hugged Jackson goodbye in Chongqing. If I allowed myself the luxury of clinging to normalcy for a few extra minutes, I figured it was justified.

Ordinarily the drive from Burlington to Nightridge took about an hour when traffic was light, but I opted for the scenic route. Which would give me another half hour to pretend I was a normal person whose house hadn't been trashed by a pissed-off poltergeist. Since Jackson hadn't been to Vermont before, I kept glancing at him out of the corner of my eye to gauge his reaction.

He tried to play it cool, but it was a losing battle and Vermont rose to the challenge, like I'd known she would. No place could touch her in the autumn, and as we entered Nightridge with its arches of elegant maple trees, displaying foliage the color of a Caribbean sunset, Jackson couldn't keep quiet any longer.

"Christ. This place is a fucking Christmas card."

"Not yet. Give it a month." Except for the bone-chilling cold I'd experienced outside Hildy's store, it had been an unseasonably warm fall, so my garden was still in bloom. I was happy Jackson was seeing my town at its prettiest, but winter, with its sparkling hoarfrost and intense sunshine, was spectacular too.

"You didn't tell me you lived in a Norman Rockwell painting." Jackson stared at my clapboard house as we got out of the Mini. "No wonder you don't want to move."

"I did my best to straighten up before I left, but like I warned you, it's still a mess." My heart ached for my little house as I fumbled for my keys. It was over a hundred years old, much too old for this shit. The things I'd put it through.

No, the things The Gift has put it through, not you. It's not like you willingly destroyed your own home.

"Hey, you've seen what a slob I am. I'm hardly one to judge. I have a hard enough time keeping my apartment clean *without* angry ghosts messing it up."

I'd been too worried about Jackson's failing health in China to notice the state of his hotel room, but clearly he'd been embarrassed about it since he'd brought it up several times since.

In spite of my resolve to be honest with him, I'd just told another half-truth. Yes, I'd put away a few things and cleaned up the worst of the mess, but otherwise I'd left everything as it was. It was important for Jackson to see exactly what he would be up against.

Dr. Death was no Yuèhai, who'd been more a lover than a fighter.

Unlocking the door, I stepped aside so he could go inside first, all the better to get the full impact.

Jackson took one step past the threshold and stopped, as I'd suspected he would. "Holy shit." His smile vanished. "A *ghost* did this?"

"I'm afraid so."

It looked every bit as bad as I remembered, maybe a little worse with the afternoon sun pouring in the windows. The lovely amber light was a sharp contrast to the ugliness within. Every kitchen cabinet was open, with at least two hanging from their hinges. Broken china in a riot of colors littered the floor. A sofa cushion had been ripped to shreds, leaving clumps of white feathers everywhere. Photo frames were lying on the ground, their protective glass shattered, but the worst were the books. My precious collection resembled something you'd see in a pulp-and-paper mill.

Jackson crept into the house as if afraid something would jump out and bite him. "Wow, this is—it's…Chernobyl. I'm so sorry, Kate."

Managing to sound more optimistic than I felt, I said, "It's okay. It's just stuff, right?"

"Jesus Christ! What the hell is *that?*"

I looked where Jackson was pointing. Two large, canted, turquoise eyes surveyed him from the gloom under the kitchen sink. I laughed. Sinking to my knees, I reached out a hand and twitched my fingers. "Come here, Nostradamus. Come here, boy. Come meet our guest."

"Nostradamus?"

Ignoring Jackson's smirk, I focused on my roommate, who was not pleased about the current state of affairs. Normally he'd have been the first to greet any visitors. It wasn't like him to hide in the shadows. "Come on, Noddy. It's okay."

My Maine Coon crept out from his makeshift cave on silent feet. Jackson's eyes widened as Noddy strutted straight to me and nuzzled my hand.

"That's the biggest cat I've ever seen in my life. I thought it was a panther."

"He's not so big for a Maine Coon." Noddy was now rubbing his entire head against my hand, and his purr rumbled through the house. "Eighteen pounds is pretty average. He's got a bit of mixed blood, though, I think. The blue eyes aren't typical, especially with the black coat."

"Him and me both." Jackson knelt beside us and held out his hand. After a few sniffs, Noddy decided he was worthy of a head butt.

"Mixed blood, or atypical?"

He rubbed Noddy's tufted ears. "Both." Jackson grinned at me. "He's gorgeous."

"That he is. Normally he would have trotted out the welcome wagon, but he's a bit spooked after last night."

"Can't say I blame him. Hey, what's this?" Jackson fingered Noddy's collar, which was inscribed with rows of silver symbols. The usual white lie sprang to my lips until I remembered who I was talking to. Jackson would understand.

"It's basically an incantation. For animal protection. It makes Noddy invisible to spirits so they can't hurt him."

There's a reason family pets always die in horror movies. Poltergeists tend to go after innocent animals because they know how much pain it causes the owners. As much as I adored cats, there was no way I would ever have adopted one without being assured it was safe.

"An incantation? As in spell? Is this your way of telling me you're a witch?"

"No, a friend of mine made it. You'll meet her tomorrow, because she's going to take care of Noddy and watch the house while we're gone."

Jackson straightened his legs and stood up, which didn't deter Nostradamus in the slightest. Noddy was content to rub against him, covering my friend's jeans in sleek, black hair. "She's coming here? To this?"

I shrugged again. "She's seen worse. It'll be fine."

Laura was the only friend I had in the industry. It was a relief to be able to be myself around her without having to answer a lot of questions. Even though she was more psychic and Wiccan than medium, she understood me in a way few people could.

"So, what can I get you? Tea? Water? Beer? Are you hungry? I could make you soup and a sandwich, or we could order pizza. There's a really good place not far from here that delivers. Or—"

"Or nothing. You're going to bed. Now."

Ordinarily, hearing those words from an undeniably sexy man would have been exciting. But Jackson didn't say it in the sexy way. He said it in the *parental* way.

"I can't just leave you here by yourself."

"Yes you can. You need to get some rest, Kate. You're exhausted."

Did I look that bad? Even though I was horrified at ditching Jackson immediately after our reunion, I couldn't put one foot in front of the other without tripping over it. "But you must be starving. I should—"

"This may shock you, but I'm a grown man. I'm capable of making my own sandwich if I get hungry."

He took me by the shoulders and turned me to face the hall, probably guessing (correctly, as it turned out) my bedroom was in that direction. "Seriously, Kate, *go*. What are you afraid of—that I'm going to mess up your house?"

"No, of course not. Not like there's much left to trash."

"That's what I'm sayin'. Can you go now, please? Noddy will help me fix up the place."

The guilt threatened to overwhelm me. "Oh, please don't! You're my guest. It's bad enough I'm deserting you. At least relax, read a book, or something."

He looked at the once-fine library now lying shredded at his feet, but wisely refrained from saying anything. "How many times did you save my butt in China?"

The corners of my mouth twitched. "Too many to count."

"Exactly. So will you get out of here and let me sweep your kitchen floor, please?"

"Since you put it that way, the broom's in the closet by the front door. I warn you, though—Noddy's not much for housework. He has a tendency to sleep on the job."

Nostradamus chose that moment to meow indignantly at me, which cracked Jackson up. There had been so many instances of uncanny timing with that cat that I was convinced he understood English.

"That's right. You tell her, Noddy. We'll show her. That tail is perfect for dusting."

I pretended to look horrified. "Don't you dare!"

He pointed to the hallway. "Good night, Kate."

"If the—"

"If the doomed doctor of doom shows up, I will kick his transparent ass, as established. And then yes, I will wake you. Now *good night*."

As much as I appreciated the humor, I worried that Jackson wasn't taking this seriously enough. I needed to warn him about the doctor, who was the most powerful spirit I'd ever encountered. I'd never experienced a soul that dark. There would be no point appealing to his better nature, as the doctor didn't have one. "Jackson, there's something—"

"Good night, Kate."

Oh, hell. I'd tell him on the flight.

~ CHAPTER SEVEN ~

MIDNIGHT CAME FAR TOO SOON. When I slammed my hand down on the alarm, I heard a muffled snort from across the room. Startled, I turned on the lamp, nervous about what I'd find. Thankfully, it wasn't the mad doctor or even the women from the spirit board, but Jackson sprawled out on my little reading chair. Noddy was doing his best to be a lap kitty, even though his back legs and head dangled over the side.

Though still tired—I was too sleep-deprived for a few hours of shut-eye to be enough—I felt more rested than I had in weeks, and now I knew why. "Jackson?" I kept my voice low, slightly above a whisper, so as not to startle him. His eyes flew open anyway.

"What's wrong?"

"Nothing. Except that we've got to be on the road in less than an hour."

He stretched his arms over his head, careful not to jostle the cat. "How'd you sleep?"

"Wonderfully, thanks to you. Please tell me you didn't spend the entire night in that chair." I'd fallen in love with it and its deep purple chintz when I'd seen it in Hildy's, but it turned out the ancients knew nothing about comfort. As a result, I mostly used it as a clothes hanger.

"I thought I should be here for you. In case…" His eyes flicked to the scar on my neck, which was a souvenir from another demonstrative ghost. "You know, just in case."

"I appreciate it, Jacks, but we've shared a bed before. I trust you. I probably wouldn't have even woken up. Wait a minute—that sounds bad. Scratch that."

He grinned, an embarrassed little smile. "That was a long time ago, though. I didn't want to make assumptions."

There would have been a nice symmetry to it. I'd used my presence to protect Jackson from Yuèhai at night, as he would have used his as a shield against the mad doctor. "Well, thanks. That was sweet of you. How are you feeling?"

"A bit stiff," he admitted, tilting his head to one shoulder and then the other. "Wait, that sounds bad too. Maybe we should stop talking."

"We have to hustle as it is. Laura's going to be here soon."

And, with her usual impeccable timing, my friend rang the doorbell. Sensing his favorite visitor had arrived, Nostradamus shot out of Jackson's lap as if the demons of hell were after him.

"Oof. What's going on?"

"Laura's here." I pulled a robe over my nightshirt as I hurried down the hall. "Be nice."

Jackson followed close behind. "What do you mean, 'be nice'? I'm *always* nice."

I opened the door.

"Oh," he said. "I see what you mean."

Giving him a slap on the arm, I gestured for Laura to come inside. After returning my hug, she treated Jackson to her patented once-over. It was the kind of look men often give women but are never comfortable receiving. I could almost feel Jackson squirm.

"So this is the guy you've been telling me about. He does have a gorgeous aura, doesn't he?"

"You tell me," I said. "You're the one who can see it."

"You can see my aura? What color is it?"

The man I'd met in China would have laughed at the idea of auras, but from the way Jackson's eyes lit up, I could tell he was genuinely interested. That interest quickly turned indignant at Laura's answer.

"It's a lovely shade of pink. It looks wonderful with your skin tone."

"Laura!" I hoped Jackson wouldn't be offended, but he didn't so much as blink.

"Are you trying to say I'm…a little limp in the wrist?"

I released the breath I'd been holding, glad he'd stayed on this side of political correctness. Well, as politically correct as Jackson got. Laura was what she referred to as a "sexual free spirit," but I'd only ever seen her date women.

"Not at all! Why are men so threatened by pink? The whole pink-blue thing is just a societal convention, you know." She smiled at him, looking like an extra from *The Lord of the Rings* with her blonde braids, which were heavily decorated with feathers and beads. "But you can relax. A pink aura means you're romantic, loving, and loyal. You're also a healer and a great communicator. Pink people are social butterflies and they're often gifted writers."

"Seriously?" He looked over at me. "That's pretty cool."

I nodded. "Yeah, it is." Laura frolicked in New Age fields where I dared not venture, and her aura reading could be eerily accurate. She also knew how to flatter the hell out of people—a necessary skill when one wanted to get paid.

"You're what I call a freedom fighter, speaking out

against injustice, poverty, and inequality. You strive to make the world a better place and will make personal sacrifices in pursuit of this ideal."

"Wow," Jackson said.

"Wow is right." I rolled my eyes. "Don't you think you're laying it on a little thick?"

"I could add that all that self-righteousness also makes you a strong-willed, stubborn pain in the ass." She winked at Jackson, and I was happy to see they were already getting along. Most people didn't know what to make of Laura, with her talk of auras and her buckskin-vest-and-peasant-dress ensembles, although those who came of age in the '60s loved her. The most common thing her friends said to her was, "I used to think you were weird," to which Laura always laughed and replied, "But I *am!*"

"No, no, that's okay. You can keep it the way it was. I liked that better."

"Thanks a lot, Laura. Now his ego is going to be so inflated there won't be room for me on the plane."

Jackson raised his hands in surrender. "Is that any way to talk to the guy who cleaned your house? Give me a break, woman."

I'd been in such a hurry to let Laura in that I hadn't noticed. Words failed me. It was spotless. Somehow, he'd made it look better than it had before the doctor's tantrum. "I stand corrected. You are more than worthy of your pink aura. Thank you so much, Jackson."

"That's better." He smirked, a dimple appearing in his cheek. "I feel redeemed."

And, just because I couldn't resist ribbing him a little, I added, "I think we should call you Pinky from now on."

He pretended to lunge at me before returning his

attention to Laura. "What color's her aura, brown?"

"Nope." My friend shook her head, sending beads, feathers, and braids swinging. "Kate has the bluest aura I've ever seen. You are in the company of an amazing person."

"Pink and blue, hey?" Jackson slung an arm around my neck. "There you go. We were made for each other."

☾

For the first time since our reunion, there wasn't a hint of a smile in Jackson's eyes, no flicker of warmth when he looked at me. We were sitting in the cozy English-style pub not far from our hotel in Venice, awaiting our second plate of cicchetti—tapas, Venetian-style.

"Is there any reason you decided to keep this from me?"

In spite of the cold front he presented—I'd bet his aura wasn't so damn pink now—I decided to risk a lame joke. Jackson was big on lightening the mood; perhaps it would work on him too. "What, how good the food is?"

"Not funny, Kate. Why didn't you tell me about Poveglia?"

I *had* told him about Poveglia, of course. Its ugly history, which got uglier the more I researched it. But that wasn't what he meant. "Because I didn't think it would be a problem once we were here."

It had been a miserable day. Jetlagged and drenched (we'd expected snow but not rain), we'd wandered the confusing streets of Venice, trying to find someone to take us to Poveglia. After receiving nothing but blank looks from the locals, Jackson finally wrote the name of the island on the back of a receipt. That helped tremendously—now we got refusals instead of puzzled expressions.

After hours of *"Why would you want to go there?"* or *"It is forbidden to go to the island"* or, memorably, the old man who'd shaken his fist at us and called us fascists for reasons unknown, Jackson had had enough. Not me. In spite of my fears for Lily, I couldn't help but be smitten by how charming and beautiful Venice was, even in the rain: its ancient cobblestone streets, the grandeur of St. Mark's Square and its astonishing population of pigeons, the gondoliers guiding their boats through green water.

"We'll find someone who will take us. Don't worry."

The waitress arrived with the cicchetti, slamming the plate down between us and rushing off before we could ask for another round. It was too soon to call, but so far Venice's restaurants had featured either gracious male waiters who provided a level of customer service I'd never before experienced, or bitter-seeming waitresses who greeted you with the same enthusiasm they would a skin rash. The contrast struck me as bizarre—perhaps men were tipped better? If so, it presented a chicken-or-egg scenario.

Jackson folded his arms, ignoring the food entirely, a sure sign he was upset. "And what if we don't?"

The day's difficulties had surprised me as well. I'd figured we'd find a local with a boat who could get us close enough for me to coax Lily away from the doctor without putting myself in jeopardy. The wall of resistance we'd faced had been completely unexpected. "We will," I assured him. "Ghost hunters have spent the night on Poveglia. Obviously there's a way to get there. We just haven't found it yet."

"Maybe they had their own boat. Or maybe their visit happened before it was private property. Face it, Kate. We're screwed."

It wasn't like him to give up so easily. The Jackson I knew was not a quitter, and I told him so, aware that the diners around us were listening to our argument with amusement. Not that they had much choice. The restaurant's lounge was the size of a changing room.

He rubbed his eyes and sighed. "You're right; I'm sorry. I don't understand what my problem is today. I think it's just—those people throwing roadblocks in our path, it brings back bad memories. It's like Harold all over again."

A lot of the tension left my shoulders. I reached for his hand across the table, relieved when he accepted mine without hesitation. Harold had caused a lot of problems for Jackson in China, but it had never occurred to me to equate that with what was happening in Venice.

"While you were sleeping on the plane, I did some reading about this doctor, and he was a bad dude, a really bad dude. Every time someone else said, 'You can't go to the island'"—Jackson raised his voice in a mocking falsetto—"I felt like shaking them, telling them they were condemning that girl to death. But of course they wouldn't have had a clue what I was talking about."

My breath caught in my throat, and I slipped a hand into my pocket for the hundredth time, caressing the reassuring form of my inhaler. I'd been flirting with an asthma attack all day. "Lily isn't going to die, Jacks. Don't even say that."

More than ever, I longed to return to our hotel and see if I could connect with her. I'd wanted to do that the second we checked in, but Jackson thought we should arrange a ride to the island first. As it turned out, he was probably right. It was clear to me now that figuring out that part was going to take a while.

"Sorry." He rubbed his forehead, and I noticed how exhausted he looked. I wondered if he was getting one of his migraines. "But what if he's hurting her? I hate that we're sitting here, helpless. I *hate* it."

"Me too. I honestly didn't think it would be this hard. I thought there would be fishermen everywhere, hoping to make some extra euros. We'll figure it out, though, Jacks. We'll have a good meal, get some sleep, and try again in the morning. Everything will seem better when we're well rested and have some food in us."

"You're probably right; you usually are." He reached for one of the little crostini, which were topped with some kind of white fish. "I just hope we're not too late."

"Would you stop it? You're starting to freak me out. The doctor thinks Lily is his patient, remember? Killing her wouldn't further his research. He wants to study her."

Jackson raised an eyebrow at me. "You know how he treats his patients. What if he lobotomizes her? What then? Christ, Kate, he's a butcher."

I gazed at my crumb-specked plate, no longer hungry. "I know," I whispered. What happened if Lily's soul was tortured or somehow altered during a sinister operation? This was uncharted territory for me. I'd helped many clients who'd been injured by angry spirits, but never before had a client's *soul* been in jeopardy. My expertise was limited to the souls of the dead. I had no idea how to help those of the living.

"Excuse me."

A woman leaned in from the table adjacent, clearing her throat to get our attention. She was young—I guessed her to be in her early twenties—and classic Italian: curvy, beautiful, and impeccably dressed. Jackson had been right to put some effort into his appearance. I'd spent a total of fifteen minutes gathering the bare essentials for this trip, and as a result had felt like a hideous slob ever since we'd left the airport. In Italy, the purses matched the shoes, which matched the gloves. Hell, half the time they even matched the Vespa. "Forgive me. I did not mean to interrupt your conversation, but did you say you wanted to go to Poveglia?" Her accent made the island sound lovely.

"We do. Do you know how we can get there?" The optimism had returned to Jackson's voice, and he sat up straighter, but perhaps that was more in deference to the interloper's stunning good looks.

The woman smiled, displaying blindly perfect teeth. "Yes, I do. My father-in-law has a boat. He'll be happy to take you. He was the Paranormal Detectives' driver."

Jackson's eyes met mine, and I could see how excited he was. The Paranormal Detectives had spent a night on the island filming their experiences, which mostly consisted of jumping at shadows and farting to freak each other out. "He's not afraid?" I asked.

We'd discovered the rumors about the Venetians' fear of the island had not been exaggerated. If I had to watch another fisherman cross himself while muttering "*Maledetto,*" I'd probably kill somebody myself.

The woman shook her head so her dark curls bounced. "No, not at all. My father-in-law is a very brave man. Besides, the stories about Poveglia are just that, only stories told to scare children."

My experience with the good ol' Doctor of Death told me this wasn't the case, but I let her comment ride. I didn't have the energy to try and change anyone's mind, assuming such a thing was possible.

"That would be great. We really need to get to the island tomorrow. Do you think your father-in-law would be available in the morning?"

I shot Jackson a look. *What is he doing? We don't know anything about this woman.*

"I don't see why not, but let me check." Hitting a button on her smartphone, she held up her index finger in the universal gesture for *Give me a minute, you impatient Americans.*

Jackson beamed at me, oblivious to the fact that I wanted to strangle him. All traces of his sour mood gone, he proceeded to inhale half of our cicchetti platter while our new friend chattered on her phone.

"*Io non lo so, padre. Fammi controllare.*" She leaned over to us again, but this time her full attention was on Jackson. "Where are you staying?"

He glanced over at me. Oh, so *now* I was important. I affected a world-weary sigh. "The Hotel Gatto Nero."

After a moment, she turned to us with a smile. "Perfect. Your hotel has a door on the canal. Papa will pull his boat right next to it. He can be there at seven o'clock. Is that early enough?"

"That would be awesome. You've really gotten us out of a tight spot; thank you." Jackson finally appeared to notice my lack of enthusiasm. He looked at me sideways. "Kate, isn't that awesome?"

"Yes." I forced a smile that felt like a snarl. "It's awesome."

~ CHAPTER EIGHT ~

LILY DIDN'T STOP RUNNING UNTIL her feet bled. She'd left the hospital far behind, and for the past twenty minutes had been fighting through thick brush. She paused for a moment, surrounded by vegetation, and listened hard. All she could hear was her own breathing, which was comforting. Dead people didn't need to breathe, right?

The moon was full, so it had been easy enough to navigate before she'd slipped into the overgrowth. Not that she had any idea where she was going, or even where she was. Her eyes had acquired a strange double vision, and by experimenting she discovered she saw something different with each one. To her left eye, it looked like she stood on a well-kept lawn bordered by hedges, but through her right eye she could see the tangle of vicious, overgrown weeds. The realization frightened her. She'd never had problems with her eyes before. Unlike most kids her age, she didn't even need glasses. Her surroundings were so creepy when viewed through her right eye that she tied a strip of cloth from her hospital gown around that side of her face. Without the double vision, it was much easier to walk.

"*Ti sei perso?*"

Lily jumped, a small cry escaping before she could clap her hands over her mouth. She turned to see a little girl with dark ringlets standing behind her. Between the curls and the rosebud mouth, she was a living doll.

"I'm sorry I scared you," the child apologized in Italian. "Are you lost?"

Was she lost? Yes, but not in any way the girl was likely to understand. "Can you tell me where I am?" She was ashamed of her own Italian, which lacked the melodic lilt of the child's. *I'm out of practice.* Her cheeks warmed as she remembered the many instances she'd gotten frustrated with Nonna.

"We're in A-MER-I-CA. Can't you speak-a de English?"

Lily's mother had been horrified and threatened to take away her smartphone for the entire year, but Nonna had only shaken her head, this sad smile on her face. "One day, you will learn the value of your heritage, *mia figlia.* Then you will be happy me and Nonno teach you *italiano.*"

If she'd known Nonna's prediction would come true so soon, she would have paid more attention.

The girl wrinkled her brow, managing to look even more adorable in her confusion. "You are in Poveglia."

"Po-veal-ya?" The name meant nothing to her, which must have shown on her face.

"It's an island, but it's part of Venice. That's where I'm from." She stared into space as if she could see Venice through the trees. Though the sky was tinged with the palest of pinks as the sun began to rise, Lily doubted the girl could see anything but forest.

"Are you here to see the doctor?" Lily asked. This girl had both her eyes and tongue, thank God, but that didn't necessarily mean anything. Perhaps she was a new arrival too.

She was surprised by how relieved she felt when the girl shook her head, sending her curls bouncing around her shoulders. "Not *him*. We do not have anything to do with him. Me and my mamma, we live on the other side of the island." The girl put her hands on her hips. "You are not with him, are you?"

Unsure how to explain to a child—a child who spoke Italian, no less—that she was trapped in this situation against her will, Lily settled for, "I used to be, but I ran away. He's a bad man."

The girl nodded so hard Lily feared her little head would pop right off her neck. "He is. A very bad man. We stay away from him." She glanced in the direction Lily had run. "This is not a good place to hide. You are not so very far away. He will find you."

The idea of being under his control again made Lily's pulse quicken. *Calm down. You have to think clearly. You're still here, and he is not.* "I'm Lily. What's your name?"

"I am Maria." She held out a pudgy hand for Lily to shake.

Of course you are. Could you be any more Italian? "Nice to meet you, Maria. Do you know a better place to hide? Somewhere I will be safe from him?"

"Follow me. You will come stay with us on the other side of Poveglia. The bad man will not be able to hurt you there."

She's seen the horrific results of his "treatment" then. She understands what I'm up against. Taking a deep breath, Lily accepted the girl's hand and was startled by how determinedly Maria led her through the bush. She had to bob and weave to avoid the clutching branches.

"Bad man hurt your eye?"

Lily had been concentrating so hard on not maiming herself that she'd forgotten the strip of cloth. She wasn't sure how to explain it, and settled for agreeing that, yes, the bad man had hurt her eye. It was close enough to the truth. He was certainly responsible. After all, he *had* brought her here.

To Poveglia, wherever the hell that was. What she couldn't figure out was *why*.

Maria stopped so abruptly that Lily tripped over her. The little girl, who was a lot sturdier than she looked, didn't appear to notice. She turned to Lily with a solemn expression on her face. "Can you run?"

Lily's bruised and battered feet called out an immediate protest. But she nodded, ignoring them. "Why?"

"This is the most dangerous part." Maria straightened her shoulders, as if bracing herself. "In here, no one can see us, but once we leave the woods, everyone can. *He* can see us."

Lily's stomach curled itself into a hard knot. "I thought you were taking me to a good hiding place. I thought he couldn't hurt us there?"

"I am. But we have to cross the field first, and the field is dangerous. Are you ready to run? It will be daylight soon. We have to hurry. *Andiamo!*"

The girl burst into the clearing with Lily following close behind. Maria was a blur, sprinting so fast Lily was afraid she'd lose her. Her lungs burned. When she got home, she was definitely going to take up jogging. And she'd thought she was in good shape! Nothing more humbling than having a little kid kick your ass.

A wooden bridge came into view, and Maria headed

for it at full tilt, head down. Standing on the other side of a canal was a tall woman. She beckoned to Maria, urging her on. Afraid she would be left behind, Lily willed new speed into her legs. She was only partly successful, but at last she reached the bridge where the woman waited with Maria, holding the child close to her side. When Lily met her eyes, the woman smiled, and waved her over the same way she had with the little girl.

Lily put her hand on the bridge's wooden rail—and stopped. Her bleeding foot hovered in the air. Frowning, she looked at Maria again. The girl gestured at her with both hands, screaming at her to hurry with an urgency that was almost theatrical. But there was something very wrong on the other side of the bridge. She could feel it, and her instincts were screaming louder than Maria.

The girl's eyes widened. She pointed at something over Lily's shoulder. "He comes! The bad man! Run, Lily, *run.*"

The uncomfortable prickling sensation she got when someone was watching her—it was like that, but so much worse. With a sinking heart, Lily turned to see the doctor closing the distance between them, fury plain on his face. As soon as he saw she was aware of him, he began to yell. Her treatment was to begin today; she mustn't leave him now; didn't she know how sick she was?

The woman opened her arms to Lily. Making a split-second decision, Lily ran across the bridge, doing her best to disregard the dread that threatened to crush her. Maria threw her arms around Lily's legs, while the woman placed a gentle hand on her shoulder.

"Welcome. I am Alessandra, Maria's mother."

"You are safe now, Lily. You are safe. The bad man can't get you." Maria pulled back from her, her rosebud mouth pursed in a pout. "But why, why did you stop running? I thought we would lose you. I was so scared."

How could she explain it? Lily didn't understand it herself. There was nothing sinister on this side of the canal to account for her dread, unless it had been her instincts warning of the doctor's approach. She really hoped Maria was right about his not being able to get to her, since the fact that she'd crossed the bridge hadn't slowed him down. *What if he has some rights to me, since he's the one who brought me here?* It was too terrible to contemplate. In any case, it was too late to do anything about it now.

The doctor gripped the railing on either side of the bridge. Lily cried out, unable to help it, but Maria took her hand again.

"Don't worry. He cannot hurt you here."

Lily was about to say that if that was true, the doctor didn't appear to be aware of it, but just then the man stepped onto the bridge. The air hummed with electricity, lifting Lily's hair. There was a loud zap from the other end of the bridge and the doctor fell backward, wincing. He retreated a few steps, shaking his hands as if he'd touched a hot stove.

"Please, Lily. I am your physician. I wish to help you, to heal you." He pointed at Maria and her mother. "These people are evil. You do not realize what they want from you. They will rob you of your soul. I only wanted to help you."

"We are *not* evil," Maria shrieked, her face flushed. "*You* are the evil one, always hurting people. You are a bad man."

"Don't listen to his madness, daughter. You know he is capable of nothing but lies," Alessandra said, resting a hand on her child's shoulder again. Her touch seemed to relax the girl, though Maria continued to shout at the doctor.

"Lily is *our* friend. You will not hurt her. You better stay away from her. Go *away!*"

The doctor held up his hands in defeat. "Fine, fine. I will go." He addressed his last words to Lily. "I hope you understand what you are doing. I hope they have been honest with you."

He left, but the dread that shriveled her insides did not. For an insane moment, she had the urge to run after him, to beg him not to leave her. *What's wrong with me? Why am I freaking out?*

It had to be a delayed reaction to seeing the blinded person in the hospital, because there was nothing to fear anymore. Maria had saved her. From what, Lily wasn't yet sure, but she was certain the doctor had planned something horrible for her treatment. Would he have torn out her own eyes and tongue? She shuddered.

Alessandra patted her arm. Her touch was as light as butterfly wings. Lily could barely feel it, but her sense of impending doom vanished. "You'll be all right now, don't worry. Please don't pay his words any heed." She sighed, looking past Lily toward the woods. "He's done terrible things to innocent people—terrible, terrible things. He's tortured so many."

"He's a *bad* man."

Alessandra smiled at the girl, smoothing her curls back from her reddened face. "Maria has tried to rescue his patients countless times. She brings them here, but the poor dears, they can hardly walk, and then when they get here, they can't cross." She peered at Lily, studying her face. "You're the first one who was able to cross the bridge. You must be very special."

Yeah, aren't I the popular one. Lily didn't want any of it. Maria's theatrics, though adorable, were already wearing thin, and Alessandra's curiosity made her uncomfortable. There was an expression on the woman's face she didn't care for at all. She didn't quite know the right word for it, but if she had, it would have been *shrewd.* All Lily knew was that Maria's mother was not the simple, honest woman she'd appeared to be at first.

Her doubts melted away when Alessandra gently tilted Lily's face toward the rising sun. "We were too late. He has already hurt you, I see." She *tsk-tsked* under her breath. "Did he take your eye?"

The thought made Lily cringe. "No, it's just hurt. I think it will be fine later."

God, I hope so. If it stays like this, I can't…I can't even.

"We can have our own healer take a look at it, if you like. In any case, that dressing will need to be changed. It's quite dirty, and dirt is our enemy, isn't it, Maria?"

Maria bobbed her head. "Dirt breeds *disease.*"

What an odd thing for a little girl to say, Lily thought. But then again, Maria *was* odd. No, that was unkind. She was unusual. She looked like something out of a storybook, and her Italian was very formal, like the doctor's. Lily struggled to understand both Maria and her mother, but they didn't have a problem understanding her. Perhaps Venice had its own dialect, and that accounted for the difference Lily was hearing.

Alessandra's words sunk in.

"There's a doctor here?" *And where was* here, *exactly?* All she could see around them were cultivated fields, as if they were standing on the outskirts of an abandoned farm. Everything had happened too fast for her to think, but she'd assumed Maria and her mother were escapees from the hospital who were hiding out on this side of the bridge. Somehow they had figured out a way to electrify it so they could control who crossed. Lily wondered why the doctor hadn't waded across the canal. It didn't look that deep.

"Of course. There are many skilled people in our village. But you, you are truly special." Alessandra gave Lily a one-armed hug that put her fears to rest again. "You are the first visitor we've had in quite some time."

How long have they been living here? Why don't they go home? Lily's mind raced. Maria had said she was from Venice. If Poveglia was a Venetian island, surely Venice proper couldn't be that far away. *Why haven't they built a raft, or—*

Alessandra slipped a hand into hers and Lily's mind cleared. She supposed it didn't matter. Maria and her mother were here, and they had saved her from the evil doctor; that was all she needed to know. Holding her hand and Maria's, Alessandra led them across the field.

"Mama, is Lily an angel?"

The question caught Lily so off guard she snorted with laughter, but when she saw the earnest expression on the little girl's face, she choked it back. The last thing she wanted was to hurt Maria's feelings. It hadn't been that long since she'd been that age, and she remembered well how it felt to be belittled and snickered at by adults who kept saying how "cute" you were. How many times had she yelled, "I'm not cute; I'm SERIOUS!" in a desperate attempt to make the grown-ups listen to her? Too many to count.

Alessandra smiled. "She looks like one, doesn't she? But I'm pretty sure she's a human girl, just like you. Only a little older."

Maria craned her head to look into Lily's eye. "I really hoped you were an angel."

"Why?"

"So you could take us home."

~ CHAPTER NINE ~

JACKSON PULLED OFF HIS TRAINERS and tossed them so they bounced off the wall.

"Shh! Do you want to wake the people next door?"

He glared at me. "It's eight o'clock."

"So? Maybe people go to bed early here."

Thus far, the opposite seemed true. The streets of Venice came alive at night. When the moon rose I could see why Venice was considered one of the most romantic places in the world. But, as my mother would say, logic has no place in a good argument.

"Would you mind telling me what your problem is?"

My blood pressure, already spiking, soared. "I don't have one."

He rolled his eyes. "Yeah, I can tell. You've been snapping and snarling at me since we left the restaurant. I thought you'd be happy."

"And why would you think that?" *You arrogant, egotistical prick.* How could I have thought he was cute? Now I wished he were still wearing that ridiculous scarf so I could choke him with it.

"Christ, Kate. We couldn't get to the island. We were screwed. And then, out of nowhere, comes this nice woman—"

"Exactly," I interrupted. "Out of nowhere. Who is this person, and why does she want to help us? What's in it for her?"

Jackson stared at me like I was someone he didn't recognize. I didn't recognize myself at the moment, but his expression of disbelief just made me angrier.

"I don't know…maybe she's a nice person? Who wants to help others because, I don't know, she's nice? Maybe it's no more complicated than that."

"She gives me the creeps, okay? I don't like her." Once I'd vocalized my innermost thoughts, I was embarrassed. But there it was, the truth. Jackson would have to take it or leave it.

"That's pathetic. Really pathetic." He shook his head as if he'd never been so disappointed in his life. The guy would be lucky to survive the night at this rate. "I expected more from you."

"Sorry to disappoint you." Venom dripped from my words. "But it's how I feel. There's something about this chick that isn't on the level, all right?"

"And I suppose this bad juju has nothing to do with the fact that she's a fox? Gimme a break."

"It's not like that." Although I had felt a twinge when Jackson flirted with her and I'd wanted to jab my fork into her hand when she'd flirted back. *What's wrong with me?* I'm not normally this insecure. "I have a bad feeling, that's all. Don't you think it's odd she happened to appear just when we were talking about not being able to get to Poveglia?"

Jackson sighed, crossing our tiny room to sit on the bed beside me. I had to give him credit for not bitching about the accommodations. Not every guy would be comfortable staying in a room that belonged in a fairy-tale palace. Cutesy gilded details were everywhere. Secretly, I loved it. "That's how it works. Come on, Kate. You've traveled a lot. The weird way things always pan out? It happens all the time when you're a tourist. You must have experienced it too. Not to go all 'woo woo' on you, but it's kind of…magic."

"Of course I've experienced it before. But this feels different. I'm not sure why, so I can't explain it, but trust me that it does."

It *was* magical how everything fell into place once you'd made that leap of faith and put your trust in the kindness of strangers. When you were hopelessly lost, you'd get directions. When you were starving, you'd be offered a meal. When your purse was stolen and you were in tears, a family would insist on treating you to a bowl of homemade goulash before taking you to the police station. It was the same the world over, leading me to believe that the true currency of travelers everywhere was blind faith.

But this wasn't magic. I'd told Jackson the truth. Something was off, but I couldn't put my finger on what it was, so it was nothing I could define. What if I was wrong, though? What if this was more of what I'd felt when I'd heard Destiny giggle over the phone? Keeping things professional with Jackson was a lot more difficult than I'd expected.

I wished I had Laura's abilities. Jackson seemed to believe that jazz about auras. What if I just told him the chick's aura had bright yellow hazard signs all over it? Would he take me seriously then? Probably not.

He opened his mouth again, but I made a frustrated

sound, a cross between a huff and a sigh, before he could say something dumb or offensive. "Didn't Destiny ever tell you about women's intuition?"

"Uh, Destiny and I didn't do a lot of talking." Jackson's smirk left no doubt as to what he meant. "And I'm beginning to think that's a blessing."

Seizing the closest decorative pillow, I beat him over the head with it. Soon we were laughing again. How could I have ever thought we'd make a good couple? We were like brother and sister, for Chrissake.

He covered his head with both hands, rolling onto his side. "Okay, that's enough—stop. *Stop.*"

I hit him a few more times anyway. It was a great stress release. When he said, "Shh, you'll wake the people next door," I lost it. Falling onto the bed beside him, I giggled until my stomach hurt. If we kept this up, we'd get kicked out for sure.

"You're really beautiful right now."

Turning my head to the side, I saw him looking at me with admiration. The laughter died in my throat. "Cut it out."

Jackson smiled, counting on those dimples of his to get him out of trouble. "What? You *are.*"

Damn it, Jacks. I sat up, feeling the anger bubbling in my chest again, and whacked him with another pillow. This one had decorative buttons on it, and I heard the click they made against his thick skull.

"Ouch! What was that for? Can't a guy give a woman a compliment anymore?"

"Other guys can, but you can't."

"Why not?"

"Because Destiny, that's why." Seeing his wounded

expression pissed me off enough to give him another clout with the pillow. He caught my wrist before I could connect.

"Stop, seriously. That one actually hurts."

"You're lucky I didn't use the one with the tassels."

"What's going on, Kate?" He kept hold of my hand, looking into my eyes. "You're playing, but you're not playing. You're seriously pissed at me, aren't you?"

I yanked my hand from his. "Give the guy a diploma."

"But why? Things were great when I got to Vermont. What changed? Was it the scarf?"

Damn him for always knowing how to defuse me. "No, it wasn't the scarf. The scarf was pretty awesome."

"Then what is it? Be honest with me. We've been friends too long to bullshit each other."

It was on the tip of my tongue to say we hadn't been friends that long, but then I realized we had. Not in terms of time, but in what we'd been through. Jackson and I had experienced a lifetime together.

"I—I just…" Avoiding his eyes, I focused on a tassel, twirling it around my fingers. "I didn't think you were that kind of guy."

He lifted my chin, forcing me to face him. "You didn't think I was *what* kind of guy?"

"You know, a player."

Jackson dropped my chin and reared back in mock astonishment. "White girl did not just call me a *playa*."

Nothing calms a woman down more than having a man mock her. "What would you call it?"

Chuckling, he shook his head. "This thing with Destiny isn't what you think."

I leapt from the bed, clapping my hands over my ears. "If

you're going to tell me it's just sex, I don't want to hear it. And, just so you know, that won't do you any favors."

"Kate, Destiny is a friend of Roxi's."

"Roxi, your sister?"

"Roxi, my *baby* sister."

"Ugh. That's even worse." I had the urge to hit him again. Where was that pillow?

Jackson pinned my arms to my sides before I could grab another weapon. "You're not understanding me. She's a friend of my sister's, and that's *all* she is."

I stopped struggling. "You're not dating her?"

"God, no. Did you hear all that giggling the night you called? A dude can only take so much."

My mind raced. I still found it difficult to believe. "Why did you say you were in a relationship with her, then?"

He arched an eyebrow at me. "Girl, I did not say anything of the kind; you assumed it. I just didn't correct you."

"But why?"

"I don't know. Maybe because being unavailable makes a guy irresistible." His dimples deepened.

Bastard. The next thing I hit him with wouldn't be a pillow. "You don't seriously believe that crap."

"Crap, hey? Is that so? Let's consider the facts for a moment. One minute, I hadn't heard from you in months—"

"Weeks." *Shit, had it really been months?*

"And the next, you're begging me to come see you."

"You jerk. You know damn well I was calling you about this job *before* I heard about Destiny."

He shrugged, releasing my arms. "Why quibble over semantics?"

Part of me was filled with relief, something I didn't

want to acknowledge. The rest of me was staggered at the enormity of what I'd learned. Easing away from him, I stared at the bed. *One* bed. Which had been weird enough when I'd thought he was in a relationship, but now…

"Jackson."

"You're worried about the sleeping arrangements. Don't be."

Looking over at him, I felt sad, though I wasn't sure why. "How did you—"

"Hey, you may be the medium, but I'm the mind reader. At least when it comes to you."

The bed occupied so much more of the room than it had before. "This is so awkward."

"It doesn't have to be. Nothing's changed. We're friends who work together, same as before. Sharing a room saves Vittoria money and gives you some protection in case the Doctor of Doom comes back."

"Doctor of Death."

"Whatever. Nothing's changed, Kate." He paused, before giving me a look that left no doubt as to his true feelings. "Although we were a lot more than friends in China."

The night I'd relived a million times and tried equally hard to forget came back to me. My cheeks caught fire. "That was different." When we'd returned to our hotel room that night in China, we were emotionally drained. We'd both needed comfort, and it was only natural we'd turn to each other, especially after what we'd been through.

"Different for *you*, maybe."

"Jacks—"

He held up his hand. "I don't want to hear it. Please don't give me the 'friends' speech. I'm feeling very fragile right now. Destiny and I just split up; I can only be dumped once in a day."

Wandering over to the luggage rack, he rummaged in his duffel, withdrawing a leather toiletry case. "In any case, I'm going to crash. If we're not going to take Sophia's father-in-law up on his kind offer, we've got some running around to do tomorrow. Either way, it's going to be a long day."

As I watched him walk away, I wondered what the hell was wrong with me. "Jackson?"

He turned at the bathroom door, looking surprisingly weary. "What is it, babes?"

"I hope you know it's—it's not that I don't like you. Because obviously I do. But you live in Minneapolis; I'm in Vermont. I can't stand the city, but the country bores you to tears."

"Like I said before, Kate—why quibble over semantics?"

Before I could respond, he went into the bathroom, closing the door behind him.

~ CHAPTER TEN ~

NOT SURPRISINGLY, I COULDN'T SLEEP. I listened as our next-door neighbors returned in the early morning hours, giggling and murmuring to each other. Guess there had been no danger of us keeping *them* awake.

Their merriment was actually a welcome diversion. Once they'd settled down, I went back to listening to the sound of Jackson's watch, which I could hear from across the room.

Tick tick tick.

I'd been worried that I'd hurt his feelings, but when Jackson had emerged from the bathroom in his pajama bottoms, he'd acted like nothing had happened. And I'd let him. *Why had I let him? What was wrong with me?*

Groaning, I buried my face in my pillow. There was no point dwelling on this now. It was irresponsible to even *think* about this now, with God knows what happening to Lily, and the girl's parents probably half-sick with the stress. Picturing Vittoria cradling her daughter's doll-like body, I forced myself to refocus. That was the important thing: Lily, not whatever was or wasn't happening between Jackson and me. We could deal with it later, on the flight or, well—later.

That decided, I swung my legs over the mattress.

"Can't sleep either, huh?" Jackson asked.

"No."

"I didn't mean for us to get into this stuff now. I know we have a job to do."

"Yeah. Can I turn on the light?"

"Go for it."

Blinking as my eyes adjusted, I brushed the sleep away to see Jackson lying with his arms over his face, blocking the glare from the lamp. I had the strongest desire to leap on top of him and show him exactly what I thought of this stupid "friends" idea, but that would mean breaking the promise I'd made to myself. Instead I reluctantly stuck to my original plan—getting the spirit board from my luggage.

"I'm going to see if I can connect with Lily."

This interested him enough to sit up. His eyes widened when he saw the old board, and for a second I wondered if he had noticed the circle of women too, but of course he couldn't see them. Jackson was a man of many gifts, but he didn't have The Gift.

"You don't normally need that stuff, do you?"

I brought the spirit board to bed with me, thrusting my legs back under the covers. The room was cold enough to keep gelati from melting. "No, but everything's different with Lily, since she isn't dead. To be honest, I'm not sure this will work, but it did before. I have to try."

Closing my eyes, I willed the women of the board (Lily's ancestors—by now I was sure of it) to step aside and make room for the girl, should she be willing and/or able to communicate. Retreating into the darkness, the women vanished from view. *Good.*

It took every ounce of willpower I had to lay my hands on the heart-shaped planchette. On general principle I hated these things, but this one was the worst I'd ever encountered. It smoldered with malevolence. *Ugh.* I wondered again, as I had many times before, how "mainstreamers" managed to shut off their instincts so completely that a rattlesnake could be sitting right in front of them, coiled and ready to strike, without their sensing any danger.

The wood was so worn it felt like silk under my fingers. Almost immediately I was overwhelmed with the pleas and demands of dozens upon dozens of spirits. I pushed past them like you would at a party when you've finally spotted the person you want to talk to. They faded into the shadows behind me.

Closing my eyes, I envisioned walking down a long, dark tunnel. At the end would be light and Lily—*if* I was able to reach her. I accepted this was a big if. The walls of the tunnel pressed closer, and I consciously slowed my breath to keep from panicking. Now would not be a good time to have an asthma attack. Cursing the spirit board, I stretched my arms out as far as they would go, running my hands along the sides of the tunnel to fight the sensation that the walls were collapsing in on me.

Peering through the darkness, I spotted a pinprick of light in the distance.

"Lily. Lily Walkins. Lily, can you hear me? Are you there?"

No answer. Good thing I hadn't expected this to be easy.

One foot in front of the other. *That's all you have to do, Kate. Keep walking; stay the course.*

A hideous face, twisted by hate and madness, burst out of the dark without warning.

"LOOK AT WHAT YOU'VE DONE! ARE YOU

HAPPY NOW? SHE'S GONE AND YOU ARE TO BLAME."

I cried out, using my arms to ward off whatever evil this was. Its hot breath blasted my hair back from my forehead and made me stumble.

"Kate! Kate, are you okay?"

Blinking until Jackson swam into focus, I noticed ornate ceiling tiles like petit fours shimmering above his head. *Damn it.* Whatever it was had startled me enough that I'd broken the connection. "No, I'm not. Something was in there, something hostile."

"In where? A different dimension or—" He shook his head. "Christ, I hardly understand half the shit I say when I'm with you."

I patted his hand. "Welcome to my world. I guess you can think of it as another dimension, but technically it's not. It's a safe place I create with my own mind where I can talk to spirits undisturbed. I'd hoped to talk to Lily."

"Let me get this straight. You were in some imaginary room in your head, and…you know what? Never mind. There is no understanding this."

"Be serious, will you? What happened just now has never happened before. This space I create, it's the next thing to sacred. It belongs to me. But from the start, there was something very wrong with it tonight. It was like the tunnel itself wanted to crush me. And then this thing came out of nowhere."

"Man, your normal is my living nightmare. I don't get how you deal with this shit."

"Practice. This 'shit,' as you so aptly put it, has been going on for as long as I can remember."

My earliest memory was of watching the faces that swirled

above my crib. They were speaking, telling me things, but I couldn't understand them yet. Some were scary faces that made me cry, but most pulled funny expressions to make me giggle. Mom had thought I was an unusually happy baby.

"What do you mean by 'thing?' Was it some sort of...I don't know...monster?"

I started to tell him monsters didn't exist, but then I realized that wasn't exactly true. "The only monsters are bad people, Jacks. What mainstr—what most people tend to call monsters are really just creatures we don't have a name for yet. This was most definitely human, or at least it was at some point during its life cycle. I think it was the doctor."

"Dr. Doom? What the fuck was he doing in your secret mind tunnel?"

"Good question." *And why could I understand him?* Whatever the thing was, it had spoken Italian. Sometimes it worked that way if I'd built a close connection with a spirit. The same phenomenon had allowed Jacks to understand Yuèhai and her father in China. But the idea of any bond, let alone such a close one, between the doctor and me was scary. Shared intentions were key to that kind of connection, and we wanted completely different outcomes. It didn't make any sense.

"Are you going to try again?"

Another good question. Jackson was hitting them out of the park tonight. The idea of that mad doctor assuming complete control over the girl's soul had been enough to drive me crazy, and yet...

"He said she's gone."

Jackson snorted. "Well, that's obviously bullshit."

"I don't think so. He was furious. He blamed me, said it was my fault, and I think he was telling the truth." For the first time since we'd arrived in Venice, I felt optimistic. "And that means she got away."

"How? Did you do something?"

"No, it definitely wasn't me. If she escaped, she either did it on her own or someone else helped her."

I only hoped Lily was smart enough to recognize a rattlesnake when it was right in front of her.

~ CHAPTER ELEVEN ~

LILY THOUGHT SHE WAS SEEING things at first. She was frightened enough to tug at the makeshift bandage covering her right eye, but Alessandra gently stilled her hand. Lily's fear melted into the ground below her injured feet.

"What you suspect is an illusion or a trick is real," Alessandra said. "There is nothing wrong with your vision."

Lily gasped as round, green mounds emerged from the field like giant turtle backs. Neither Alessandra nor Maria appeared to be concerned. Instead, Maria skipped toward them, letting go of her mother's hand. She twirled in the sun, singing a tune that sounded vaguely familiar.

"What are they?" Lily asked.

"That's the village." Alessandra's voice carried a hint of pride. "We make our homes with sod so they will be undetectable from a distance."

They were close enough now that Lily could see Alessandra was telling the truth. No ancient turtles slumbered in the fields. She smiled in spite of herself when she spotted the little rounded doors and windows. "Oh, how cute! They're hobbit houses."

"You are mistaken, I'm afraid. No one by that name lives

here."

Lily scrutinized Alessandra's face, expecting her to smile, but the woman remained impassive. *Oh my God—how can she not know about "The Lord of the Rings"?* Everyone *knows about it.*

Before she could explain what a hobbit was, people began to emerge from the huts. Soon a small crowd had gathered and stood watching them, waiting. Something about it gave Lily the shivers, though she realized that was silly. They were just people...what was there to be scared of? Still, she slowed her pace to a crawl, dropping farther and farther behind Alessandra until she stopped walking altogether.

The doctor's warning kept playing in her mind like an MP3 on repeat. There had to be some reason she was feeling this much anxiety.

"Lily?"

She snapped out of her reverie to find Alessandra staring at her, her brow etched with concern. "What troubles you, dear?"

"I—I..." She glanced at the rows of villagers again. With the pretty sod houses behind them, it was like a scene from a fairy tale gone wrong. *I don't know if I can trust you.* "I'm not sure I'm welcome."

Lily could tell by the skepticism on Alessandra's face that she didn't believe her for a second. The woman attempted to close the distance between them, but Lily shied away. Every time Alessandra touched her, she went into this warm and sleepy state where all was peaceful and calm. If she was going to meet the villagers, she wanted her wits about her.

She tried not to be bothered by the hurt in the older

woman's eyes. Alessandra's hand, which had been about to touch her shoulder, hovered in the air for an awkward moment. "You are more than welcome, dear. Your arrival is cause for celebration."

This only increased Lily's discomfort. "Why?"

"Well, everyone misses their children, you see. It's been a very long time since they've been allowed to go home and see their loved ones. We rarely get visitors, and over the years, we've grown weary of seeing each other's faces. Anyone new is welcome."

"I'm hardly a child." Lily straightened her shoulders, but at five foot two, she wasn't that much taller than Maria. Not to mention she'd never felt more like a child. All she wanted to do was go home and hug her mom. If she could somehow manage to be reunited with her family, she'd be such a good kid it would blow their minds. She'd never argue with her mother again. Well, at least not for a week or two.

"Lily, come! I want everyone to meet you."

Lily craned her neck to see Maria, who stood in the middle of the gathering with her hands on her hips. "Come *on*. They're waiting."

"Please, I beg of you, do not disappoint her. You're the one new friend she's made in such a long while. She looks up to you. As you will see, you are the closest to her age of anyone here."

Lily assessed the villagers and saw at once that Alessandra hadn't misled her. Maria, spinning faster and faster so her tattered dress swirled around her ankles, was the only visible child. "But I don't understand. Where are the rest of the children?"

The tall woman sagged, her face seeming to age at least

ten years. "They didn't make it, I'm afraid."

"Didn't make *what?*" Alessandra wasn't easing her nerves. A village where children were welcome but not present— it was more than a little creepy. Once again, Lily wished for her own mother, a woman who could be counted on to make pasta with butter and cheese when she was sad, or tell her a funny story when a nightmare startled her awake. At the thought of her own bed, Lily wanted to weep.

I don't want any of this. I don't want to meet the rest of them. I just want to go home.

"There was an illness on the island years ago, a terrible disease. A couple of our villagers had it, and that was all that was required for it to spread. We lost many of our people, especially our elders and our children. They were not strong enough to survive." Alessandra's voice cracked, and Lily felt guilty for doubting her.

"And Maria?"

They both watched the girl, who continued spinning in circles, her dark curls soaring behind her like a flag.

A wan smile flickered across Alessandra's face. "Maria was different. She's a fighter. Her spirit is stronger than most." The smile vanished. "Still, I do fret about her more than I should."

"She looks healthy to me." Lily had meant the comment to be reassuring, but Alessandra's frown deepened.

"Not all is as it seems. In time, you will understand."

Maybe it was the lack of sleep, but it took a moment for Alessandra's words to sink in. *A disease that kills people. That kills kids!* The doctor had insisted she was ill. Perhaps he was right. Was she already sick?

"Is the—is the disease still here? Am I in danger?"

The woman's smile, however frail, returned. "Not to fear,

dear one. We've never had a newcomer fall ill. The colony is the one at risk."

Strange. Lily had never heard of such a selective disease. Maybe it was like an allergy, where only certain people were affected.

Maria ran over to them. "Why are you standing here? People are waiting to meet you."

Her outrage made both Lily and Alessandra laugh.

"Well? Will you stay?" Alessandra asked, her dark eyes pleading.

"What are you talking about? Of course she's going to stay! She's my friend. Right, Lily? You are my friend, right?"

The anxiousness on the little girl's face made Lily feel ashamed. What was wrong with her? Maria and her mother were the first kind people she'd met since she'd arrived. There was no reason for her to be suspicious. Maybe her father was right; maybe she was becoming a "dreaded teenager."

Maria held her hand toward Lily and she took it without hesitation, resolving not to be such a jerk in the future. "All right, I'll stay. At least until I can figure out how to get home."

☾

The cooking fire wavered in front of her. Lily rubbed her good eye and blinked, but her vision refused to clear.

The circle of people sitting around her was a blur as well. At least if she went blind, she wasn't doomed to wander alone. The villagers had been every bit as welcoming as Alessandra had promised. Many of the women even hugged her. And Lily, who hadn't let her mother embrace her in weeks, let herself be hugged. It was nice to be part of a group that was genuinely happy to see her, unlike her family, who treated her like a pain in the ass more often than not. Her brother, always the wit, had been quick to pick up on this, and now he called her PITA all the time.

She maybe missed her mom—a *little*—but she didn't miss that.

Struggling to see, Lily tugged at her makeshift blindfold and immediately felt a soft hand on hers. "Don't do that, dear. That poor eye of yours needs to rest."

Alessandra's face was a blurred blob perched on another blurred blob, but her voice was easily recognizable, as was the feeling of peace that filled Lily at her touch. Lily's eyelid sagged. Maybe if she put her head down for a minute or two, she'd feel better. The stew had been hearty and thick, and heavy meals always made her tired. In her exhausted stupor she wondered what kind of meat had been in it, since she hadn't seen an animal anywhere on the island.

But then again, Alessandra and Maria hadn't had a chance to show her the entire village yet. The animals had to be somewhere. In any case, the dinner had been tasty, and Lily was glad she hadn't let her paranoia get the best of her again. It was only natural that people would stare at her like that. They hadn't had a visitor in a gazillion years, apparently. Alessandra had assured her that newcomers were always treated like royalty, though, and given the finest food and the most comfortable place to sleep. She could use the latter now, she thought, doing her best to stifle a yawn and failing miserably.

A man chuckled. Lily thought it was the one they called Stefano, but she couldn't see well enough to be certain. "You'd better get that child to bed, Alessa, before she tumbles face first into the fire."

"Maria, why don't you show Lily to the bed we made for her this afternoon? Our healer will examine your eyes tomorrow, dear child, and we'll find a fresh bandage for you. I'm sure they will feel better in the morning."

Lily nodded, waving good night in the general direction of the people clustered around the fire. Even that took more energy than she could spare, and her arm fell back against her side as if it were weighed down with stones. She heard more laughter, but it was kind. They weren't mocking her; these people were her friends.

I can trust them.

Maria's tiny hand closed on hers, pulling her upright, and Lily staggered to her feet. With the energy Lily was just getting accustomed to, the little girl dragged her away from the others.

"Lift your feet here," she said after a moment. "You don't want to hurt yourself."

Following Maria's direction, Lily stepped over a threshold. Cool air hit her cheeks and she realized they were outside. Through her blurry eyes, the world was a Monet painting seen underwater.

"You'll like your room. I worked really hard to make it extra pretty, and I gave you my favorite doll to sleep with. She'll keep you safe."

Lily was touched. "That's nice of you, Maria. What's her name?"

"Mary, but not after Mother Mary. I named her after my best friend, who used to live across the street from me. I haven't seen her for a very long time—ages and ages and ages." Her voice took on a wistful tone. "Maybe you could be my best friend now?"

Lily gave Maria's hand an extra squeeze. "I'd like that,"

she said, reminded of the kids she used to babysit. Except those kids had dozens of dolls and more friends than they could count. Some of them had birthday parties with over a hundred guests, which meant over a hundred presents. *Poor Maria. She must be so lonely.*

A door creaked, and the girl helped her over another threshold. Lily barked her shin only once before she felt something soft hit her around knee level. Maria guided one of her hands lower, lower, lower, until Lily could feel a blanket under her fingers. She'd never felt anything so soft.

"You have to step up here. Take my hand; I'll help you." Maria half-pulled, half-pushed her into the bed, which seemed to be on some sort of platform. There was a slight musty smell, and every now and then, a fly buzzed around her head, but other than that, it was perfect. Lily's eyes began to close as soon as her head settled on the pillow.

Maria tugged at her arm, and then something cold was wedged between Lily's elbow and her body. "This is Mary. She'll protect you."

"Hi, Mary. Nice to meet you," Lily slurred, although some part of her mind insisted that it wasn't nice to meet Mary at all. Mary stunk. In fact, Mary *reeked*—and she had hard edges that dug into Lily's skin and made her feel like she was bleeding.

But that's silly. It's just a doll. A doll can't hurt me.

"You'll still be here in the morning, won't you?"

With the last of her ebbing strength, Lily pawed the air, groping for Maria's hand. The poor girl sounded so worried. "Of course. Why wouldn't I be?"

It came out as, "Mmm-muh. Ugh oooldn't oob," but somehow Maria managed to understand her.

"My last friend ran away in the middle of the night. I

woke up and she was gone. You won't do that to me, will you?"

"Brufff. Umm ugh eerf." *No. I'll be here.*

"Good, because I like you better than her anyway. You're a lot prettier." Lily felt Maria's lips on her forehead, followed by a loud, smacking kiss. "Good night! I hope you feel well tomorrow."

Lily was tired of talking. There was a brief moment of relief when she heard Maria's steps skip away and the creak of the door and soft thud as it closed behind her. Babysitting was exhausting.

Kids! Where did they get all that energy?

She wrinkled her nose. *Ugh, what was that smell?* It was worse than before. The flies seemed worse too. She could hear the low hum of their buzzing. Opening her eye, Lily searched for an explanation, but her vision was blurrier than before. All she could see was a flurry of black spots that winked in and out of view.

Brushing the insects from her face, Lily managed to heave her body onto her right side, shoving Mary away from her. She heard a clunk as the doll hit the floor. The smell and the fly situation immediately improved. Too tired to ponder what that might mean, Lily closed her eyes and slept the dreamless sleep of the dead.

~ CHAPTER TWELVE ~

IF I HAD TO DEFINE the Hotel Gatto Nero's general manager in one word, that word would be reluctant. It was in the slump of his shoulders and the hang of his head that morning as he shot us vaguely resentful looks. He did everything but drag his feet like a stubborn child in a cartoon.

"I do not understand why you want to go there," he said for what had to have been the tenth time. "It's a bad place." When he spoke, he added an 'ah' to every English word, which made it sound like he'd said, "It's-ah bad-ah place-ah." I normally found this tendency charming, but it was the ass crack of dawn and I hadn't had my coffee. *Nothing* was charming.

"It's an important part of Venetian history, Marcello," I repeated, for what also had to have been the tenth time. "Jackson writes books about the gritty underbelly of some of the world's most beautiful places."

Marcello widened his eyes at the words "gritty underbelly." I wondered what meaning he'd taken from them—dirty stomach below? *Christ, I need coffee. I'm going quietly mad.*

The Great Writer himself was no help. He was

preoccupied, pacing in front of the wooden doors that apparently led to the canal. "Apparently" because Marcello had said so, but also because we could hear water lapping against them, which made it a safe bet.

Every time a boat had approached, Jackson had jumped from his chair as if he'd just gotten an electric shock. Eventually he'd given up on sitting down. Hence the pacing, which was getting on my nerves. "Are you *sure* we'll know when they arrive?" He cast a doubtful look at the heavy double doors, which were constructed around the time Mussolini's great-granddaddy was in diapers.

"Yes, yes. I tell you, there is big doorbell. Very loud. Even at the front desk, we hear it," Marcello assured him.

The problem, which I would have happily explained to Jackson if we'd been alone, was not whether we would hear the boat when it arrived. The problem was it *hadn't* arrived, and we didn't know if it ever would. It was almost thirty minutes late. I'd suggested, first gently and then a little more firmly, that it was time to start figuring out a Plan B, but Jackson wanted to wait. *Fifteen more minutes,* I promised myself. *Fifteen more minutes and his time is up.* We were in this together, but Vittoria was *my* client. I wasn't about to risk losing her daughter because Jackson had something to prove.

"It is illegal to go there," Marcello said, which was his favorite argument against our plans. I had to admit, if solely to myself, his warnings were making me nervous. What if we were arrested for this? Would Vittoria be able to bail us out? As glamorous as Italy was, I had a feeling their prison jumpsuits weren't made by Armani. I pictured ending up in a peeling, mildewed cesspool full of rats and the spirits of long-departed thugs.

"Come on, Marcello. Many American television stars have been there. I've seen proof. They couldn't *all* have gotten permission from the owner."

I don't know about many, but the Paranormal Detectives had been there, and if it was okay for them, it was definitely okay for us.

The manager leaned close enough that I could smell the stale coffee on his breath. I was almost jealous. His bizarre goatee was trimmed to a sharp point, which lent him an unfortunate resemblance to a silent-movie villain. "It is dangerous there. You must not go. The spirits there, they do not rest."

Before I could respond, Jackson did. "We have no choice, okay? We have to go. I'm on deadline."

His attitude was a bit over the top. He was certainly letting this "I'm an important writer" act go to his head, but it did the trick. Marcello retreated, raising his hands in surrender.

"Fine, fine. You do not listen to what I have to say; you do not care for my advice. I go now. I will return when the boat is here."

We both watched as Marcello left in a huff. I hoped it wouldn't bite us in the butt later. Making an enemy of a hotel manager is not the smartest idea, particularly when you were staying in his hotel.

"Jackson—"

"Don't say it, okay? Don't say it. You were right and I was wrong. I get it. So why don't *you* decide how to get to Poveglia, since you're the one who has it all figured out? I'll stick to schlepping the luggage around."

I felt like my eyes were going to pop out of my head. *What on earth was going on with us?* We'd gotten along so well in China, but now we were always seconds away from ripping out each other's throats. "I never said—"

"It doesn't matter. You were thinking it."

"I wasn't aware you were a mind reader. Good to know."

"Can the sarcasm, Kate. I'm serious. I am not in the—"

An earsplitting *BONNNGGG* reverberated through the hotel and my head, interrupting Jackson's rant and vibrating my fillings. Marcello pushed past us, his call to duty higher than his obvious annoyance.

"Your boat," he announced unnecessarily. "It is here."

Grasping the metal rings, he heaved the doors open. On the turquoise waters beyond bobbed a sleek speedboat, its driver concealed behind tinted windows. Marcello moved a wooden ramp over to the entrance, then looked a question at me.

This is your boat, yes?

Good question. I joined Jackson in peering through the smoky glass in a futile attempt to see who was at the wheel. Before either of us could speak, a familiar figure emerged from the passenger cabin.

"*Buona mattina*, American friends! I've brought you a surprise." Sophia lifted her hands to the sky, displaying two familiar green-and-white cups that made me want to weep with joy.

"*Buona mattina*, Sophia," Jackson said, grinning at me.

🕊

Poveglia was a lot prettier than I'd expected. As Sophia's father-in-law, a man who limited his communication with us to grunts and nods, sidled his boat snugly to the dock, I was surprised to see a variety of well-dressed people going about their business. Pretty, well-kept homes featured pretty, well-kept lawns. *What the hell?* This bore no resemblance to the creepy abandoned island I'd read so much about online.

Jackson turned to me, raising an eyebrow. I was willing to bet he was thinking the same. Before either of us could speak, Sophia gave us a wave and hopped out of the boat.

"Well, this is me. It was nice meeting you both. I hope you find what you are looking for on Poveglia."

"What do you mean, 'this is you'? Aren't we all getting off?" Jackson asked. There was an edge to his voice I hadn't heard him use with her before, and I suspected Sophia's bloom was beginning to fade.

Her tinkling laugh struck me as a tad more patronizing than usual. "This isn't Poveglia, silly. This is Lido, where I live. My father-in-law will take you the rest of the way, don't worry."

Jackson glanced at me, and that silent exchange spoke volumes. I'd had faith that the mind meld we'd experienced in China still worked, and I was not disappointed. "I think we'd both feel better if you came along," he said. Sophia had explained that her father-in-law's English consisted of *hello* and *yes*, so we'd been counting on her to translate. "If something goes wrong, it would be good to be able to communicate."

She laughed again. She was lucky she was out of the boat so I couldn't smack her. "You Americans! You worry too much. You need to learn to relax. My father-in-law is very skilled. Nothing will go wrong."

I knew better than to tempt fate like that. We were going to the world's most haunted island. Plenty of things could—and probably *would*—go wrong.

"He knows we need to keep Kate at a safe distance,

right? He can't drive up to that island like he did here."

"Yes, yes, we've gone over this. He knows, I know, everything will be okay. Please don't worry. I need to get to work now."

Work. Why hadn't she mentioned this before? I was relieved Jackson had reminded her of my limitations, as I'd nearly had a heart attack when Vincenzo pulled up to the dock. The lack of pain I'd felt during the approach should have told me this wasn't Poveglia.

"Can you tell him again, just to be sure? It's really important," Jackson said.

Sophia sighed, but she leaned into the boat and said a few lines of hurried Italian to her father-in-law. Vincenzo smiled, displaying a bright gold tooth, and gave us the thumbs-up.

It was less than reassuring.

"Okay, I have made sure. He understands. You are happy now?"

Apparently we didn't have much choice, for she vanished down the street in the time it took Jackson to open his mouth. Vincenzo nodded at Sophia's rapidly departing backside and tromped on the gas, flinging me against the seat.

Bracing his hands on the ceiling of the cabin, Jackson staggered over to sit beside me. He intertwined his fingers with mine, holding tight to my hand.

"I'm so sorry, Kate. You were right; I should have listened to you. I don't have a good feeling about this."

There were many things I could have said, but for better or worse, Jackson and I were in this together. "I'm sure it will be fine," I yelled over the roar of the motor. "Sophia told him what we need, right? It'll be okay."

"Nice try, but this is me, remember? You're scared as hell and I don't blame you. This is seriously fucked up."

Vincenzo gave us another thumbs-up accompanied by a hearty, "Okay!"

"How far away is Poveglia?" Jackson said in my ear.

"I'm not sure. It's about twenty minutes from Venice, but I wasn't expecting this detour." We'd been distracted by Sophia's chatter during the first portion of our little adventure, so I wasn't certain how far off course we were. Checking my watch didn't help; it was stuck at 7:45. *Perfect.* Great time for the battery to die.

Soon we were on open water again, leaving the picturesque island of Lido behind. The sky and lagoon were a reflection of each other, a cold, blue slate. Jackson grabbed on to the doorframe and poked his head out of the cabin, surveying the sky. "Looks like a storm's coming."

"Of course it is." I mentally cursed my lack of preparation. My fingers were already numb in their thin, woolen gloves. If it rained, I'd freeze. At least I'd brought a jacket.

A loud knocking sound erupted from the duffel bag resting on Jackson's lap. He jumped and the bag slipped, nearly hitting the floor. I caught the strap with two fingers and set the duffel on my other side. The knocking intensified until I felt the wooden seat underneath us vibrate.

Even Vincenzo noticed, looking at us over his shoulder. "Okay?"

I returned his thumbs-up, relieved when he went back to watching the water. Perhaps operating a boat on this deserted portion of the lagoon didn't require as much concentration as driving a car, but I'd still prefer he kept his eyes on the road, so to speak.

"What the fuck is that?" Jackson asked, scooting over on the bench so he was as far away from the bag as possible.

"Consider it our own spiritual Geiger counter. We must be getting close."

Keeping a tight hold on the strap to stop the bag from sliding again, I was careful not to touch the duffel itself. It was obvious the spirits of Lily's family had a lot to say. If not outright warning me, they were definitely anxious, and I wasn't in the mood to placate them at the moment. Besides, tell me something I didn't know. *You're preaching to the converted, sisters.*

I felt Poveglia before I saw it. A heaviness crept into my stomach and crawled up my insides, invading my chest and turning the remnants of my morning coffee into bile. The knocking from the bag intensified.

"Can't you get them to shut up?"

Ignoring Jackson, I ducked my head to peek out the window. Sure enough, the famous bell tower loomed against the gray sky, every bit as ominous as predicted. Just the sight of it made me shiver. At least the window where the doctor had jumped to his death was boarded up—or *had* he jumped? I had my doubts. Those who'd killed themselves usually knew they were dead. If the doctor was a suicide, he was an unusual case.

Jackson's face appeared beside me, his cheek brushing mine. "Shit. That's it, isn't it?" His voice had that *what-are-we-getting-ourselves-into* tone that perfectly matched the distress churning in my gut.

"Afraid so."

"Holy fuck! Why is he going so close?" Jackson leapt from his seat, covering the distance between Vincenzo and us in a split second. As the two men argued in a mix of

Italian and English gibberish, the boat continued to bring us closer and closer to Poveglia.

And this is why you never put your life in the hands of someone you don't know, kiddies.

Good thing I still had my sense of humor. I could die laughing. And then it dawned on me: the tightness in my stomach and chest hadn't gone anywhere, but it hadn't intensified either. There was only that sense of discomfort. *Strong* discomfort, yes, but no pain. Nothing like I'd expect from an island where thousands of people had been tortured, where many souls had suffered so greatly. The bag beside me mustered another *tap tap tap* before falling silent. Perhaps Lily's ancestors had tired themselves out. Or maybe the danger had passed, at least for now.

"Stop! Do you understand anything, man? I said *STOP.* Um, *arreti-vous!*"

Jackson made wild cutting gestures to Sophia's father-in-law, who was bent over the wheel as if his life depended on it. Biting back a laugh at his attempt to speak Italian, I had to call Jacks several times before he heard me.

"Jackson, it's okay. I'm okay. Really."

He made his way back to the cabin, forehead creased in confusion. "Are you sure?"

"Of course I'm sure. I feel a little pressure here," I said, touching my breastbone. "But it's nothing I can't handle. No worse than heartburn."

"That doesn't make sense. If as many people died on that island as you say, being this close to it should lay you out."

Few people understood that being a medium wasn't as simple as *"I see dead people."* While experiencing the agony of getting stabbed, shot, or burned could never be described as a fun time, I was used to it (as much as one could get used to something like that). When I was a little girl, encountering the violent death of a single spirit could send me into the fetal position. These days, I could handle as many as six at a time, but any more would threaten my own life, as Jackson had witnessed in China. The human body could only take so much pain.

Lord knows what it was doing to my soul. Sometimes I pictured my own spirit riddled with holes from gunshots and stabbings. Laura had chided me for being silly when I'd confided this fear, but I wasn't so sure it *was* silly. Everything I'd experienced over the years had to have made its mark on me somehow.

Poveglia's dock was long gone, so Vincenzo brought his boat to a stop alongside the island itself, which was reinforced with concrete. Scowling, he flapped his hands at us. "You go now, go! Get off my boat."

Hmm. His English had improved by leaps and bounds. Something was foul in Poveglia.

"When will you come back for us?" Jackson asked, but Vincenzo grew more agitated. He stood up, making the universal "get the fuck off my boat" gesture.

I raised my wrist, pointing to my watch. "*A che ora?*" With my limited Italian, "What time?" was the most I could manage. Yelling it again, I hoped for the best. Vincenzo was going to come back for us, right? I mean, he wouldn't actually abandon us here…would he?

"You wanted Poveglia. Here is Poveglia. Now, get off. Go!" Vincenzo's face reddened until he resembled a beet with hypertension.

Knock. Knock knock knock.

I had to agree with Lily's ancestors. Time to get the hell out of Dodge. "Come on, Jackson. This isn't working."

Sweat dotted his forehead, even though the air was freezing. "But what if he doesn't come back? What if he just leaves us here?"

"Sophia won't let that happen," I said, though I had my doubts. "And if she does, we'll figure it out. Let's go."

It was easy to see from Vincenzo's expression that we'd long overstayed our welcome. "Jackson, let's *go*. Now."

Seeing we were leaving, Vincenzo morphed from a man consumed with murderous rage to the friendly fisherman we'd met that morning. He even offered his hand to help me up the steps of the boat onto dry land.

"You realize you are alone on this island," he said, his eyes searching mine. Was it my imagination, or did I see a hint of regret?

"Yes." I wasn't alone, but not in any way a mainstreamer would understand.

Vincenzo's hand lingered on mine for a moment. "Goodbye."

I'd never heard the word sound so final before, but I didn't have a chance to consider what that meant for us, as the sky opened with a loud crack. Yelping in shock as the freezing rain hit our skin, we ran for the closest shelter, not bothering to make sure it was safe first.

The ravages of time had created an unintentional skylight in the building we chose, letting in water that pounded on strange metal structures coated with rust. The result was cacophony, like standing in the middle of a *Stomp* performance. My heart banged along with it, but The Gift told me there wasn't anything inside the structure that wanted to harm us. I felt a gentle curiosity, nothing more.

Jackson put his arm around me, pulling me close. I hadn't noticed how much I was shivering. "Are you all right?"

I nodded, and then remembered I'd need to give him the same reassurance my gift had given me. "We're safe. There's nothing to worry about, at least not here."

He exhaled, but as I rested my head against his chest, I could feel the tension in his body. Couldn't blame him there. This racket would put anyone on edge. "What the hell was that about, do you think?"

Did I stick to my resolve to tell him the truth at all times, or was it better to spare his feelings? His next words decided me.

"Level with me. I can handle it."

"Honestly? I don't think Vincenzo has anything to do with it. I think Sophia told him to leave us both here. And I don't think he'll return for us, either."

To my great relief, Jackson didn't argue. "But why? I don't get it. It doesn't make any sense. What's in it for her?"

I'd been asking myself the same thing as I struggled to figure out what it was about Sophia that had set off every alarm bell I had. "I have no idea, and unless one of her dearly departed is hanging out on this island, I'll probably never know."

"I'm sorry, Kate. I feel like this is all my fault. If I'd listened to you…"

"Well, then you wouldn't be a guy."

He swatted at me before drawing me into his arms again.

Whatever had been fueling our pissing contests on the mainland had to end. We were on an island where, theoretically, I shouldn't be able to survive for longer than an hour, and even that hour would feel like a lifetime of torture. There was absolutely no benefit in playing the I-told-you-so game.

"It's no one's fault, really. We both wanted to get to

Poveglia, and Sophia happened to be in the right place at the right time. Anyone would have done the same."

"You wouldn't have—you didn't. But how did you know?"

I shrugged. "I'm not sure. Maybe it was just that—that she happened to have the solution exactly when we needed it. I know, I know, the magic of travel and all that, but this was a little *too* perfect. Where I come from, nothing is that easy. Think about it. We spent an entire day getting shot down by anyone and everyone, and then the second we sit down for a breather, there's a woman who has the answer? And for free? It was a bit suspicious."

Even though I was telling him the truth, there was more to it than that. It was like having a bad connection with a spirit, where they wavered in and out of focus. Whenever Sophia spoke I swore I could glimpse something in the shadows behind her, trying to get my attention, but *what*? Once more I wished I had Laura's gift instead of my own. Then we wouldn't be in this mess.

I leaned my head against Jackson's chest again. His heartbeat had slowed considerably. Perhaps he too sensed that this was a safe space. Or maybe he was actually listening to me for once. Stranger things had happened.

"How are you doing? I'll never forgive myself if something happens to you because of my fuck up."

"Oddly enough, I'm fine." The tightness I'd felt in my chest and stomach when we'd arrived hadn't eased, but it was nothing close to what I'd expected. "But that's not necessarily a good thing."

He let go, gaping at me like I was insane. "What do you mean, it's not a good thing? It's a *fantastic* thing."

"Jacks, listen…" The atmosphere gained weight, as if the

ceiling would collapse on our heads at any second. "Let's find a better place to talk about this. Somewhere I can try to contact Lily again. It should be easier now."

Maybe she was watching us. Someone certainly was. The skin on the back of my neck prickled with such intensity that I longed to shake it off, but I refused to give whatever it was the satisfaction.

"Where do you suggest?" Jackson quirked an eyebrow as he indicated our rubble-strewn surroundings.

Water still poured onto the floor from the hole in the ceiling, but it never reached us since there was a similarly sized hole in the floor. Beside the front door was an alcove with a stone staircase. Each step was ragged, as if it had been bitten in half, but it appeared sturdy. From the looks of it, it only led to the roof, though, and with this rain, that wouldn't be the best option.

"There has to be something. Come on."

Leading the way past the building's unintentional water feature, I picked my way through broken stone, shattered glass, and twists of old electrical cord and rusted metal. As usual, our species had left a hell of a mess to clean up, but Mother Nature was trying her hardest to beautify it. Nurtured by the rain, a tree had sprouted through the hole in the floor. There was something striking about seeing new life in the midst of these ruins.

The spacious entryway led to an even larger room. A great hulk of machinery stretched from floor to ceiling, running from one wall to the other. Rust had turned the paddles, pulleys, and giant springs a dull red.

"What the hell is that?" Jackson asked.

"I'm not sure. I've never seen anything like it before."

"Well, it's freaking me out. It looks like some kind of

medieval torture device."

"No one was tortured here. That much I can tell you. I'm not getting any pain from this building at all."

Plenty of fear, but no pain. What was going on? What had happened here?

"What were you so afraid of?" I murmured under my breath.

"What's that?" Jackson spun around, and I could tell without having to touch him that his heart rate was off the charts again. He was picking up on their fear as well, without understanding what was agitating him.

Holding up a hand so he'd give me a minute, I placed the other one on the wall, fingertips first, and closed my eyes.

The ceiling was solid above our heads. No tree grew in the middle of the floor, which was gleaming white tile instead of dust-covered stone. Free of their coat of rust, the paddles moved back and forth, back and forth. The combined fumes of antiseptic and bleach stung my nostrils with every breath.

At first the room was empty of everything but the false life of the machines, but then they burst into view: dozens and dozens of women wearing white dresses and smocks, their hair scraped back into little caps. Some wore surgical masks over their faces, and all wore gloves.

They were of a time and place I could not recognize, and yet they were familiar to me—the sensible white shoes, the harried pace, the intense and wearied expressions of women whose work will never be done.

Removing my hand from the wall, I turned to Jackson, who was standing as close to me as it was possible to do without actually touching me. The sight made me smile. "You can relax."

"Why, what is it? You saw something, didn't you? What did you see?"

"Nurses. I saw lots and lots of nurses."

He cast a dubious eye on the gigantic metal contraption. "This doesn't look like any hospital I've ever seen."

"I don't think it was a hospital. This was where they did the grunt work. As ominous as that thing appears, I believe they used it to do industrial-sized loads of laundry." Too many women had rushed past me holding bundles of linens for it to be a coincidence.

"Wouldn't they have had aides or something to do that for them?"

"I guess not. I'm thinking Poveglia wasn't the most sought-after place to work. Probably only the truly dedicated and desperate came here."

Desperate to feed their families, to escape scandal, to feel like they were doing some good in a world turned increasingly dark. Around the time Poveglia's asylum was in use, Mussolini had seized power, stealing the people's rights and freedoms bit by bit; the shadow of Hitler loomed on the horizon. Perhaps a forgotten island in the Venetian lagoon, surrounded by the unwanted and the mentally ill, had seemed like the safest place to be.

But why the fear? What were they so afraid of? Had they known the war was coming? Could they sense how bad it would get, how evil? Or was it something else?

"Any sign of our doctor friend?"

"Not yet, and I'm not looking forward to that reunion. Come on, let's go."

Seeing light at the end of the room, I hurried toward it, as much as anyone could hurry on a floor strewn with debris. A door hung open in front of us and I plunged through the gap, taking huge gulps of fresh air. Directly ahead, another building waited, but a canopy of trees had grown within the space between, providing leafy cover from the rain.

"This is better," I said after I'd caught my breath. The space felt free from prying eyes and listening ears, either from this world or the other.

"I don't know about you, but I'm thinking we should find this Lily chick and then figure out how to get the hell out of here." Flipping the hood of his sweatshirt over his head, he stamped his feet to warm them. "How do you retrieve someone's soul, anyway? It's not like we can just grab it and run."

"It's not going to be easy. I have no idea how he got her here to start with. Lily doesn't belong in this time, or in this place. By yanking her out of our world and into his, he's disturbing the natural order of things."

"It seems crazy to ask you what's wrong, but I feel like something is. I'm right, aren't I?"

"It's just…This is going to sound weird, but I figure we're way past that." My mind raced on ahead as I fumbled for the best words to explain an extremely complicated concept. "You know how people talk about having the 'will' to do something?"

"Yeah, like willpower."

"Kind of, but not exactly. More like when people say their will is strong and stuff like that."

His brow furrowed, but he let me get through it, which I was deeply grateful for. "Well, that 'will'—the part of you that dictates your resolve, your inner strength, your resilience—that's actually your soul."

Jackson shook his head as if something had flown into

one of his ears. I reached out and touched his elbow, careful not to startle him. "Too much?"

"No, it's just…I'm still trying to wrap my head around the fact we even *have* a soul."

"The word 'soul' is a religious conceit. You can call it a person's essence, if that makes you feel better."

"Oh yeah, that makes me feel *way* better."

"The point of my telling you this is to explain why this situation bothers me so much. In addition to the obvious, of course. What some people call the soul is really their will, which means it's extremely difficult to make a soul do something the person wouldn't."

"What are you saying, Kate? I'm listening, but I'm not quite following."

"Have you seen *The Exorcist?*" "Who hasn't?"

That movie was the bane of my existence. If I had a buck for every time a priest had called me about a demonic possession, I'd have been able to get heated seats for my Mini. "Well, contrary to what movies like that would have you believe, it's practically impossible to possess someone and mess with their soul. I've only seen the very ill or desperate taken over the way Lily was, and even then, she's an extreme case. And according to her mother, before this happened she was a happy, healthy twelve-year-old girl."

"So you're saying Lily *wanted* that death doctor to bring her here?" I saw my own disbelief and horror reflected on Jackson's face.

"At least part of her did, yes. And that means it's going to be a lot harder to bring her back."

~ CHAPTER THIRTEEN ~

IN RESPONSE TO HER MOTHER'S voice calling from downstairs, Lily rolled over and pulled the pillow over her head. It was no use, as the voice seemed to echo from within her own mind.

Lily. Lily. Lilllly, are you there? I need to talk to you.

Pressing the fabric against her ears, Lily squeezed her eyes shut. "Go away; I'm sleeping." It couldn't be time to get ready for school yet. She'd just drifted off.

Where are you, Lily? Are you with the doctor?

As her situation came rushing back to her, Lily sat up so fast it made her dizzy. It wasn't her mother calling her, because her mother wasn't there. It wasn't the light from her bedside lamp at home shining in Lily's face—it was the blue glow that emanated from the red-haired woman.

Please tell me where you are. Are you with him?

"No," Lily said, her voice coming out as a strangled croak. "No, other people saved me."

Other people? What other people?

"Alessandra and Maria. Alessandra is Maria's mom. They've been very nice to me."

The light surrounding the woman flicked from azure to navy. *Where did you meet them? Are they patients of the doctor?*

Remembering that she'd been able to communicate with the woman without speaking, Lily lowered her voice to a whisper. Pink-tinged daylight had begun to creep along the edges of the window above her bed, but not enough that she could make out many details. Others could be sleeping around her, and she didn't want to wake them— partly out of politeness and partly because she wasn't ready to answer questions about the woman in blue. How could she explain something when she didn't understand it herself? "I don't think so. They're just people. They live on the other side of the island."

She described how she'd escaped from the restraints and ran away from the hospital, and how Maria had found her hiding in the shrubbery and brought her here.

The woman's light grew darker still, until it was a shade of midnight blue. *I can only hear you this time; I can't see you. Are you all right? Did the doctor do anything to you?*

"No. He was going to, but I got out before he could. There's something wrong with my eyes, though."

What do you mean?

When Lily told her what had happened the day before, the woman's frown vanished, though the color surrounding her remained dark. *It may be difficult for you to believe, but there's nothing wrong with your eyes at all. Actually, the opposite is true. Something incredible has happened to them that is letting you see things as they once were.*

Now that she was awake and thinking about her eye problem, Lily realized how much it had worsened overnight. Her vision had been blurry the previous day, but she hadn't been in any pain. Now her right eye burned something awful and there was an uncomfortable pressure.

As the woman continued talking, Lily's panic grew.

Something was wrong. Really, *really* wrong.

I want you to take the blindfold off. Take it off and slowly look around. I need you to look around and tell me what you see. Cover the other eye if you have to. When Lily didn't respond, the woman cocked her head to the side. *Can you do that for me?*

An icy sweat broke out on Lily's forehead as she moved her hand to her eye. "I can try," she whispered, wishing she could remember the woman's name.

I'm Kate. What's wrong? Something's changed since you told me about your eye. What happened?

They—

Lily's fingers grazed the thick cloth that was wrapped tightly around her head, pressing painfully against her eye. "They changed my bandage. Alessandra said they would, but I thought they'd wait until I was awake."

How could she have slept through something like that? They would have had to lift her head up, for starters. Resentment filled her at the thought of Alessandra touching her without her permission, as if she were an invalid, or a doll.

You're right to be angry. They shouldn't have done that while you were sleeping. Can you take the bandage off?

Her fingers felt thick and clumsy as they followed the fabric to the knot at the back of her head. She picked at it but couldn't find an opening. Her arms ached from the effort, and before too long she was unable to hold them up. "It's too tight. I can't undo it."

Don't worry; it'll be okay. I'm sure they did what they could to help.

Although the woman sounded like she was trying to be comforting, Lily could hear her doubts loud and clear, even in her thoughts. She hadn't known thoughts had a tone to them, much like voices did. Then again, she'd never been able to read anyone's mind before.

Yes, I'm worried, but not about this. I honestly think your eye's okay, really.

Crap. She'd forgotten Kate could read hers too.

Can you pull the bandage off?

For a moment, she felt renewed hope, but that was soon dashed. The blindfold was fastened so tightly she couldn't budge it. Some of her hair was caught in the knot, and she bit her lip to keep from crying out as her efforts yanked several strands from her scalp. "It's too tight. It hurts."

The dizziness overcame her again, and her head began to throb.

Can you lie down? Just lie down for a little bit and try to relax, okay? I'm on the island with my friend, and we're going to come get you and bring you home.

Halfway to her pillow, Lily was jolted upright again by the news. "You're here? Where?" She was struck by a wave of longing for her mother so intense tears dampened her blindfold, trickling down the cheek under her one good eye.

Your mother misses you too. She's been so worried, Lily. She loves you so much.

"Can you really bring me home?"

Yes. We just have to find you. Can you tell me anything more about where you are?

Her thoughts swirling like pinwheels, Lily pictured the village with its hobbit-like houses sprouting from the field. *Be careful, though. I think the bridge is electrified.* Remembering what had happened to the doctor when he'd attempted to cross, she willed that image to Kate.

The woman's light darkened further still, until filaments of black sparkled amid the blue. Lily thought it looked like the night sky. *It's okay, Kate. He's not here, and Alessandra says he can't cross no matter what he does. So I'm safe until you find me.*

Sometimes when her father got frustrated with her, he would say she was "too smart for her own good." Lily had never understood what that meant, but she did now. "I'm not really safe, am I?"

She could feel the woman sigh, just like her father had sighed when he was tired of answering her questions.

I'm glad you got away from the doctor. That was smart. He's a dangerous man who wanted to hurt you. But don't be too quick to trust others, either. Rather than listen to what they say, pay attention to what they do, and if you see anything that worries you, start making your way back to the hospital as quickly as you can. Do you remember where it is?

"Yes, I think so."

Good. Make up some kind of excuse. Say you're going to pick berries or you left something behind, whatever story you think they'll believe. Act casual. If you can, slip away when they're not paying attention.

"But what about the doctor? As soon as I cross the bridge, he can grab me again."

Let me worry about him. I do need to ask you something, though. Is there some reason you wanted—

"Good morning, child! We're overjoyed to see you awake and looking so well."

Lily started. Alessandra stood in the doorway, her hand resting on her daughter's shoulders. Though she sounded friendly as ever, her smile didn't meet her eyes. Maria's lips were pursed in a ferocious pout that would have been comical if Lily hadn't been so nervous.

"Who were you talking to?"

There was a delay while Lily's mind translated Alessandra's words into English. Just as Nonna had warned, she wasn't able to *think* in Italian, and until she could, she'd never be truly fluent.

She felt weak with relief when she saw Kate had gone back to wherever she'd come from. "I'm sorry; I don't understand. There's no one here but me."

"Ah, but there was someone here," Alessandra said, walking over to Lily's bed so she towered over her. "And I would like to know who it was. You are an invited guest in our home, and we have a right to be informed if that invitation is extended to anyone else."

"I told you, there's no one. Can you untie my blindfold, please? It's too tight. It's hurting me."

"I'm sorry, dear, but it's for your own good. Our healer has applied a poultice. If the bandage were any more lax, his treatment would escape."

Lily gritted her teeth. "Well, his poultice *stings.* I want it off."

"Sometimes we have to endure minor discomforts for our own good, dear child. I'm sure your mother would tell you the same."

"My mother would never say anything that stupid. Now take this off me."

Alessandra only smiled, her calm demeanor provoking Lily to new heights of fury. "You seem to be in a terrible temper this morning. Did you not sleep well?"

"You better watch your tongue or Mama will wash it with soap." Maria scowled, folding her arms across her chest.

How could I have ever thought that little brat was endearing?

"That's enough, darling." Alessandra stroked her daughter's shoulder, pulling her close again. "Remember, Lily is our guest and she's come a long, long way to visit us. It will be a while before she gets accustomed to our way of doing things."

Lily wasn't sure what frightened her more: Alessandra's words or her eerie calmness. *What way of doing what? What had she gotten herself into?* "Actually, I think I'm tired of visiting. I'd like to go home. My own mother is worried about me; I've been away for too long as it is."

She swung her legs over the thin mattress, careful to avoid Alessandra's touch. The last thing she wanted was to have that woman's hands on her. She needed every bit of energy she could get.

Alessandra shook her head. She had that sad little smile on her face that Lily had already grown to hate. "I'm afraid that's not possible."

"Then let me go back to the hospital."

"You're not making any sense, child. You need more rest to clear your mind. We helped you escape from that terrible man. Why ever would you want to go back there?"

"Thank you for helping me. I really appreciate it. But he's my doctor," Lily said in a burst of inspiration. "I never should have let another physician treat me. I have to go back."

"Perhaps you should have thought of that before you accepted my daughter's invitation."

Lily stared at the little girl. She longed to smack that smug expression off Maria's face, but had the sense to restrain herself. "She told me she knew a place where I could hide, where I could be safe. She lied to me."

"She didn't lie at all. Maria told you the truth. You *are* safe."

"Not if I can't leave! That means I'm a prisoner."

Alessandra rolled her eyes heavenward as she stroked her daughter's hair. "I've already explained this. You're not a prisoner; you're a guest in our community. We've done nothing but take care of you since you arrived. How can you be so ungrateful?"

"Thank you again for your kindness." Lily's jaw tightened so that her teeth ground against each other. "But I would like to leave now."

"You must be exhausted. I believe I've explained more than once that this is not possible."

"This is ridiculous. I'm done talking to you. You're not my mother; you can't keep me here." Lily swung her legs over the mattress on the other side, out of Alessandra's reach. Her feet felt strangely numb, and as soon as she put weight on them, they splayed to one side. She had to grab the bed frame to keep from falling. It was easy to see the problem. Both feet had been bandaged as tightly as her eye.

"Oh, but I can. Have you forgotten what happened to the doctor when he tried to cross the bridge without our permission? It won't be any different for you."

She limped toward the door, giving Alessandra and that daughter of hers as wide a berth as possible. "Then I'll swim."

Lily froze when she heard the woman's next words.

"Not if you want to keep your eye, you won't."

"What did you do to it?"

Now it was Alessandra's turn to smirk. "Nothing that can't be cured, *if* you stay on our side. Once our healer is convinced you have seen reason, he will repair the damage.

Until then, you will remain as you are, in pain and half-blind."

The strength went out of Lily's legs, and she slid to the floor. "But why? Why are you doing this to me? I don't understand. All I want is to go home." She looked up at Alessandra, whose face betrayed no emotion. The kindness she'd seen in the woman's eyes yesterday was long gone. "Imagine if someone took Maria from you. How would you feel?"

Alessandra's fingers tightened on her daughter's shoulders. "No one will *ever* take her from me. I'm a good mother. Perhaps if your mother had cared about you the way I care for Maria, you'd still be with her."

"Don't say that! Don't talk about my mom that way, you dumb bitch. She's a better mother than you'll ever be."

"I think we should let Lily rest today, darling. She's obviously not in the mood to play right now, but I'm sure she'll feel better later."

Putting an arm around the little girl, Alessandra guided Maria toward the door. Desperate to do something, to say anything that would get a reaction, Lily blurted out the most hurtful thing she could think of. "Are you kidding? I'll never play with her, never! I can't stand the sight of that little bitch. She's as ugly as you."

Alessandra shook her head and sighed, but Maria's face darkened with rage. "You better be nice to me, or you'll end up in tomorrow's stew!"

"Now, darling, what did I tell you about threatening our friends? There's no need to lose your temper. Lily's a smart girl. She'll figure out the rules soon enough."

But Lily, still crumpled on the floor with her throbbing feet tucked uselessly underneath her, didn't pay any attention to Alessandra's admonishments. Instead, she was thinking of the stew she'd eaten last night, thick with sweet, white meat. She was remembering how she'd wondered where the animals were, and how she hadn't seen any. Her stomach churned. *No, it couldn't be—it wasn't—they're just messing with you. That's all. They're trying to get to you and it's working. Don't let them.*

"It's one of the wonderful things about our little community, which you'll soon appreciate," Alessandra said. This time when she smiled, Lily noticed how sharp her teeth were. "Everyone has a purpose here. Your role is to be my daughter's friend, but if you really feel that's too distasteful, well…there are other ways you can prove useful."

There was a terrible moment of reckoning when Lily realized Maria's outburst wasn't just a childish threat. Moaning, she leaned over and threw up, vomit and saliva clinging to her mouth in thick strings. The smell of it made her queasier, and as she retched and heaved, she could hear Maria's childish laughter.

"See, what did I tell you, my darling? Your friend is just sick, that's all. I'm sure she'll be feeling better tomorrow. Won't you, Lily?"

Without waiting for an answer, they left the room, closing the door behind them.

~ CHAPTER FOURTEEN ~

"**A**RE YOU CRAZY? THAT'S THE weirdest thing I've ever heard. And believe me, that's saying something."

I hugged my knees to my chest, hoping to stop the trembling. The contact with Lily had been troubling, to say the least. And I wasn't sure I had the time or the words to make Jackson understand. "I totally get why you'd feel that way, but you don't understand. Everything has changed."

He shook his head. "I guess it has, if you want us to now seek out the dude we were trying to avoid. Can't you at least give me a reason? Especially since Lily isn't even with him anymore?"

"I can't explain it, and I might be wrong. I just think he could hold the key to this whole thing."

Getting to his feet, Jackson reached out a hand and pulled me up. "If you say so. You're the boss."

"Thanks for at least being willing to give it a try." I brushed dust off my jeans. We were tucked in a corner of the laundry, where there was enough light coming through the door to see the spirit board. As Jackson was putting it back in the bag, I caught hold of his arm. "Just a minute." Grimacing, I moved the planchette to *Good Bye*. "Better safe than sorry."

"And all this time I thought these things were a goof." He zipped up his duffel with the board inside and swung the bag over his shoulder. "I've never seen one work before."

"Just because no one answers the phone doesn't mean there's nobody home."

"Touché. So where are we going, boss?"

I gestured to a door that was partly visible through a tangle of trees. "The asylum."

We left the relative safety of the laundry, crunching through dry leaves to the building next door. Poveglia's asylum loomed over the island, an immense brick structure supported by corroded metal scaffolding, but I got a feeling of sorrow rather than danger from it. Every impression I'd had of this place, of its history, had been wrong. The fact that I could stand so close to the site of the doctor's horrific experiments without falling to the ground in a writhing heap made me wonder if there had been any truth in what I'd read at all.

I'd noticed the rotting wooden door the first time we'd come out here to get some air, and I headed toward it now without hesitation, hoping that whoever had Lily would remain preoccupied for the time being.

The wood had swollen with rainwater, sticking it firmly in place. As I shoved it with both hands and forced my way inside, flakes of paint scraped my skin and showered the toes of my boots. Jackson followed me shoulder first, ignoring the door's squeal of protest.

We stood in a large room, dark except for the feeble light that crept through windows shuttered by Mother Nature. Trees and climbing vines were everywhere.

"Let there be light," Jackson whispered, turning on his

phone's flashlight.

"Careful it doesn't drain your battery. We may need it later."

"It's all good. I've got a power bank." I heard a patting sound as he double-checked his jacket pocket.

"Spirits are skilled at diverting that kind of energy to their own use. I wouldn't count on it."

"Hey Kate, no offense, but is this place actually haunted? I mean, you're fine, and aside from what you say happened to Lily, nothing even mildly spooky has occurred since we got here."

"I think that's about to change."

Though Jackson's app didn't stretch to the corners of the cavernous room, I didn't need light to see the small shape huddled in one of them. A young girl had pressed her body as tightly as she could against the wall. Hunching her back so she formed an almost perfect circle, she kept her face hidden in her knees.

"Hello," I said, cursing my lack of Italian. Without anyone to translate for me, this was bound to be a disaster. *Ciao* was too modern for this child, I was certain. She wouldn't understand it. "*Buongiorno?*"

As I crept closer, tears filled my eyes and spilled over my cheeks. This little girl had not had a happy life. Searing pain shot through my temples and my mouth, and I inhaled deeply, squaring my shoulders and taking it. *Did that bastard give her a lobotomy? Perhaps my original research was right after all.*

She didn't respond, but she wanted to. I could feel it. "*Buongiorno. Come va?*"

"You're wasting your time. She cannot speak."

Biting back a cry, I whirled around to see the doctor

emerge from the darkness.

"Even if she were able, I doubt she would. She's quite distraught at the moment, aren't you, Abelie?"

To my horror, he walked over to the girl and knelt beside her, reaching out as if he planned to grab her.

"You get away from her. Don't you touch her!"

Jackson nudged me. "Who are you talking to, Kate? Who's here?"

Imbuing the words with as much scorn as possible, I sneered at the hateful spirit. I'd tried to give him the benefit of the doubt, but it was difficult when just being in the same room as him made my skin crawl. "The good doctor has joined us."

"He has? Oh, that's great. Perfect. How am I supposed to kick his ass if I can't see him?"

"Tell your ill-tempered friend that when he is in my hospital, he will show me the respect I deserve. That applies to you as well."

"He *is* showing you the respect you deserve."

"Is he talking trash at me? What's he saying?" Jackson asked.

With a weary, I-don't-have-time-for-this sigh he could have cribbed from modern physicians, the doctor straightened. While I couldn't sense any emotion from him, his posture and the lines around his eyes gave him a defeated air. It wasn't the demeanor I'd expected from the spirit who'd trashed my house.

"I believe you already suspect I was not the one responsible for that overwrought display of temper at your home. You have been so quick to portray me as the villain that you closed yourself off from the truth."

"Oh? And what would that be?"

"The truth, my dear woman, is that I am a learned man, a man of science. I have taken an oath to heal, not to wound. If your little friend had stayed here, she would have had nothing to fear from me."

"If that's so, why is *she* afraid of you?" I indicated the child cowering on the floor.

"Oh, it's not me she's afraid of." Crouching down to her level again, he spoke to the girl. I suspected from his tone that he was coaxing her into something, but of course I had no idea what. The doctor looked over at us. "I have asked Abelie to show you her face. You will find it difficult to see, but for obvious reasons, I must ask you to control your natural reaction. Can you do that?"

I nodded, not that sure I wanted to see her. My chest tightened and I automatically slipped my hand into my pocket, reassuring myself that my inhaler was still there.

"What's going on?" Jackson said in my ear, making me twitch. For a moment, I'd forgotten he was there.

"He has a child with him, and he wants me to see her face."

"Okay…that makes absolutely no sense."

"I'll explain later."

"Are you quite finished?" the doctor asked, but he sounded amused rather than impatient.

"I'm sorry. He can't hear you."

"I gathered. I do feel it's important you see this—*if* you are ready."

"I'm ready," I said, bracing myself for the worst.

The doctor continued to talk to the child, resting his hand on one of her arms. Though I couldn't understand what he was saying, I was struck by how gentle he sounded when he spoke to her. Apparently he saved his frustration for me.

Finally the girl lifted her head from her knees. With the utmost care, he cradled her chin in his hand, turning her face in my direction. Thankfully I was biting my lip too hard to scream.

There were empty sockets where her eyes should have been.

"*Apri la bocca, Abelie. Far loro vedere.*"

The poor child opened her mouth, and I clapped my hand over my own. My eyes stung with tears again.

"Who did this to her?"

"*Grazie, Abelie. Hai fatto bene. Si può riposare adesso.*"

As the girl huddled close to the wall again, the doctor patted her on the hand before getting to his feet. "I believe you know."

"Are you telling me the people who have Lily are responsible? What reason would they have for doing something like this?"

"What reason would be good enough?"

It was all I could do not to weep. I finally felt the doctor's pain: a second of overwhelming panic, followed by crushing agony that made me sink to my knees on the rubble-coated floor.

"Kate, are you all right? What is he doing to you?" Jackson yelled, but I barely heard him. I was so focused on the doctor that I didn't even realize my friend was lifting me off the floor.

"You had a terrible death," I said, understanding how important it was to acknowledge the suffering of those left behind.

The doctor's haughty tone softened. "I do not like to discuss it."

Remembering the shrieking fury of the thing that had interrupted me when I'd initially attempted to contact Lily with the spirit board, I shook my head. I had been so blind. The signs were all around me, and yet I'd ignored them. "You weren't the one who used the spirit board to frighten me off, were you?"

"You already know the answer to that."

"And you weren't the one who destroyed my home."

He raised an eyebrow, managing to look incredulous and offended at the same time. "I would never do such a thing. Whatever would the profit be in harming or provoking you? As much as we might both find it distasteful, we are allies in this situation."

That was going a bit too far for me. "Allies? Let's not get ridiculous."

"Are you still under the illusion we are at cross-purposes? We desire the same outcome and, like it or not, that makes us allies. I see absolutely no gain in continuing to spar with each other when a more threatening enemy looms."

"Cut the patronizing crap, *Doctor*. We don't 'desire the same outcome.' I want to bring Lily home. You want to turn her into one of your zombies." I tilted my head toward the girl, now just a shadow among shadows. "I'd hardly call us allies."

"And to think I was beginning to give you more credit. Not that I expect you to listen to reason, since you are so clearly incapable of it, but I would like nothing more than for you to take Lily 'home,' as you call it. I no longer have any desire to treat her."

"You can stop the bullshit anytime, Doc." I folded my arms across my chest, gripping the insides of my elbows to keep from embarrassing myself. It is, after all, impossible to punch a ghost in the face. Much to my great regret. "She told me you were talking about treating her. You were examining her head, and I'm well versed in what your 'treatments' entailed. So let's not pretend you wouldn't stick a drill through her brain the first chance you got."

"Christ," Jackson said. "The guy's a butcher. Why are we listening to him? Let's get out of here. I don't have a good feeling about this place."

"Perhaps I considered it at one time. It is devastating to see a child in so much pain, especially when the treatment is simple and highly effective. But her mind is already weak. The last thing I would want is to weaken it further."

"Don't you dare say that about her. She's not weak. There's nothing wrong with her mind."

"Oh no? Then perhaps you can explain why she is in this predicament. Either she is weak or she is mentally disturbed, and I believe you will agree the former is better than the latter."

"And why would you say she's in pain unless you wanted some excuse to perform another one of your barbaric lobotomies on a child? She's not in pain. She was a happy, healthy kid before this happened."

The doctor closed his eyes. I could almost hear him counting to ten in his mind. "Tell me, how did you arrive at this brilliant diagnosis? Did Lily's mother inform you of her daughter's happiness and sound mental health? Or did Lily lie to you herself?"

A sharp reply sprang to my lips, but guilt gave me pause. Since I'd encountered Lily in a crisis situation, there had been no time for chitchat. I was the supernatural equivalent of a Saint Bernard, charged with rescuing her from disaster and bringing her back to her family. It would, as always, be the family's responsibility to deal with the aftermath, whether that resulted in counseling, a concentrated effort to strengthen their relationship, or simply a new awareness of the dangers the unseen world could present.

The doctor had no doubt been offended by the insults I'd hurled at him, and had struck back at me in retaliation, but he wasn't far off the mark. I *had* taken Vittoria's word for it that Lily had been a normal, relatively well-adjusted preteen before everything went to hell.

Completely disregarding the fact that normal, relatively well-adjusted preteens weren't typically drawn to spirit boards. And if they were tempted into using one, usually at a party with friends, they either got bored when nothing happened or rejected the board if something did.

Their self-preservation instinct would kick in long before their own spirit could be kidnapped and dragged halfway around the world. The fact that it hadn't with Lily should have told me something, but I was too preoccupied (probably with the prospect of seeing Jackson again, let's be honest) to ask the questions I should have been asking.

"How did you know? About her pain, I mean?"

"These people—and I use that term *very* loosely—are only attracted to those they can manipulate, and they have manipulated Lily very well, as you've seen. Before I could help her, they got her away from me, to a place I cannot go. They are manipulating her still, toying with her mind. As for her pain, all you need to do is look at her arms. They tell the story her mother refuses to acknowledge."

Had Lily tried to commit suicide? If so, I could strangle Vittoria for not telling me. That would have given her daughter more than a toehold in the other world, especially if she'd flatlined. It also explained how Alessandra and

Maria had gained control over her so quickly.

"What do you mean, 'a place you cannot go'? How are they stopping you?"

"The area of the island where they reside is strong with spiritual energy, both from their victims and from the poor souls who perished there during the nightmare years of the Black Death. Somehow they have learned to harness this force and use it to their advantage." The doctor frowned. "I cannot enter and they will do everything they can to keep Lily from leaving. I attempted to warn her, to tell her not to cross the bridge, but by then, they'd poisoned her mind against me. Now it is too late."

"No, it's not. We came here to find her and bring her home, and that's exactly what we're going to do." I reached for Jackson's hand and was relieved when his fingers entwined with mine. It must have been unnerving for him, listening to me have a conversation with someone he couldn't hear or see. "We're not leaving without her. They've already done something to one of her eyes." I hoped it wasn't the same thing they'd done to the doctor's young patient. "Please tell me where we can find them."

"You are still of the physical realm. Perhaps you have a chance, but it will not be easy." He sighed. "If you insist on going through with this, you will need to understand what you're up against."

~ CHAPTER FIFTEEN ~

LILY SWOONED THEATRICALLY AS HER brother Garrett set the table, managing somehow not to break any of Nonna's good china. "You weren't kidding. You guys really did miss me."

Her brother growled. "Don't push it." But he was joking, and their mother smiled through her tears, wrapping her arms around Lily for what had to be the five hundredth time that day.

"Of *course* we missed you, *patatina*. To celebrate, I've cooked all of your favorite dishes."

"Great. I'm starving." Lily patted her non-existent belly, which was flatter than usual after her time in the hospital. Her stomach rumbled on cue, and everyone laughed.

Why did I ever want to escape? Why did I hate them so much? These are good people. As they headed to the kitchen, Lily rested her head on her mother's shoulder. Her mother had lost weight during the ordeal as well, and it hurt to see her so tiny and frail. There were streaks of white in her hair now. "I'm sorry, Mama."

"Don't talk nonsense. You have nothing to be sorry for. You're home, everyone's happy, and everything's good. Let's enjoy our time together. We were fortunate to get a reminder of how precious it is. Not everyone gets a second chance."

For a change, Lily didn't feel like arguing. She returned her mother's smile. "Okay, let's eat."

Her father grunted. "Finally. That's the smartest thing anyone's said all day."

"Yeah, enough of this mushy stuff. You two are going to make me lose my appetite," Garrett agreed.

They'd wanted to seat her at the head of the table, like they did on her birthday, but Lily had declined as gently as possible, sliding into her usual chair beside her brother. "I want everything to go back to normal. Let's pretend I never left."

"Will you at least let me serve you the first piece?" Her father readied Nonna's sterling silver server over the pan of lasagna.

"*That* honor I can accept." Lily held out her plate, breathing in the savory steam. "It smells amazing, Mom."

"Thank you, sweetheart." Her mother beamed, even when Garrett made gagging noises and stuck his fingers down his throat.

"That's enough, Garrett." Dad tried to sound forbidding, but he was too happy to pull it off. "Not at the table."

The piece Dad gave her was so heavy her arms shook as she took back her plate. She couldn't wait to dig in—it had been too long since her last real meal. Without waiting for the Caesar salad or garlic bread, without even waiting for everyone else to be served, Lily cut a corner of the pasta off with her fork and popped it in her mouth.

As she chewed, she glanced down at her favorite treat. Mom must have changed her recipe. The sauce was much redder than usual. It was a different consistency too. Lily stared as the sauce poured from the cut she'd made in the noodles.

That doesn't look like tomato sauce. It looks like—

When her teeth broke through the coating of crusty mozzarella cheese, an intense metallic taste filled her mouth. The sauce was slimy on her tongue. Her stomach lurching, Lily grabbed a napkin and spat the pasta into it.

"What's wrong, sweetheart? Don't you like my lasagna anymore?"

Her mother's chin dripped with the deep-red sauce, but she appeared not to notice. She smiled at Lily, her teeth tinted pink. Lily's body trembled as Garrett and her father bared their own rose-hued teeth in identical grins.

"Eat up, honey," Dad said. "It's getting cold."

Unable to stop herself, Lily looked at her plate again. Something slid from the layers of pasta and lay amid the carnage, glistening.

A human fingernail.

Lily screamed.

"It's all right. It's only me."

She opened her eyes to see a pair of mud-caked Mary Janes and dusty ankle socks. With a cry, she pulled away from Maria, who stared at her with her head cocked to one side, as if Lily were an interesting bug she'd managed to trap.

"You threw up," Maria announced, wrinkling her nose. "Stinky."

Lily pushed herself up from the floor, her gorge rising again when she caught sight of the pool of vomit she'd been lying beside. The resident flies were going to town, and by the smell of it, she'd gotten some of the puke in her hair.

"Is there someplace I can clean myself off? I feel disgusting."

The little girl shook her head. "Mama says you're not allowed to leave the cabin. She doesn't want you to hurt yourself."

"But that's silly. Why would I hurt myself? I just want to get clean, that's all." Lily used her most cajoling, persuasive tone, even though she wanted to shake the girl until her teeth rattled.

"Mama says you're not allowed to leave." Maria stamped one of her tiny feet, sending up an equally tiny cloud of dust.

"Can you bring me some water and soap then? I'm supposed to be your friend, and I'm sure you don't want such a stinky friend. Do you?"

For the first time in her life, Lily hoped she reeked.

The girl's brows drew together. "I thought you didn't want to be my friend. That's what you said."

"Well, I was very upset. People say things when they're upset that they don't really mean," Lily said, parroting the words she'd heard her own parents say a million times. "Of course I want to be your friend. That's why I came here in the first place, remember? So we could be best friends forever and ever."

For a second, Lily worried she'd gone too far, had laid it on a little too thick. Maria may have been annoying as hell, but the pint-size drama queen was far from stupid. Lily sagged with relief when the shy smile returned to the girl's face.

"Really? Forever and ever and ever? You mean it?"

"Sure I do. Your mama scared me, that's all."

"You're sure you're not lying? Mama says that new

people can't be trusted. She says they always lie."

Lily sighed. "Even if I were lying—which I'm not—what could I do? I can't leave the village, right? It would be pretty easy to find me. There's nowhere I can hide."

Maria studied her face intently, and once again Lily had a moment of panic where she was sure the child could see right through her ruse. The little girl turned on her heel to leave the cabin.

"Wait! Maria, where are you going?"

"To ask Mama for a bucket. I will tell her Maria doesn't want any stinky friends."

As the cabin door shut behind the girl, Lily bit her lip to keep from grinning.

☾

Her joy evaporated when Maria returned ten minutes later with her mother following close behind.

"My daughter informs me you have changed your mind," Alessandra said, giving Lily the same once-over Maria had.

Cold sweat trickled down the back of her neck. If she hoped to stay alive, she had to make Alessandra believe she was sincere about being Maria's playmate. "I didn't need to change my mind," she said, meeting Alessandra's eyes. "I always wanted to be Maria's friend. That's why I came to the village with her."

"I thought you came here to escape from the mad doctor. You were using my daughter for your own purposes, were you not?"

Lily remembered her first experiences with the spirit board, when she'd made contact with her grandmother. Before long, her cherished Nonna had introduced someone else: a wise, older man. He'd claimed to be a healer, telling

Lily that she didn't have to be in pain all the time—that he could help her. What an idiot she'd been to believe him, to believe anything the spirits of the board had said.

She wasn't sure how she could be here, on some godforsaken island off the coast of Venice, when she was from Nightridge, Vermont. Her last memory was of having some silly fight with her mother, and the next thing she knew, she was here.

But one thing she was sure of: she was tired of being bullied, of having people threaten her and control her and tell her what to do. She couldn't figure out what this Alessandra woman's game was. Did she really want a friend for her daughter, or was she just a sadistic bitch? Lily leaned toward the latter, but it didn't matter what the woman's intentions were. She had to start, as her mother would say, setting some limits.

Lily straightened herself to her full height, deciding to use whatever tiny bit of leverage she had. "No, I was doing fine on my own, thank you. I escaped from the doctor on my own, and your daughter found *me*. She asked me to come with *her*, not the other way around. I don't know where you get off saying I used her."

"You silly little girl. The doctor would have had you back in his clutches within the hour. You saw how quickly he came after you. If my daughter hadn't brought you here, he'd be drilling a hole through your brain right now. Perhaps that's what you deserve."

The memory of the doctor caressing her temples with his long fingers made her shiver. Since her nonna had taught her Italian, she didn't know many swears. She'd had to rely on her cousins for that. Narrowing her eyes, she hit Alessandra with the one she did know. "*Cazzo!*"

Alessandra hit back, literally. Her hand shot out and smacked Lily hard across the face, bringing tears of pain and shock to Lily's eyes. No one had ever struck her before. The pressure behind her bandage increased to unbearable levels.

"Mama, don't hurt my friend. She's *my* friend." Alessandra's hand was raised, poised in the air for another shot, and Maria jumped to bring it down. "Leave her alone!"

"I'm sorry, honey, but I think we made a mistake. This girl isn't the right friend for you. We'll find someone else to be your playmate, don't worry."

"But no one else comes here! It's already taken forever, and I'm *bored*." Maria's whines made Lily's head throb. As much as she was terrified by what Alessandra's grim pronouncement might mean, she wished the girl would just shut up already.

"There are already three more on the island, two women and a man. Perhaps you would like a boy for a friend this time."

Oh God, has she seen the red-haired woman? Does Alessandra know she's here? And who are the other two?

"Those are big people. I want another small person, like me." Maria sulked. "And they won't even be able to see me like this. Lily can 'cause she's different."

What the hell is she talking about? Why wouldn't they be able to see her? How am I different? The conversation interested Lily to the point she'd temporarily forgotten about the slap. She'd have to get Maria alone again so she could ask her.

"We can discuss it later." Alessandra glared down her nose at Lily, as if she'd never seen anything more revolting in her life. "Why don't you give your 'friend' her washing water? No matter what we decide to do with her, she's no use to us like this."

Lily was about to tell Alessandra what she could do with her washing water when she noticed Maria's face. A ribbon of blood trickled from her nose, splashing on the front of her pretty pink dress. "Maria, what happened to your nose? You're bleeding."

The little girl's huge, dark eyes grew even wider. "Mama? It's happening again."

Taking the wooden bucket from her daughter's hands, Alessandra set it down and pressed a handkerchief to Maria's face. Blood bloomed on it, spreading like the petals of a deadly rose. "It's the stress. It's not good for you. We've talked about this, little one. You have to stay calm."

Alessandra cradled the back of her daughter's head so she could apply more pressure. As she held the cloth to Maria's nose, the girl's body shook with sobs. "Mama, I'm scared. My tummy hurts."

"I know it does, baby, but there's nothing to be scared of. You're having a bad day, that's all. Try to relax and it will pass, as it always does. You'll feel better tomorrow."

Lily felt sorry for Maria in spite of herself. It wasn't her fault her mother was a monster, and it *was* a shocking amount of blood. It seemed to go on and on and on. Soon the handkerchief was saturated and Alessandra took the scarf from her own head. "What's wrong with her?"

Hot embers glowed in the woman's eyes, and Lily stumbled back so quickly she tripped, nearly losing her balance.

"*You're* what's wrong with her. It's because of you this is happening. If you hadn't upset her, she'd be fine."

"I doubt this has anything to do with me. She's obviously

sick. Can't the village doctor do something to help her?"

Alessandra returned her attention to her daughter. The scarf was turning red as well, but not as quickly. "There is nothing he can do for us."

"What about the doctor on the other side?"

"You are referring to the monster you escaped from? I would never let that butcher touch my daughter."

Lily didn't know what to believe. There had been such worry and fear in the doctor's eyes when he'd warned her not to cross the bridge. And now here she was with a woman who'd threatened to cook her for supper. *Which one is really the monster?* "He told me he's a famous physician, a great healer. He might be able to do something to help. You don't have anything to lose, if you think about it. The villagers would easily overpower him if he tried anything."

"Mama, don't let the bad man touch me." Maria whimpered, her lower lip protruding. "I'm scared of the bad man."

"Don't worry, sweetheart. No one's going to touch you. Remember my promise? No more doctors and no more needles." Alessandra frowned at Lily. "I'll thank you to keep your suggestions to yourself. Maria is *my* responsibility, no one else's."

Chastened, Lily raised her hands as if in surrender, backing up until she felt the bed behind her. "All right, fine. I was only trying to help my *friend,* because that's what friends do. She's obviously in pain. I don't know why you won't take her to the doctor."

Was Alessandra one of those weirdos who didn't believe in modern medicine? Lily hoped not. If so, it didn't bode well for her eye.

"Mama, can I stay with Lily until dinnertime?"

Alessandra removed her scarf from Maria's nose, using a clean corner to wipe the rest of the blood from her face. "I'm not sure that's such a good idea. Lily will need to sleep for a bit, and she won't want you here."

"Actually, I'd love it if she'd stay. It gets lonely in here by myself." Lily mentally crossed her fingers. If Maria continued to think of her as a friend, Alessandra wouldn't dare hurt her. The girl was her best chance of survival until she could figure out how to get away.

Alessandra looked from her daughter, who was laying it on thick with her pleading eyes and pout, to Lily.

"*Please*, Mama."

"Well, I guess it would be okay if you stay here for a while. But if she tries anything or attempts to hurt you in any way, scream as loud as you can." She narrowed her eyes at Lily. "I won't be far."

"Of course I'm not going to hurt her! *I'm* not the monster." Lily felt wounded by the mother's mistrust. In all the time she'd babysat, no parent had ever suggested she'd hurt their kids. It was absurd.

Maria acted like she hadn't spoken. "Okay, Mama."

"Very well, then. I'll see you both at dinner. You can help Lily get ready."

When Alessandra left, it felt like air returned to the cottage and Lily was able to breathe again. "How are you feeling? Are you really okay?"

Maria was already busy exploring the cottage. She hunkered down and grabbed something from the floor— the doll. *So that's what I tripped over.* The sight of it made Lily feel sick. Maria was welcome to it.

"I'm okay. I used to be really sick, but Mama says I'm fine now."

Mama says? Jesus Christ. "Do you think you're fine, Maria?"

The child shrugged. "Sometimes. But sometimes the blood comes back and my stomach hurts and I get scared."

She hummed a song Lily didn't recognize as she straightened the doll's dress and pulled up her teeny stockings. She didn't look well. Her cheeks had lost most of their color, and her nose had a darkish spot on the tip. Come to think of it, Maria's fingers were purplish too, as if she'd spent time in the cold.

"Maria, let me see your hands."

Still clutching the doll, the girl extended one of her pudgy hands to Lily, who took it in her own. The violet coloring started at the second knuckle, extending down the finger to the nail. Maria's fingernails were a light shade of blue. Lily lifted the hand to her mouth and blew on it, rubbing briskly to warm it. "Are you cold?"

"Not really." She pulled up Lily's sleeve. "What happened to you?"

"My cat scratched me." Lily could feel her cheeks growing warm and hoped the girl wouldn't notice. It had been a while since anyone had asked her about the scars. Usually people just made fun of her, which was why she wore long sleeves, even in the summer.

"Your cat?"

"Yeah. Haven't you ever seen a cat? They have long claws, like this." She curled up one of her hands and swiped at Maria's nose, careful not to actually strike her. The child shrieked with laughter.

"It must be a bad cat."

"It is. It's a very bad cat."

The doctor's words echoed in her mind. *You do not have*

to feel this way, Lily. The pain you are struggling with, it is not normal. I can help you, but you have to trust me. Will you trust me?

Lily brought Maria's hand to her lips and blew on it again. "These scars are why I'm here. It's the cat who got me into this mess," she said.

~ CHAPTER SIXTEEN ~

THE DOCTOR'S OFFICE WAS A crumbling ruin like the rest of the asylum. To get there we had to traverse a winding stone staircase full of gaps, missing steps, and half stairs that reminded me of broken teeth.

Jackson insisted on leading the way, holding on to my arm whenever things got dicey. I didn't need his help, but I accepted it anyway. It was nice not to go it alone for once.

"Tell me again why we're trusting the bad guy?"

"I'm not so sure he *is* the bad guy anymore. There's a lot more going on in Poveglia than I originally thought."

"What about the girl missing her eyes and tongue? That's pretty fucked up, you have to admit."

I was beginning to regret I'd told Jackson about her; I should have waited until I'd heard the doctor out. But Jacks was anxious to know what was going on, and I didn't blame him. I couldn't expect him to follow me through an abandoned asylum at the behest of a man I'd painted as a violent poltergeist and the Italian version of Dr. Mengele without some sort of explanation.

"What the fuck is this?" Jackson burst into the doctor's office, plunging through the man himself without noticing, and snatched an ugly, beaked mask off a desk. The sight of it made me shudder, but I'd seen enough of them in my research to know what it was.

"The plague doctors wore them. Isn't that right?" I asked the doctor, who regarded Jackson with a bemused expression on his face. There's never any telling how spirits will react when you invade their inner sanctum, but I suspected the doctor was used to it. Judging by the graffiti and the broken beer bottles, the place had seen quite a few parties in its day.

"Yes. There is a filter here to protect the wearer from contracting the disease." He tapped the bridge of the beak with a long finger, but Jackson didn't react even though he still held the mask. *Must be nice to be a mainstreamer.* "You are aware, of course, that the plague virus may remain active on the island. There's no telling what spores escaped when they burned the bodies."

The ludicrousness of a ghost wearing another ghost's mask against a disease that could no longer hurt him struck me, and I didn't know whether to laugh or cry. Should I be honest or humor him? Then again, subtlety had never been one of my strong points.

"You do realize you're dead?"

This time Jackson reacted, shooting me a funny look and returning the mask to the ruins of the doctor's desk.

"I may have lost my corporeal self, but I have not lost my mind. Old habits die hard, like old physicians, I suppose. If it makes me feel better to wear it, I see no harm. Everyone has a coping mechanism of some sort."

"You're sure it's not because you enjoy scaring the shit out of people?"

A smirk toyed at the corner of his mouth. "Death has a decided lack of amusements. Purgatory, even less so." He waved his hand at two rotting chairs that had miraculously survived the raves. "Do sit down. You two are making me nervous, hovering over me like ghosts."

More black humor. It was something I'd never encountered before. Spirits could be devastated, vengeful, deranged or furious, but I'd never before met one with a sense of humor. Then again, the doctor had been a most unusual man.

"Please, sit. And ask your angry friend to do the same, if you will. He seems to be a bit hard of hearing, the poor fellow."

I raised my eyebrow at the doctor, unsure whether or not he was serious. This time his smirk was more pronounced.

"Yes, Miss Carlsson, I am 'having you on,' as they say. I am pulling your leg. Or, as Lily prefers, you've been punk'd." The slightest of frowns creased his forehead. "But perhaps that last one is not appropriate. Suffice it to say I am well aware you have an ability your friend does not. I must confess I have wondered more than once why you brought him along. He appears to be nothing more than dead weight."

Rolling my eyes, I groaned. "You're here all night; try the veal."

Now it was his turn to raise an eyebrow. "Pardon me?"

"It's an English expression. It means you fancy yourself a comedian."

By this point, Jackson was staring at me like I'd lost my mind. The conversation had definitely taken a turn for the bizarre. It was a good thing more ghosts didn't crack jokes. A few more experiences like this, and I'd be seeking a new line of work.

The doctor stroked his chin. "Hmm. I can't claim to

understand it, but I will say you should never joke about veal with an Italian, especially one who lost his ability to enjoy a fine meal almost a hundred years ago. On this side of the island, spirits do not eat."

An icy chill crept over me as his meaning sunk in. "And on the other side they do?"

"Oh yes. You would find their appetite voracious, I should think. Not to mention vulgar and abhorrent. But I will say no more with you both hovering over me like shadows."

Taking a deep breath, I looked over at Jackson, who was leaning against the doorframe.

"Well? Did you two finish your chitchat?"

"He wants us to sit down."

He widened his eyes as he took in the pitiful state of the doctor's office furniture. "Then he's crazy. That piece of kindling isn't going to hold me."

"Jacks, please." Picking my way over the rubble, I closed the short distance between us. "He still feels this is his office. Let's show him this little respect, please."

"Okay, but I hope he starts getting to the point, which is saving Lily's soul, remember? This place gives me the creeps."

"The girl is fine. Her safety is assured as long as Maria keeps thinking of her as a friend," the doctor said. "Fortunately, Lily was clever enough to figure this out and she's playing her part admirably. It has bought you a bit of time."

"He says she's okay because she's made friends with someone," I told Jackson, hoping to reassure him.

"How do we know he's telling us the truth? I don't trust this guy."

I was thankful he kept his voice down as we carried the dust-coated chairs to the doctor's dilapidated desk. Before I could explain it was a hunch I'd developed through years of interacting with all sorts of spirits, the doctor spoke. "Your friend has a point—that may be the most intelligent thing I've heard him say yet, so I will respond. You can trust me because we have a common enemy. I don't want Lily in the clutches of those vermin any more than you do."

Repeating his words to Jackson, I said a silent prayer and sat down. The chair creaked, but it held my weight. Jacks leaned forward, keeping most of his on the balls of his feet. Smart.

"Before we begin, can you ask your friend to put his device here?" The doctor pointed to the top of his desk.

"Oh no—we need it for light, and to get back, and probably for a million other things I'm not remembering."

"I promise not to drain it. And you have one as well, do you not? It's just easier."

Sighing, I turned to Jackson once more. "Can you put your phone on the desk?"

"Why?"

"Trust me."

He shrugged as if to say, *What the hell? I've come this far.* "On or off?"

"Airplane mode will be fine."

"I have to tell you, Kate—life with you is never boring." Adjusting the settings, he put his sleek, state-of-the-art phone on the doctor's ruin. Rather than gush with gratitude, the doctor merely cleared his throat until I pushed it closer.

Jackson lunged forward as if to retrieve it. "Hey!"

"Trust me," I said again. "He won't hurt it. It makes it

easier for him to communicate."

Sure enough, the doctor's form was already less transparent. He had been a handsome man in a bland sort of way, with dark, wavy hair swooping over his forehead in the style Cary Grant had made popular. So much more appealing than the assortment of Bieber clones ubiquitous today. His eyes were surprisingly kind when they weren't behind that evil-looking mask, with a hint of laugh lines when he smirked. He had been young when he'd died, no older than me.

Always the mind reader, the doctor showed off his skills.

"You flatter me, but the Italian genes are misleading, I'm afraid. I was forty-one when I was murdered."

"You were *murdered*?"

"We can go anytime, Kate," Jackson said. "*Any*time."

"Hang on—this is important." I gestured for Jacks to be quiet, figuring I'd make it up to him later. "My research indicated you took your own life, Doctor."

That sad little smirk returned. "I am certain it did, just as I am certain they did not give me credit for the great advances I made in the treatment of mental illness."

I hoped he was joking, but it was obvious he wasn't. He fairly swelled with pride whenever he spoke about his treatments. Like many intelligent men, his ego was out of control.

My usual MO when encountering an overinflated male ego was to pop it and watch it go hissing around the room. Why should this guy be immune just because he was dead? "No offense, Doc, but your treatments were more like torture. Thankfully, medical science has managed to advance without your intervention."

His eyes lit up. "Really? Then depression has been cured?"

"Um…no, not yet."

"What about mania?"

"We call it something different, but it still exists. I never said we were perfect."

"Do people continue to suffer from nerves? Hysteria? Dementia?"

"Yes, of course."

"Schizophrenia must have been cured, though, surely."

"There are better treatments now, but it hasn't been cured, no."

He leaned back in his chair with an expression of astonishment. "Well, then. If these conditions continue to torment the innocent, what are the advances you speak of?"

"We don't go around drilling holes in people's heads, for starters."

"And electric shock? Is electricity no longer used to treat mental conditions?"

Shit. "Not as much."

"Would it surprise you to know, Miss Carlsson, that before our common enemy came to the island, I had incredible success with leukotomy?"

I snorted with as much derision as I could. "It's hardly surprising that drilling holes in a person's head would change their personality."

"You make it sound so barbaric. Are these the hands of a barbarian?" He waved his long, graceful fingers.

"I can't say I've met enough barbarians to make a study of it."

"What *are* you guys talking about?" Jackson blurted. I was shocked he'd stayed quiet for this long. I probably wouldn't have been able to.

"The good doctor is explaining how wonderful his practice of drilling holes in people's skulls was. Once they'd been turned into zombies, they were no longer depressed. Go figure."

"*One* hole, Miss Carlsson. Singular, never plural. And my patients were not 'zombies,' as you so inelegantly put it. They were whole, happy people, something they had not been for some time before they came to me, if ever in their lives."

"And the girl downstairs? She doesn't seem whole or happy to me."

The doctor curled his lip in a snarl. "I had nothing to do with the state she is in. I already told you that."

"You have, but it doesn't make any sense. Why would the others on the island do that to a child? And who are they?"

"Get him to make it quick. I want to blow this joint," Jackson added. I was thrilled to see we were once more on the same page.

The doctor's flicker of temper vanished as quickly as it had appeared. He leaned back in his chair, steepling his fingers under his chin. "When I arrived here as a young man, I had already earned some renown for my work with the mentally ill in Rome and Venice. Even in Paris and London. This was the next natural step, an opportunity to expand my work with patients removed from the outside world. Here on Poveglia, I could closely observe their treatment and recovery. And they *did* recover, Miss Carlsson."

"If you say so." As flippant as I sounded, which was a reaction to his arrogance more than anything else, I already knew people hadn't suffered here. Not in any great numbers, at least, which gave credence to the doctor's claims that he hadn't tortured his patients, as history would have one believe. His nurses had been terrified, though… but of what? I suspected he was about to tell me.

"I do. Long after the plague victims had met their sad fate, Poveglia became a place of peace and fellowship, a place where, no matter their condition when they arrived, people could live out their days in comfort. It wasn't only those with mental conditions who were brought here, you understand. Children with clubfeet, cleft palates, hemangiomas, deformities of any kind—they were dropped here, as if this were some human wasteland. I used my skills to give them back their dignity."

Children had been abandoned on this terrible island because their own parents couldn't stand to look at them? It was enough to break your heart. "It didn't stay a place of peace, did it, Doctor?"

"No, it did not. *They* ruined it." His voice grew rough with contempt.

"Who are 'they'?"

"I am certain the world has not changed in this respect. Call them administration, government, boards, management. The faceless 'they' who are tasked with making decisions but who seldom fail to make the wrong ones. You are familiar?"

The Gift had ensured I'd never put in time at a regular day job, but I'd heard enough horror stories to know exactly what he was talking about. "I am."

He sighed. "I am not surprised. I am also not privy to the reason these great minds decided the island should become a repository for the criminally insane, because they did not discuss it with me. In fact, they did not even do me the courtesy of letting me know."

I reached for Jackson's hand, and once again felt relieved when he entwined his fingers with mine, his warmth reassuring in the darkness beyond the doctor's phosphorescence. "You mean…?"

"Murderers. Rapists. Child torturers. Fiends of all kinds, deposited on our shores without so much as a warning."

"Oh my God." No wonder the nurses had been scrambling around in fear. And those poor children! "What happened?"

"We were able to contain them in the beginning. Thankfully, the majority had lived in captivity for so long they had become institutionalized, so our rules were not unfamiliar. As you can understand, we did not have sufficient security or the manpower to protect our patients, and eventually the situation became dire. I needed to return to Venice and plead my case, but I dared not leave the nurses on their own."

"That's understandable."

"I used every means at my disposal to prolong the inevitable. We kept the most dangerous in a complete stupor, and in restraints whenever possible. *That* you may properly refer to as barbaric, and it surely was, but I felt I had no other recourse. My responsibility was to my patients, and to my staff, the good-hearted women who believed in my work so much they were willing to live a life of isolation out here."

The pain in his voice was palpable, and I realized the sadness of the island came not from his patients, but from him. "You did the best you could."

"Thank you, but you praise me too highly. I had already learned that one's mental condition does not correspond to one's intelligence. I had given lectures to that effect. And yet, I completely discounted the criminals' ability to plot against us…and to mobilize. That was my failing. That is why I will never forgive myself."

And that's why you're still here. You can't accept this failing and let go.

"The day they made their escape to the other side of the island, they took many of my patients with them. I am aware of what became of those poor befuddled souls, of course, though it would be better for me if I were not. But by then it was too late for me to protect them."

Squeezing Jackson's hand, I waited for the doctor to gather the strength to tell the last of his story.

"I'm sure you have noticed the tower."

Of course I had. With its boarded-up windows, it loomed over Poveglia, intensifying the island's already abandoned and somewhat ominous air.

"It has served many purposes over the years, but long before it was a lighthouse, it was the bell tower of a church. I always felt that lent it a lovely tranquility, and I was at peace up there, looking over the island and the lagoon. My staff and patients knew I liked to go there to think."

He gazed down at his desk, shoulders slumping with the weight of his story. "It is difficult to accept, even now. That I, a man of science, a man renowned as an expert of the human brain and all its various perversions, could be fooled by a common criminal is shameful. In my own defense, all I can say is that, cunning as they were, they chose the lone person among them who had my sympathy. This sympathy had a great impact on my judgment."

The doctor lifted his head then, meeting my eyes, and as his own welled with tears, his form wavered in front of me. Jackson's phone was losing power. "And that is why you see me like this, a man who never ages, in a hell of his own making, instead of an old codger snug in his bed somewhere who has long forgotten about this terrible place.

"She arrived with the criminals, the only woman among them, and she was radiant. She was also pregnant. In my vast ignorance, I assumed she had been ravished or otherwise taken advantage of, and I pitied her. This was no place to birth a child, let alone raise one. Her future would be very difficult, or so I thought. But any man who dismissed her as the weaker sex did so at his folly."

I could scarcely breathe. There was only one woman with a child on the island that I was aware of. "What happened to you, Doctor?"

He looked past me as if he were reliving the moment in his mind. "She said she had come to plead their case. In a last-ditch attempt to save my remaining patients, we had cut off the criminals' supplies, hoping that if we starved them out, they would return the poor souls back to my care. Little did we know they had acquired a readily available source of food."

His upper lip drew back in revulsion, but I wasn't sure what was behind this reaction and I wasn't ready to ask.

"The death itself was fairly anticlimactic, I'm afraid. She calmed my nerves—cajoling, flattering, appeasing me—until I let my guard down. The second my attention slipped, it was only a matter of giving me one strong push. The last thing I recall is the earth rushing up to greet me, so I suspect my neck snapped on impact. Or perhaps my skull shattered. In any case, I should be grateful that at least my physical body did not suffer.

"Sadly, my patients were not so fortunate."

That his death had been painless was not news to me. It was the reason I could be in his company for prolonged periods without suffering.

"You realize, of course, why I am telling you this. My demise is of no concern to you—it is ancient history. However, the identity of my killer *is* of concern. You came to Poveglia to rescue the girl's soul, believing she was in danger in my care.

"I hope you now understand that her situation is much more precarious with them than it ever was with me."

~ CHAPTER SEVENTEEN ~

IT WAS WHILE SHE WAS playing with Maria that Lily figured out how to solve her problems. Well, one of them, at least.

Like many of the girls Lily had babysat, Maria was obsessed with playing house. Thankfully, the child was content to take on the role of mother while Lily pretended to be the dad who spent his days working in the fields, only to barge in the house and demand dinner, which never failed to make Maria giggle.

This gave Lily the perfect excuse to avoid the "baby," which repulsed her to the point she felt like throwing up whenever she looked at it. She didn't understand why the doll affected her so strongly. Though she'd never cared for them—they were all a bit creepy, with their unseeing eyes and frozen grins—she hadn't *hated* them before. Maria's doll appeared to be perfectly normal, as far as dolls went. The one thing that made it unusual was its age, which was understandable under the circumstances, and its realism. It was as close to looking like a real infant as any doll was ever going to get.

It's the smell. That's all it is, Lily told herself as Maria thrust the doll into "Daddy's" face for yet another good-night kiss. Lily felt her gorge rise. "For heaven's sake, woman, I'm the man of this house," she said, deepening her voice. "I don't have time for such nonsense. Now go get me a snack."

To her relief, Maria squealed in delight and cuddled the doll to her chest, automatically compensating for her husband's lack of parenting skills.

The smell, and the flies.

As before, a small cloud of the bothersome insects followed Maria's doll wherever it went. Lily suspected whatever had been used to stuff the toy was rotting, but what could produce such a horrible stench? Maybe Maria was used to it, because she didn't seem to be repulsed by the smell or even to notice it.

Lily cleared her throat in a masculine way. "That daughter of ours carries a foul stench, wife. I think you need to change her."

The child's brow furrowed. She brought the doll to her nose, inhaling deeply while Lily cringed at the thought of having that thing so close to her face. "No, she doesn't. She's clean. I just changed her before dinner."

Oh well. It had been worth a try. "If you say so. Now I'm going to read the paper while you clean the house. Fetch my slippers, will ya?"

Maria frowned, saying the words Lily had begun to suspect she'd never hear. "I don't want to play house anymore. Being the mother is boring."

"Okay. What do you want to play instead?"

Lily sighed with relief when Maria left the doll on a chair, far enough away that the smell didn't reach her.

"Do you know any songs you could teach me?"

"No Italian songs, but—" As the thought popped into

her head, Lily hesitated. *Was she brave enough? Or stupid enough?* It would be like poking a sleeping tiger with a stick, especially if Alessandra found out. "I could teach you a game we play back home."

Maria clapped her hands. "I love games! Games are lots of fun. How do we play?"

"Well…you may not like *this* game. It's for adults, really. You have to be a grown-up to play it. And we have to sit in a circle very quietly and not move around too much."

"I can do that. I'm very mature." Maria crossed her arms, her cherub-like pout belying her words. Lily bit her lip to keep from laughing.

"I can see that. That's why I suggested it. But if I show you how to play, you have to keep it a secret. No one else can ever know we played."

Maria's eyes swallowed her face. "Is it a *bad* game?" she whispered.

"No, not at all. It's just secret."

No child she'd ever met had been able to resist a secret, and she hoped Lily would be the same.

"Please tell me. I won't tell anyone else, I swear! I want to play."

"Okay. Let's sit here."

They faced each other on the cabin floor, avoiding the stain of Lily's earlier shame. The little girl regarded her somberly, keeping as still as her doll.

"It's called Truth or Dare. If I ask you a question, you have to swear to tell me the truth, no matter what it is. If I dare you to do something, you have to do it. And the same goes for you with me. Do you think you can handle that?"

Maria nodded. "Yes. I can do this."

"Are you sure?" Lily raised an eyebrow, trying her best to

look doubtful. "It can get...*intense.*"

"I am sure. I will win this game."

She thought about explaining that no one won Truth or Dare, not really, but decided against it. Better that she engage Maria's competitive instincts. "Would you like to go first?"

"No, you. You show me."

"Okay, which do you want—truth or dare?" *Pick truth, Maria. Please pick truth.*

"Dare."

Shit. "Okay. I dare you to...hide your doll somewhere I can't find her."

Maria wrinkled her nose. "That's not much of a dare."

"It's best to start you off easy. It's your first time. This game can get super difficult."

The girl pushed herself to her feet. "Close your eyes so you don't see where I put Mary."

Lily closed her uncovered eye and waited, smiling as Maria scampered over to her doll. A good deal of rustling and shuffling followed while she prayed Maria would ask for truth next. She cursed herself. Why hadn't she told the girl the game was called Truth and Truth? At least she wouldn't have to see the doll anymore, but other than that, dares weren't going to do much for her.

Maria gave her a kick, her tiny foot jabbing against Lily's insole. "Now I get to dare *you* to do something."

Rather than correct her, Lily decided to go along with it. "Okay, go. What's your dare?"

"Show me how you escaped from the doctor."

"What?"

The girl's eyes gleamed in the dimming light. "Mama says no one was able to get away from him before without her help. I want to see how you did it."

Lily's mind raced. "I—I don't know how to show you that. There was nothing to it, really. I just waited until the doctor was asleep…"

Maria shook her head. "The doctor don't sleep. He doesn't need to."

"Oh. He wasn't around, anyway. It was dark, so I thought he was asleep. I felt my way around the hospital until I found the door, and then I ran. That's when you found me."

"Weren't you tied up? Mama says he keeps his prisoners tied to their beds so they can't run away."

She'd forgotten about the restraints. That night felt like it had taken place a lifetime ago. And that's when it occurred to her—could the trick the redhead showed her work on other things? She suspected it could.

Lily's enthusiasm for continuing the game was gone, but she knew Maria's was only getting stronger. She would have to tire the girl out.

"Oh yeah, he had these big cuffs on my wrist. They were too loose, though. I pulled my arms out, like this." Lily mimed yanking her arms back.

"That's it?" Maria asked. "That doctor doesn't seem too smart."

"I guess even doctors make mistakes. Okay, your turn! Truth or dare?"

"I pick…truth!"

Whew. Now the question was where to begin. There were so many things she wanted to know. "Where are the other children? How come you're the only child on the island?"

Maria shrugged. "Mama says they got sick and died."

Gambling that Maria wouldn't call her on asking more than one question at a time, Lily risked another. "What kind of sick, do you know?"

"Something from the island. A lot of the villagers, they died, but Mama says we're stronger than the sickness."

"Is that why your nose bleeds? And your tummy hurts?"

"Sometimes I'm scared, and I think I'm sick again, but Mama tells me it will go away and it does."

"Will your mama hurt me, Maria?" It was what she most wanted to know, and what she was most afraid of knowing. Lily held her breath, waiting for the girl's answer.

"If you're my friend, Mama will never hurt you. She only gets mad when people betray us."

"How do they betray you?"

Maria screwed up her face. "Isn't it my turn yet?"

"You're right; I'm sorry. How about another dare?" She prayed Maria wouldn't ask anything else about her miraculous escape from the hospital. She'd never been a very good liar.

"No, I want truth too."

"Okay. What do you want to know?" Lily braced herself.

"Do you *really* want to be my friend?"

Her pulse pounding in her ears, she answered without hesitation. "Of course I want to be your friend."

"Mama says you're pretending. She says you're trying to trick me."

"That doesn't make any sense. Why would I pretend to be your friend?"

"So we won't eat you."

⚄

Lily waited until the only sound in the room was Maria's

breathing. The girl's nose had started bleeding again that evening, and now and then Lily heard a muffled snort, as if air couldn't quite make it through.

As it turned out, she hadn't lied to Maria after all. That had been the most intense game of Truth or Dare she'd ever played, and she didn't care to repeat it. In fact, it was her new mission in life never to play that game again.

She'd suspected the truth, of course. Alessandra's hints that morning had been unmistakable, and combined with the lack of livestock and the strangely plentiful meat, it was simple enough to put two and two together. But suspecting it and hearing a child say it so matter-of-factly—as if it were the most ordinary thing one could say—was totally different. Lily had heard of cannibals (there were a few illicit books that had been passed around her group of friends) but as far as she knew, it was normally a last resort, something done out of desperation, for survival. The villagers had a farm, and presumably there were fish in the lagoon, judging by the nets she'd seen outside the hospital. There was just one conclusion she could come to.

Maria and her people ate human flesh because they *wanted* to.

Lily's stomach churned, and she pushed the thought away. It wasn't helping her focus. She had no idea if she could master the water trick with her head—heads were different from arms and legs, obviously—but she had to try. She could only skip dinner for so long.

My head is water. My head is water. Lily concentrated, picturing her face melting under the blindfold and dripping off the mattress. *Head is water; head is water.*

Each time Maria snorted in her sleep, it broke her concentration and she had to start over again. She wished the girl hadn't insisted on staying with her, but the child was determined not to leave her side. For once, Lily had rooted for Alessandra to win an argument, but when it came to her daughter, the woman had a difficult time saying no.

Focus. What else do you have to do? Head is water; head is water. It seemed like she had been picturing the same thing for hours and hours. If her teachers knew she was capable of this kind of commitment, they'd have a whole new respect for her. *Wait—why am I thinking about my teachers? Christ, Lily, FOCUS. Head is water; head is water.*

Finally it happened. It was the slightest change at first, so slight that Lily wrote it off as wishful thinking. The pressure on her eye eased, and along with it, the dull headache that had thrummed in her brain all day. She forced herself to remain calm, breathing slowly the way the red-haired woman had shown her.

In…out. Head is water. In…out. Head is water.

The fabric sagged like a deflated balloon and Lily seized it, ripping it over her head before the effect wore off.

What the hell?

Aside from the fact that her head no longer felt like it was being crushed in a vise, nothing had changed. She still had tunnel vision, as if something were covering one side of her face. Lily strained to open her eye as wide as she could, but nothing happened.

Waiting until she heard Maria's soft snoring again, Lily reached up with a trembling hand. *Maybe it's another bandage. That's probably it. They put a smaller one on in case the blindfold fell off. That's all it is. Relax, girl—you're on the homestretch.*

She wasn't brave enough to go right for the eye at first. Instead, she touched the skin around it, and was relieved to find it felt completely normal. Inching her index finger up to the corner of the eye, she couldn't feel anything other than skin. No bandage then, unless the villagers had managed to perfect some insane medical technology, which she seriously doubted.

Her heart racing in her chest like it wanted to make a break for it, Lily took a deep breath and touched her right eyelid. At the base, where her eyelids met, was a ridge. It felt bumpy and rough under her fingers, and she was rewarded by an immediate flare of pain. Not all of the soreness had been due to the tightness of the blindfold, then. They'd done something else—but what?

It took her brain a minute to process the information her fingers were giving her.

The ridge she was feeling was her own skin—skin held together by thick thread.

My eye is sewn shut!

~ CHAPTER EIGHTEEN ~

JACKSON BREATHED DEEPLY, CLOSING HIS eyes as he filled his lungs. I knew exactly how he felt. The air in the asylum was oppressive. It was a relief to be back outside, away from the murdered doctor and his terrible burden. An immense weight lifted from my own soul, even though we were no closer to rescuing Lily. The heaviness of the doctor's despair was enough to crush anyone. I resolved to help him before we left the island, but Lily came first.

Stretching his arms above his head until his spine cracked audibly, Jackson turned to me. "Man, I am so glad that's over. I thought I was going to suffocate in there."

"Yeah. It's not a happy place, that's for sure. But at least we get to leave. Imagine what it's like for those who are stuck here forever."

"What about the dude who bought this island? He'll tear down the asylum, right?"

"I would think so. He'll probably build a resort or something." I couldn't imagine anyone wanting to vacation here, where the hopelessness had seeped into the atmosphere like a pall, but stranger stuff had happened. Some people might even come here for that very reason.

Just look at Aokigahara. Tourists went there all the time, hoping to find a body or see what effect the infamous forest would have on them.

"And when the asylum's gone, those spirits will go too, right? They'll have no reason to stay here anymore."

Ah, if only it were that simple. "Not necessarily. You know how that room we were in looked to you?"

"Yeah, it was full of old junk, with mold all over the walls. Half the ceiling was caved in, and I was scared shitless waiting for the other half to come down. That place is a hazard."

"Well, to the doctor, it's his office. He sees it as it was on the day he died: pristine, neat, everything in order. The ideal place to have a difficult conversation. It's his sanctuary."

"So even if the asylum is burnt to the ground…"

"As far as he's concerned, it would still be here, yes."

Jackson held his forehead as if his brain were about to explode. "Are we talking parallel universes here, Kate? Because I'm not sure how much more of this I can take. I'm still kind of hung up on the soul-kidnapping poltergeist thing."

Good thing I hadn't told him about the cannibalistic ghosts. Yet.

"More like an alternate reality. We're in the same dimension, but in many ways, ghosts see what they want to see. That's how some can persist in believing they're not dead. Of course, they conveniently neglect to notice that their world is stagnant and nothing ever changes, but I suspect they avoid thinking about it too much."

"I can understand why." He ran a hand over his head. "This is seriously messed up. I don't know how you keep it straight."

I smiled. We were walking toward the laundry to regroup and decide on our next move. The doctor had been more open with me than I'd expected, which was a good thing, but now I had to figure out what to do with his information, which was unrelentingly bleak. "Remember, I've had a lifetime to process this. You're getting hit with it all at once. I think you're doing remarkably well, considering."

"Gee, thanks." He bumped his shoulder against mine.

"Seriously. Now you can understand why I don't talk about this stuff with mainstreamers. Too many questions."

Jackson froze in midstep, an expression of exaggerated horror on his face. "Hold the phone. Hold the fucking phone—did you just call me *mainstream*?"

I laughed. "Don't be offended. It's an expression, that's all. People like Laura and me use it to refer to people who… well, aren't like Laura and me."

"I am the furthest thing from mainstream you're ever gonna find."

"Okay, okay." I raised my arms in surrender. "I stand corrected. You're as big a freak as I am. Better?"

"Much. So, does that guy get that he's dead?"

"Most definitely. He remembers his murder in painful detail."

"He knows he's dead, but he can't see that time has passed. You realize this doesn't make any fucking sense. You do realize that, right?"

"Hey, I don't make the rules." Poking my head inside the brick building that had already begun to feel familiar, I was about to lead the way to the alcove where we'd used the spirit board when I paused at the stairwell. "Want to go on the roof? It isn't raining anymore."

"Sure. Better outside than in."

"Okay, watch your step." Steadying myself against the stone wall, I climbed the crumbling stairs to the roof. The sky was the color of a robin's egg and the air was surprisingly warm in spite of the brisk wind. Oh, to be a tourist poking around St. Mark's Square, nibbling on a cone, instead of hanging out on the world's most haunted island. I had a desperate urge to get the rescue over with so we could enjoy the rest of our time in Venice. "I haven't been able to figure out if it's arbitrary or a conscious decision, but some spirits who linger see the world as it truly is, and others see it as it was at the time they left the physical plane. What I can't tell you is why."

"But that guy believes he's seeing things as they really are, right?"

Remembering how the doctor had insisted we sit on those decrepit, rotting chairs, I nodded. "I'd bet money on it."

"So how do we know that *our* reality is reality?"

"You've watched *The Matrix* too many times." I socked him on the arm before I saw the concern on his face.

"No, seriously. Hear me out. What if we died in China, and the past year has been some kind of afterlife delusion?"

"We're not dead, Jacks."

"But how do we *know*? Lots of spirits don't, right? So we could be dead and not know that we're dead."

"We're not dead, trust me."

"How do you know?"

I sighed. "I guess it's a moot point, because it's impossible to ever know these things for sure. Now can we get back to figuring out how we're going to get Lily away from those *gaki*? You're making my head spin."

"What the hell are *gaki*?"

I quickly explained my suspicions that Lily's new "friends" were a particularly nasty kind of spirit, the kind that could devour souls. Since Lily wasn't dead, they couldn't touch her physical body. But without the girl's soul, her body would be a lifeless shell dependent on nourishment from tubes. If anything was worse than murder, it was that, since Lily's soul would cease to exist.

"Are you sure they're dead?"

"Yes. They all got very sick. The plague victims were buried on the side of the island where the psychotic criminals settled, so the virus might have still been active. They could have stirred things up when they cultivated the land for their farm."

"You're absolutely positive? Because, depending how old they were in the thirties, some of them could still be alive."

"Thanks for the math lesson. But yes, I'm sure. We have to go and get her, Jacks. It's already the afternoon. I'm sure neither of us wants to spend the night here."

He drew away from me. "What's this 'we' bullshit? You aren't going anywhere near that place."

"What are you talking about? I have to go."

"Kate, have you lost your everloving mind? People died of the plague over there, maybe hundreds of thousands of 'em. Then a band of cannibal killers settled there, torturing and eating people. If you go anywhere near that place, you're history. The only reason you're alive right now is that the dock is on this side of the island."

I'd steeled myself against this reality. It definitely wouldn't be a pleasurable experience, and I couldn't stay more than an hour, but that should be enough time to retrieve Lily's soul and send it back where it belonged. "I have to go. I'll just deal with the pain."

"Deal with the pain of hundreds of thousands? I saw what happened to you in Hensu, Kate. I almost lost you, and the numbers were infinitesimal compared to this. No, it's too great a risk."

"Don't you think I realize that? Why do you think I called you? You can help me. If the situation gets to be too much, you can get me out of there."

"The situation is too much now! It was too much before it started. Jesus Christ." Jackson paced the roof, glowering at me. Then his expression brightened. "Hey, wait a minute—I think I've figured it out. If they're dead, then they can't hurt me, right?"

"That's not necessarily true." I pulled aside my hair to show him my scar, the one darling Isabelle had decided to give me as a parting souvenir. "Remember this? Some spirits can definitely hurt the living, or even kill them. You saw what happened to my house. You think they could destroy my place and not hurt a person?"

"Shit. I was kinda hoping that just applied to mediums."

"Sorry to disappoint you."

"What if I try hard not to believe in them again? Won't that make a difference?"

"It doesn't matter if you don't believe in the devil; the devil believes in you. Also, you'd have to find Lily's soul, retrieve it, and send it back on your own. Unless you have talents you haven't told me about, I suspect that might pose a problem."

"Ah, fuck. Well, that settles it. You'll have to contact Lily's mother and tell her we couldn't do it."

"Are you crazy? I'm not going to *leave* her here, Jackson."

"Well, I'm not letting you go on this fucking suicide mission, Kate."

We glared at each other, chests heaving. For a second, I regretted getting him involved, but there was no way I could get to Lily without an ally. Jacks was right, as much as I hated to admit it. Even with his help, the odds were against my reaching her. Alone, I would have no chance.

Taking a deep breath, I struggled to control my temper. I needed him on my side, and standing here ranting and raving wasn't going to do anything but drive him further away.

"Wait a minute. What the fuck is that?"

I turned to look in the direction Jackson was pointing, and instantly understood the reason for his shock. "It appears to be a boat."

"I got that much on my own. Does that boat look at all familiar to you?"

It didn't, but since we'd only been on one boat recently, it was easy to follow his line of logic. Assuming you could call any of the workings of Jackson's mind logical. "You think it's Vincenzo's?"

"Of *course* I think it's Vincenzo's. You don't?"

"I'm not sure. They all look the same to me."

"That's because you don't know boats." Jackson began listing every feature that made Vincenzo's boat unique until I was tempted to jump from the roof—or push him off.

"If it's Vincenzo's, what's he doing here?" I asked in a futile attempt to change the subject.

"Maybe he's come to pick us up." I didn't miss the hopeful tone that had crept into Jackson's voice. So he still thought there was a chance Sophia had been trying to help us. Well, I guess one of us should see the best in people.

"If he's here for us, what's he doing over there?" The

sleek craft was waiting at a dock on the other side of the island, which was why we hadn't seen it when we'd left the asylum. "He couldn't possibly have predicted we'd climb onto the roof and check out the view."

"It's the direction we have to head in anyway if we're going to get Lily, right? There's no harm in checking it out."

I wasn't so sure about that. I didn't trust Vincenzo or his daughter-in-law. But if it got us closer to Lily, it was better than standing here arguing. "Okay," I said, mentally crossing myself for luck. "Let's go."

☙

Once we'd rounded the corner of our favorite brick building, it was obvious why the secrets of Poveglia had remained secret for so long.

"Christ, it's a jungle back here. I don't suppose you thought to bring a machete?" Jackson cursed, bringing his arms up to protect his face, but it was too late. The vicious thorns that had taken over this part of the island had already done their damage. His skin was crisscrossed with bleeding scratches. The part of me that had watched too many horror movies hoped his blood wouldn't unleash some ancient evil—and then I realized we were already up to our asses in ancient evil.

"Sorry, I left it back with my Weedwacker."

"Figures. Motherfucker!" he yelled as another branch clawed its way across his face.

"Did it ever occur to you there's a reason these things are here? It's like Mother Nature's way of saying, 'YOU SHALL NOT PASS.'"

"I've been saying that all along. Call Lily's mother and

tell her the jig is up."

There was no point arguing this time. I knew he didn't mean it. Jackson couldn't leave Lily on this godforsaken island any more than I could. This was no place for any soul, or anyone who had a soul, for that matter.

We quickened our pace as we neared the island's cavana. With its lagoon floor, the boathouse looked eerily like a cottage for sea monsters. From our vantage point on the laundry's roof, we'd seen Vincenzo's boat was docked slightly beyond it.

Just before we cleared the cavana, my hackles rose. I stopped short, causing Jackson to bump into me. Before he could say anything, I signaled for him to get down. We crouched in the thorns, the only sound our stifled breathing. An agonizing minute passed, and then another.

"What are we waiting for, exactly?" Jackson murmured, but I shook my head. It wasn't safe to talk yet. I don't know how I knew, but I'd learned through painful trial and error to trust my instincts.

After a few more minutes, my thighs were screaming. Every now and then I could feel Jackson's sigh on the back of my neck. Tilting my head at an awkward angle to whisper in his ear, I braced myself on his shoulder to keep from toppling over. "I've changed my mind. I don't think we should go over there."

He arched an eyebrow. "Why not?" In spite of the fact that my inner alarm bells were clanging, his breath on my earlobe made my entire body tingle.

"I can't explain it. It's just something I feel." I took it for granted he would appreciate the gravity of such statements now, at least coming from me.

"It might be our only way home, Kate. What if she had

second thoughts and came back to help us?"

It was my turn to pull the arched-eyebrow routine. "Do you really believe that?"

"Stranger things have happened."

"It's a hell of a risk if you're wrong, and it's not only our asses on the line here, remember?"

"Of course I remember. But what other choice do we have? We have to pass that way to get to where Lily is. So why not check out the boat while we're here? Kill two birds with one stone."

He had a point, as much as I hated to admit it.

"Okay, but let's keep our eyes open. Something about this situation stinks, and it's not the lagoon."

"Right behind you."

Ducking under the branches with their treacherous tangle of thorns, I led Jackson toward the water again, my apprehension growing with every step. I'd never ignored such a blatant warning before, and I wasn't about to now. But before I could tell him we had to turn around, he edged past me.

"There's no one here."

I wanted to scream at him to get back, that it was a trap and the boat was the bait, but I soon saw he was right. Vincenzo's skiff wasn't exactly a pleasure yacht. The only way someone could hide there would be to crouch in the corner beside the driver's seat, or to lie on the floor of the cabin, and it was immediately apparent both areas were clear of stowaways. My heart pounding in my throat, I sank down on one of the boat's padded bench seats. It was a relief to sit on something that wasn't in danger of collapsing under me.

"Do you think he went to the asylum looking for us?"

Jackson asked.

A hint of something green caught my eye, and I bent to pick it up. "You mean *they*." I held the Starbucks cup with its lipstick print turned where he could see it. Sophia had taken her morning coffee with her when she'd ditched us, but this particular cup hadn't contained coffee. A thick, dark sludge coated the bottom. It appeared black, but as I tilted it to the light, I saw that it was crimson.

I sniffed it, recoiling at the sharp, metallic stink and the sudden image of a man, his carefree grin widening into a scream. *I know that guy,* I realized with a start. *He was one of the refugees selling knockoffs near St. Mark's Square.*

Jackson had moved into the driver's area to investigate further. Before I could show him what I'd found and explain the implications, I heard a sound that made my skin crawl.

"Well, there you are. I've been looking all over for you. Where's your partner in crime?"

To my relief, Jackson didn't so much as glance in my direction. "She's still searching the asylum. I'm so glad you came back. I was wondering how I was going to get the hell off this island."

Lowering myself slowly to the floor of the cabin, I edged under a bench as much as I could, hoping the seat would block her view from the window.

"She let you off the leash? I'm surprised. She doesn't seem like the type to relinquish her hold so easily."

"No one let me off nothing. We're just friends."

Sophia's laugh made my blood pressure soar. "Sure, you keep telling yourself that. Maybe someday you'll even believe it."

"Where's your father-in-law?"

The boat swayed underneath me as Jackson climbed out, but it was too soon to get complacent. She could peer through the windows and discover me at any time.

"That old lush? Probably at the *bacari*. It's not like I need him to hold my hand. I'm perfectly capable of driving this barge myself."

"Awesome. What time are we leaving?"

Christ, Jackson, shut up. We were nowhere close to figuring out how to get Lily away from those who had ensnared her, and we couldn't leave without her. I didn't believe Sophia was actually here to take us to the mainland—not with a man's blood in her cup—but it wasn't wise to call her bluff, just in case.

"Soon. Shouldn't we get your partner?"

"Screw it. She can find her own way home."

Another tinkling laugh. "Oh-*ho!* So there is trouble in paradise."

"Let's just say I could use some space at the moment."

"Fair enough. Hey, don't feel bad. Poveglia can have that effect on people. It tends to heighten emotions, tension."

"Great. So let's get the hell off it."

"Not yet. I have someone I want you to meet."

"I thought you said you came here on your own." Jackson was doing a great job of sounding nonchalant, but I could hear the current of fear running underneath.

"What I said was that I didn't need anyone to help me drive the boat, but that's okay. You're forgiven for jumping to conclusions. I want you to meet my grannie, and she didn't come with me. She lives here."

Lives here? No one lived on Poveglia. My research indicated it was a privately owned island, and even the owner didn't bother to visit.

"You mean she's *buried* here, right? I can't imagine anyone actually living here."

Good job, Jackson. I waited with interest to hear Sophia's answer. This grandmother story had to be a trap. It was too bizarre to be anything but. The question was, a trap for what? What did she want from us?

Sophia laughed again, scraping my nerves raw. "Oh, Grannie is very much alive. She's a most unusual woman, as you'll see when you meet her. Poveglia is her home, so it doesn't have the same effect on her that it has on everyone else. She loves it here."

"So you come to the island to visit her?"

"Every day. She needs the company, and she loves young people, especially *new* young people."

"Fair enough. Let's go. I'd like to meet this grannie of yours."

Jackson's voice was already fainter. He was leading Sophia away from the boat, giving me time to escape. Rising into a crouch, I peered out the window to see his broad back disappearing into the bush. Then they were gone.

Willing my heart rate to return to normal, I considered my options. I couldn't leave Italy without Lily, true, but I *could* go for help and return. Vincenzo's keys were in the ignition. I'd never driven a boat before, but if Sophia had managed it, how difficult could it be? But what would I tell the *polizia*? That Sophia had murdered a refugee? What was my proof? The blood in the cup proved nothing. The Italian police weren't always reasonable when dealing with foreigners—look what had happened with Amanda Knox.

Not to mention Sophia would hear the boat's engine, which might put Jackson in danger. She'd know she'd been tricked, and I was willing to bet she was one hell of a sore loser.

No, I had to see this through on my own. I'd gotten Jackson into this, so it had to be me who got him out. Sophia was an unexpected complication, but by the time I explained the situation to a police officer, my friend could be dead…or worse.

Vincenzo's water taxi was dishearteningly spotless, but there had to be something I could use as a weapon. In desperation, I tried to lift one of the cabin's benches and almost cheered when it rose easily. *Yes!* Among the various manuals and a bag of soggy-looking snacks was a long pole with a hook at one end. Just holding it gave me more confidence. Flipping up my hood to protect my hair from the thorns, I left the boat and went after Jackson.

~ CHAPTER NINETEEN ~

"IT'S FOR YOUR OWN GOOD, you know."

Maria's tiny fingers traced circles on Lily's back in an attempt to comfort her, but Lily, who lay crumpled on the cottage floor in a fetal position, was in no mood to be comforted.

"How can it be for my own good? They took my eye, Maria. I'm blind." As she said the words, she began to cry, her tears soaking the new bandage Alessandra had tied on.

"You're not blind. You still have one good eye." The girl's voice took on a chiding tone, as if she was growing weary of Lily's distress. Lily hoped so—she desperately wanted to be left alone with her misery. "Your eye was sick, or the healer would not have removed it."

"Do you always believe everything your mother tells you?"

Maria's hand stopped in mid-caress, and Lily wondered if she'd gone too far. Her survival depended on being Maria's playmate. If she acted up too much, she'd lose a lot more than her eye. She shuddered at the thought of becoming the evening's mystery meat.

"Do you hear that?"

"Hear wha—" Lily began to ask, but then she did. Two

voices, a man's and a woman's, drifted over to them from the direction of the bridge. They were much louder than the muted murmur of the villagers, almost unbearably so. She'd gotten used to the quiet.

But Maria showed no such discomfort. She bounced to her feet and seized Lily's wrists, pulling her off the floor.

"What's going on? What is it?"

"My...*friend* is here, and it sounds like she's brought a guest! I want you to meet her. You'll love her."

A friend? If Maria already had a playmate, why did she need Lily? Lily wrapped her arms around herself to keep from shivering, but curiosity led her to follow the child out of the cabin, even though she was terrified of being replaced. Maybe this new friend could help her escape.

As usual, Alessandra was lurking outside, but she smiled as Maria yanked Lily past. "Have a good time with Sophia," she said. "Tell her hello from us."

Sophia. Alessandra clearly knew about this mysterious visitor, which meant she wasn't a threat.

"Must you move so slowly? Walk faster," Maria said. Lily quickened her steps.

Before long, the bridge came into view, and with it, the people who belonged to the voices she'd heard. A gorgeous woman dressed like a fashion model chatted with the man walking behind her. She led him by the hand like Maria was leading Lily, and Lily thought he looked every bit as happy to be here as she was. In contrast, the woman seemed thrilled. Lily hated her instantly.

Their clothes were blindingly bright. They made her remaining eye water. Even the woman's leather jacket was too shiny; Lily's head hurt whenever she looked at it.

Dropping Lily's hand like it was yesterday's trash, Maria

ran toward the newcomers with her arms outstretched. "Sophia! You returned."

The woman returned the embrace. "Of course I did. You know I always do." Her Italian was as flawless as her makeup. Lily twisted her nose, but then quickly smiled, hoping it appeared genuine. Judging by her excitement, Maria obviously adored this person. It wouldn't do to alienate her. "And I've brought a friend. This is Jackson."

The man recoiled, although Lily could tell he was struggling to be polite. A nerve in his cheek twitched as he forced a smile even more fake than hers. "*This* is your grandmother? But she's—"

Maria switched to English effortlessly. "Ancient is the word I believe you're wanting, young man. I am nearly a hundred years old, but I assure you there is nothing wrong with my mind—or my hearing. I am actually Sophia's great-great-grandmother. She only calls me Grannie to flatter me."

Nearly a hundred years old? Great-great-grandmother? Lily stared at the little girl standing in front of her, her mind reeling. What weird game was Maria playing? But neither Sophia nor the man called Jackson appeared surprised. Jackson followed Sophia off the bridge and gently shook Maria's hand.

"Nice to meet you…"

"My name is Maria. If you don't feel comfortable calling me Grannie, you can call me that." She turned and gestured to Lily. "I've made a new friend as well, but you probably can't see her, can you?"

Lily's skin prickled as both Sophia and her friend peered in her direction, squinting as if they were trying to see through a shroud of fog. "No, Grandmamma, I can't, but I believe you. I'm happy you have a friend. You've been so lonely lately."

Maria giggled. "Can you blame me? Poveglia is a lonely place, but Lily and I've been having lots of fun. Haven't we, Lily?"

Was it her imagination, or did the man stiffen when Maria said her name? There'd definitely been a reaction, but why?

"I guess you don't need our company then. I'm sorry, Grandmamma. We can go."

"Oh no, don't be silly. I'm *delighted* to have you here, and to meet your new friend. I don't want Lily to get too... tired of me. And she's different from you two, you know. One foot in this world and one in the other."

Sophia flashed her teeth in Lily's general direction, in what Lily supposed was meant to be a smile. There was no kindness in it, though, no warmth. The woman's beauty, so dazzling at first, was hollow.

Thankfully, Sophia couldn't see her. Or, at least, Lily didn't *think* she could. She'd simply acknowledged the place Maria had pointed to. Lily retreated another step, just in case.

"How interesting. I'd love to hear how Lily ended up on the island. Can she tell us?"

Lily's lip curled before she remembered to hide her disgust. Sophia and her friend may not be able to see her, but there was nothing wrong with Maria's eyes. Still, this woman was so fake, so transparent. How could Maria be taken in by her? Sophia probably didn't even *like* her.

"Oh, I don't think she's in the mood for talking very much right now. She's been quite upset about her eye. I'm not certain you could hear her, in any case."

The woman shrugged. "Oh well. Another day then."

Her friend stepped forward. He was just as beautiful, but he didn't come across as phony like Sophia. His face was extremely serious, as if he were angry…or afraid. "What's wrong with her eye?"

"Um, well…"

Lily's good eye widened as she watched Maria fumble for a rational explanation of what had been done to her. She'd never seen the girl look uncomfortable before. Maria twisted her fingers, actually wringing her hands. It would have been pathetic if she weren't so clearly terrified.

"It became infected. Our healer had to remove it, I'm afraid, but he sewed it up good as new. She still has her other eye, and once she has some time to adjust, she'll be fine. Isn't that right, Lily?"

This time Lily couldn't help sneering at her, and didn't much care what Maria did in repercussion. *Just fine—right. Maybe I should poke out one of your eyes and we'll see how "just fine" you are.*

Sophia's expression remained as bland as ever, but the man's jaw twitched. His hands clenched into fists. "He took out her eye? Why would he do that? You don't remove an eye because it's infected. That's barbaric."

"Sweetheart, medical care's a little different on Poveglia. Do you see any hospitals around here? Any that aren't abandoned, that is." Sophia laughed at her own joke, showing off predatory teeth. "I'm sure the healer did everything he could for her. It could have been much worse. You should have seen what things were like back in Grandmamma's day, when Dr. Abbandonato was still practicing his 'cures' on the island."

She snaked a hand around the man's arm, but Lily was

elated when he shook her off and stood apart from her.

Maria pretended to shiver. It looked more like a shimmy. "Don't mention that man's name, please. It's enough to bring back nightmares."

"That's no excuse. The mainland is what, twenty minutes away? Vincenzo could have taken Lily to the hospital. What your man did to her is monstrous." The man glowered at Maria from his full height, which was considerable. Lily bit her lip to keep from cheering. Finally someone was on her side! It was about time.

"Vincenzo *could* have taken her, if we'd known. This is the first I've heard about her." Sophia sidled closer to him again, but he pulled away.

"I thought you said you visit your grandmother every day. There's no way you didn't know about this."

"She's telling the truth, young man. There's no need to get so snippy. You're my guest on this island, remember. Since you seem to be the type who needs to know everything, I'll tell you that time is different here. While it may appear to you that you've been on this island for just a few hours, Lily has been here for days—even though she didn't arrive much earlier than you. That's why Sophia didn't know about her."

"So you own this island now? Is that what you're telling me? Because, as far as I know, the owner is an Italian businessman, which you obviously are not. I can't be your guest because you're an illegal squatter. You shouldn't even be here."

Lily sucked in her breath, and she saw the woman do the same. Sophia grabbed the man's arm again, but this time it was a protective gesture.

Only the man appeared unconcerned, obviously unaware

whom he was talking smack to. He shook Sophia off again with a little more force. "Don't touch me. This is sick, and if you agree with her, you're sick too."

Maria's laughter rang across the island. Lily wondered if the doctor would hear it and return for her. She was still scared of him, but nowhere near as scared as she was of Alessandra. Maybe, between the two of them, they could figure out a way to get her across the bridge. Especially if this man agreed to help. "My, you are very entertaining, young man. I can see why Sophia likes you so much, and why she brought you here. I myself came to this island when I was just a child, and I have lived here all my life. It is my home, and therefore, you are my guest. Titles and deeds mean nothing to me. Your Italian businessman can rot if he thinks he can remove me."

"They may mean nothing to you, but they mean an awful lot to us folks in the real world. What are you going to do when they build a resort here, Granny? Park your wheelchair by the pool and scare away the kiddies?"

Sophia gasped. "Jackson, you're being rude. She deserves your respect."

He turned as if noticing her for the first time. "Why, because she's old? Respect needs to be earned. And if she sat by while her 'healer' took that girl's eye, what she's earned is my derision." The man returned his attention to Maria, whose skin was flushed red. "In plain terms, you can both kiss my ass."

Maria sighed. "The earth beneath your feet grows thin, young man. Be careful it doesn't open up and swallow you."

She did sound like a much older woman now. It was so strange. Before Sophia had arrived with all of her

"Grandmamma" talk, Maria had been an ordinary, if old-fashioned, child. What the hell was going on?

The man called Jackson ignored her, looking past Maria's shoulder to a spot close to where Lily stood. "Don't worry, Lily. Your eye will be fine once we get you home."

Her heart began to pound, so hard she felt a bit dizzy. *Home.* How did this man know she longed to be back there, with her mother and even her bratty brother? And was it true? Would she regain her sight? It was almost too much to hope for. Oh, to wake up from this terrible nightmare and be in her own bed again!

Maria's face twisted into a snarl. "This *is* her home."

"Bullshit. She has a real home, with people who love her. Which is more than I can say for you. Lily, can you hear me?"

Pressing both hands to her chest to keep from bursting, Lily found her voice. "Yes!" She sounded rusty, as if she'd recently recovered from a bad case of strep throat.

The man's expression didn't change, and Lily's heart sank as she saw he couldn't hear her. Still, he held out a hand. "Lily, if you can hear me, take my hand. I'm going to get you out of here."

"How can you take her anywhere? You can't even see her." Maria laughed again, making Lily long to smack her. "You don't have the power. You're just an ordinary man."

The man grinned. "That's true, but I have powerful friends."

"I know all about your friend the red-haired woman, and she can't help you. Do you have any idea how many people have died on this soil? Thousands. Tens of thousands. *Hundreds* of thousands. She can't get anywhere near our village. Crossing that bridge would mean instant death."

"And how many of those thousands are dead by your hand, I wonder?"

"Jackson!" Sophia shrieked, looking horrified, but Maria waved a hand dismissively.

"It's quite all right, honey. Clearly your friend is better informed than either of us believed. He's not falling for my sweet-little-old-lady act, which is fine. It gives me a toothache, to tell you the truth. So much better to be honest, don't you think? There's more than enough artifice in this world as it is."

"Your sweet-little-old-lady act sucks. You're a ghoul, and that's exactly how you come across."

"And you're no friend of my granddaughter's. If I were a betting woman, I'd place my odds on your being a spy, here for Lily and no one else. Well, you can't take her away from me—no one can. She's *my* friend. Having her around keeps me young." Maria tittered, a repulsive parody of an elderly woman's laugh.

"And you're a selfish bitch. If you cared about Lily, you never would have let anyone hurt her. You wouldn't trap her here on this wretched island. You'd help her get home, to her family."

Maria rolled her eyes. "Please, spare me your maudlin fantasies."

With Maria distracted, Lily seized her chance. She ran to the man and took his hand in both of hers, squeezing it as hard as she could. He felt real and yet not real, as if he were wearing several pairs of thick gloves, but she kept squeezing, willing him to feel her.

His fingers curled around hers. "Lily, is that you? Don't let go, okay? I'm going to get you out of here."

Maria chuckled. "Oh, he is *so* amusing, Sophia. Well

done. This keeps getting better and better. Where exactly do you think you're taking her, may I ask?"

"I told you, I'm taking her home. That's where she belongs, not here. The only one who belongs here is you. And maybe your granddaughter."

"And what makes you think we'd let you leave, young man?"

His hand clutched hers tighter, and it was all she could do not to cry out in joy. She could feel him, *really* feel him. He could help her. He was going to bring her home!

Now it was Jackson's turn to laugh. "Who's going to stop me, you old witch? You?"

Lily flinched at the unmistakable sound of a gun being cocked.

"No," Sophia said. "That would be my job."

~ CHAPTER TWENTY ~

THE TIGHTNESS BUILT IN MY chest, every breath an effort, until I sounded like a whistling teapot.

"Are you all right?"

The doctor's voice made me jump. I'd been so preoccupied with Jackson's predicament that I hadn't been paying attention, and in a place like Poveglia, such carelessness could be fatal.

Nodding, I signaled for him to wait while I dug in a pocket for my inhaler. A single blast of the reliever medicine, and my lungs began to clear. After a minute, I could speak again. "Asthma."

He gave me a sad little smile. "I'm a physician, remember? Sounds like it's fairly serious."

"I don't get attacks often, but when I do, they can be bad. I need to always have this on me, unless I want to join the spirit world myself." I tucked the inhaler back into my jacket pocket.

The doctor turned his attention to the bridge then, staring into the distance with a wistful expression. "Your friend appears to be in trouble."

I sighed. If only Jackson had pretended to be friends with the old crone and Sophia, made nice a little while longer until I could figure things out. But that wasn't his way. Maybe people with pink auras weren't capable of artifice. I'd have to ask Laura, assuming I saw her again. "That's the understatement of the year, Doctor."

"Can I help?"

While I still didn't trust him, he sounded sincere. And what choice did I have? "I'm not sure. You can't go across either, I take it?"

"Sadly, no. One of the first things they did was devise that infernal system to keep me out."

Even here, hidden in the brush several feet from the bridge, I could feel its power. It hummed with the dark intensity I'd experienced near battlegrounds like Thermopylae in Greece, where thousands had lost their lives. Taking on the suffering of that many souls at once would be the equivalent of stepping into a nuclear meltdown. "How am I going to get Jacks out of there before they kill him?" My mind reeled. When I'd originally decided to bring him along, it had never occurred to me he would be in any danger. The threat on the island came from the dead, or so I'd thought. I hadn't anticipated a living, breathing human with a gun.

"They will do more than kill him."

"What are you telling me, Doctor?" *Could the women do something terrible to Jackson's soul, dooming him to remain on the island forever?* But even as I considered the possibilities, I knew he was referring to a more immediate menace. I kept thinking of the Starbucks cup I'd found in Vincenzo's water taxi, and the horrified expression on the poor refugee's face.

"I am afraid I may have misled you when I insinuated their community died from the plague. A disease did take their lives—that much is correct—but the sickness resulted from a practice considerably more nefarious than farming."

"Cannibalism."

The doctor lowered his head, unwilling to meet my eyes. "Yes. When they first arrived on the island, two of them had this compulsion and had been diagnosed as criminals of the most dangerous and repulsive sort. Whether they coerced or influenced the others after their escape, or if it was simply a means of survival after we cut off their food supply, I do not know. What I can tell you is how my own patients were treated in their village—not as members of the community, but as a source of nourishment.

"What I had taken for mental illness turned out to be the initial stages of the disease that later killed them. The two affected would burst into laughter at the most inopportune times and were unable to stop. Often they would laugh until they made themselves physically sick. It was disturbing to watch, to say the least. I suppose it was some morbid justice that those who started it were the first to perish, and were themselves consumed, but in time the entire village was afflicted. From my position in the tower, I watched as they staggered around, so beset by tremors they could barely walk. When they grew weak to the point that they could no longer stand or feed themselves, I was relieved that their reign of death and brutality would soon end. But one survived long enough to have children of her own, children who left Poveglia but not the way of life they'd learned at her bosom."

"Maria."

"Yes, a most formidable woman. I suspect you see her as she truly is, correct? A creature of advanced age."

"You could say that." It wasn't her wrinkles or age

spots that disturbed me. There was something inhuman about Maria, as if she were an ancient lizard wearing an unconvincing costume.

"To Lily, she appears as an innocent child. While I imagine she looks as she did many years ago, the innocence itself is a well-practiced act. No offspring of Alessandra's was ever innocent. Maria was in the womb when her mother murdered me."

As I pushed myself to my feet, branches scraped across my hood, their thorns scratching at the fabric. The doctor rose as well, his eyes betraying his confusion. "Where are you going? What are you going to do?"

"I'm going after Jackson."

"But you will die!"

"I have to do something, and I won't die right away." I brandished my boathook. "I'll have at least a few minutes before the pain overwhelms me."

"But will that be enough to save the girl and your friend? I beg of you, Miss Carlsson, please reconsider. You are no use to them if you are dead. They need you to survive."

He was right. I'd be lucky if I could *find* Jackson and Lily before I was overcome. Even standing this close was doing not-so-nice things to my psyche. My chest tightened again, warning of another asthma attack. But what else could I do? The doctor couldn't cross, so I was the only person capable of saving my friend's butt and Lily's soul. I cursed Jackson under my breath. He never should have let Sophia lead him to Maria. Of course, he'd thought he was doing the right thing, but—

But he saved your life.

I didn't want to admit it or acknowledge it, but the truth was, he had—by putting himself in danger. If Sophia had discovered me in Vincenzo's water taxi, she probably would have insisted on introducing us both to Maria, which would have signed my death warrant.

My mind reeled. There must be *something* I could do, some way around this. What if I contacted Lily with the spirit board? Could she do something from the inside? I thought of the symbols Laura had sewn onto Nostradamus's collar, protecting him from harmful spirits. Could I remember the symbols well enough to make something similar for me? And would it be enough if I did?

It was wishful thinking, but that seemed to be all I had. Even if I could remember them, the symbols wouldn't do much good against Sophia and her gun or her evil granny. I was pretty sure I could take down the granny and Sophia, but doubted my chances against the firearm. Shit. What a hopeless mess.

"It is not as hopeless as you might think."

I'd been so deep in thought I'd almost forgotten the doctor's presence. "Would you please stop reading my mind? It's annoying."

"Don't you understand? We are linked now. You followed me here to the island."

"I was following Lily, not you."

He shrugged, unflustered by my anger, which made me even angrier. "It does not matter *why* you came, only that you did. You are here, on my side of the island, which makes us linked."

"Great. Hooray, I'm happy for you. So what? How does that help me?"

"I am unable to go to that side of the island in this form, and you are unable to cross the bridge as you currently are."

"Brilliant summation, Doctor. Will you stop wasting my time, please? I need to think."

"I have a point, I promise you. You can take on a spirit's pain, communicate with them, even be *touched* by them, but have you ever truly let one in?"

Uh-oh. I didn't like where this was going. "What do you mean by letting them in?"

He leaned forward as if to press his forehead to mine. I stumbled back into the bush, getting a scratch across the cheek for my efforts. "I mean, let them take over. Let their mind become yours, your body become their vessel."

That's what I was afraid of. "You're talking about possession."

"Not really. You'd still be in complete control. It would be more like I was a…a passenger."

"You were more than a passenger of Lily's. I saw what you did to her. Under your influence, she attacked her mother. She terrorized that house." Remembering my first encounter with the doctor, I took another step away from him. In his own way, he was as much of a monster as Maria and her kin. I'd have to be careful not to forget that. On this island, his powers to charm and persuade were considerable.

The doctor's lower lip protruded. "I thought you finally understood. I thought that, after meeting me and speaking with me at length, you recognized it was not me who caused Lily to do such things. She was under another's influence."

"Who, Alessandra's? That doesn't make any sense. What link does Alessandra have with Lily?"

"All I know is that the girl's soul began to materialize here. Not completely—she was still tethered to your realm. I saw Alessandra controlling her like a puppet. I also saw immediately that Lily was ill. I recognized many of the symptoms, familiar with them from treating my own patients. It was the illness that gave Alessandra power over the young girl. I knew that if I could treat her, heal her, Alessandra's dominance over her would end."

I rolled my eyes. "There you go with your God complex again. Lily is not sick. She's a typical preteen girl. She needs you like a hole in the head. She needs your hole in the head like a hole in the head. Which is to say, not at all."

"Really? Before you dismiss my professional assessment with your layman's blather, perhaps you should examine the girl's wrists."

There was that reference again. My breath caught in my throat. There had always been one aspect about this case that had nagged at me. Lots of girls played with Ouija boards, but Lily was the only one I'd ever heard of whose soul was kidnapped as a result. In order for that to happen, she had to have voluntarily given her will over to the spirit realm, and to the spirit or spirits who were communicating with her. But why would any sane person do that? The answer had been staring me in the face all along.

I'd dismissed the doctor's obsession with treating Lily as just that: a crazy, over-the-top fixation with mental illness that resulted from his own megalomaniac beliefs that he could cure the world.

But he wasn't the one who was mentally ill.

Lily was.

"She does not want to die. It is quite the opposite, in fact—she wants to live. It is the pain that is killing her, and she expresses this by assaulting her own body. If you still find it challenging to believe me, ask to see her wrists. The evidence is there. As well as on her arms. And her legs."

Shit. "She's a cutter." Damn Vittoria for not telling me the full story of her issues with Lily. I couldn't bring her daughter back if Lily didn't want to go.

The doctor's face contorted as if he'd bitten into something sour. "Pardon me, she is *what?*"

"A cutter. That's what we call someone who mutilates herself." I had a strong desire to whack my head repeatedly against the nearest tree. An impossible situation had just gotten a hell of a lot more impossible. Jackson was risking his life and I was about to risk mine, all to rescue a girl who very likely didn't want to be rescued.

"Well, that is charming. No wonder she has such a highly developed sense of self-worth."

"Sarcasm doesn't become you, Doctor."

"Alessandra's hold on the girl was growing. That is why the girl acted out against her mother. It was Alessandra's rage and violence she was expressing, not mine. You have seen me; you have spoken with me. Am I a violent person?" He extended his hands as if to demonstrate he had nothing to hide. "I am the one who was murdered, if you recall. My life was dedicated to healing people, not hurting them."

That was a matter of opinion, but I decided to let it go for now. Arguing with the doctor was wasting precious time, time Jackson might not have to spare, and *he* wanted off the island even if Lily didn't. "So what's your idea, assuming you have one? You said the situation wasn't hopeless."

"If you let me in as Lily did, we can fight Alessandra and her evil together. Don't you see? Our individual weaknesses will be overcome. If we remain separate, the situation is indeed hopeless, but together we can demonstrate a power unlike anything Alessandra has ever encountered."

"I'm not interested in power. The only thing I care about

is getting Jackson the hell out of here. And Lily, assuming she wants to go." The idea of letting this man's spirit get any closer to my own made my stomach twist with nausea, but I decided to hear him out. What choice did I have?

"Forgive me if I bear a slight grudge against Alessandra for taking my life and the lives of my patients, but we need power in order to rescue your friend and the girl, correct? As it stands now, we are power*less*."

"Suppose I agree to this crazy plan. How would I know I could trust you? How could I be sure you'd let Lily go?"

"This I cannot answer for you. You will have to decide for yourself if the risk is worth it. All I can provide you with is my word that I have recognized my mistakes, and that I fully acknowledge it was my zeal to treat Lily, to cure her of her terrible illness, that led her into Alessandra's clutches and landed her in this situation. If I had let her be, she may have figured out the truth on her own. I was wrong to bring her here, and I was wrong to underestimate Alessandra and her daughter." He smirked, but there was no humor in it. "It seems my great failing, both in this life and the other, has been underestimating Alessandra."

I could feel sympathy tugging me toward him, while Jackson's voice in my head screamed at me not to trust him. Had the doctor caused this situation? Was he really the one to blame? Partly, but perhaps without his intervention, Lily would have been lost to Alessandra and Maria a lot sooner. There was no way of knowing. If he was telling me the truth, his intentions had been pure. But that was the problem—that big, stinking *if.*

If I did what the doctor suggested, the devastating pain and suffering of the victims would no longer pose a threat to me. His soul would be in control of my body, and since he was already dead, he wouldn't feel any pain. Whatever glyphs or other strange magic they'd used against him on the bridge wouldn't be able to stop my body, so by "wearing" me, the doctor could cross over into the village and reach Jackson and Lily.

But that still didn't solve the problem of Sophia and the gun.

Should we cross that bridge when we came to it?

Closing my eyes, I sighed, thinking of all the times Jackson had driven me crazy since we'd been reunited. *I must really like this guy.* "Do you promise to relinquish Lily's soul to me when this is over, assuming we're successful?" I opened my eyes again, staring at the doctor in what I hoped was a threatening manner, wishing I could read *his* mind.

"As much as I believe she could benefit from my treatment, I accept she is better off at home, among her people. Her severe reaction to my hospital was proof of that."

"Yes or no, Doctor."

"Fine, then—*yes.*"

There were other considerations. The doctor had been stuck on Poveglia for several lifetimes. What if he used my body to leave? Would I be able to stop him?

I didn't have to ask the question. His face darkened. "I would *never* leave my patients, Miss Carlsson. Do you really think so little of me that you believe I would abandon Abelie? Or my nurses? My place is here."

Maybe I was too trusting, but I believed him. I'd seen his affection for the tortured young girl, his great sorrow for the patients who had been lost. His place *was* on Poveglia, for better or for worse. He belonged here.

"All right. Will you promise to keep in mind that, unlike you, I *can* be killed and therefore you need to be extraordinarily cautious in how you proceed? No running into a hail of gunfire or anything like that?"

He sniffed. "Of course. I am not a complete dullard, Miss Carlsson."

"Just because a person is intelligent doesn't mean his actions will be. Do I have your word?"

"I give you my word that I will treat your physical form much more carefully than I treated my own." He reached out for my hand, and as we shook on it, he felt more solid than I'd expected. He had none of the warmth or vibrancy of a living form, but he wasn't as ethereal as an average spirit, either.

"Good, because I have no intention of making Poveglia my final resting place. And I'm sure you wouldn't want to get stuck with me for eternity, either. Make no mistake—if you screw this up, I am going to haunt the hell out of your ass."

A ghost of a smile twitched at the corner of his lips. "Understood, Miss Carlsson. I will not fail you. Let us go back to my office. I have more influence there."

I must be insane to agree to this. "Okay," I said, steeling myself for the unpleasantness to come. "Let's do this."

~ CHAPTER TWENTY-ONE ~

"**D**ON'T YOU FEEL EVEN THE slightest bit ridiculous?"

"Shut up, Jackson," Sophia said, twisting her pretty mouth into a sneer. Although it wasn't pretty anymore; nothing about her was. Lily couldn't believe she'd ever thought the woman was beautiful.

While the sight of a gun had terrified her, she felt much safer holding the man's hand. He didn't seem to be afraid. He was doing what the woman told him, but Lily got the sense he was biding his time. She hoped he wouldn't get them both killed.

"This isn't the Wild West, for Chrissake. Venice is right over there." The man gestured in the direction of the bridge. "You can't hold people hostage with a gun and expect no consequences. You're going to die in jail, Sophia. If that's even your real name."

The woman gritted her teeth. "For the last time, shut *up*. You're starting to piss me off."

"Only starting? I'll have to try harder then."

Lily tugged on his hand, hoping he could feel her warning. Maybe he wasn't scared of Maria and this awful woman, but he hadn't met Alessandra yet. The worst was definitely still to come.

Maria cackled, pressing one hand to her chest as if her heart hurt. It was disconcerting to hear the much older, world-weary voice emanating from the childish body. "Your tours have really paid off this time, Sophia. This one is so entertaining! I might actually miss him."

The man whipped his head around to scowl at Maria, keeping his hold on Lily's hand. "Tours? What tours? If this is a tour, I want my damn money back."

Sophia kept checking the ground as she walked, and to Lily, it appeared that she was struggling to hold the gun steady and negotiate the lumpy field at the same time. Maybe she'd make a mistake. Lily crossed the fingers on her other hand, sending a silent wish to God. "He wasn't part of a tour, Grandmamma. I picked him and his annoying girlfriend up in a *bacari*." A smug smile lit up her face at the memory. "Vinnie and I had dropped by to relax, and there they were, whining about how they were ever going to get to Poveglia. At first I couldn't believe what I was hearing. They just fell into my lap."

"Hasn't anyone ever told you chicks it's rude to speak a language in front of someone who doesn't understand it? If you're going to discuss my demise, you could at least use English."

Lily's mouth dropped open in surprise. She hadn't noticed when Sophia switched to Italian. She'd switched right along with her. She'd been around Maria and the villagers long enough that she'd begun to *think* in Italian. If only there were some way to translate for Jackson.

Maria tittered. "Very well. We'll stick to English from now on, although I'm warning you, you may not like what you hear."

"I haven't liked anything I've heard since I arrived on this godforsaken shit heap. So what's new?"

Lily recognized the expression on her "friend's" face all too well. Maria was building up to a full-scale tantrum. Throwing her weight against the man, Lily tried to give him a warning nudge. In response, the pressure on her hand increased. *He understood her!*

"This 'shit heap,' as you call it, is my home. I admire your spirit, young man, but try not to say anything you'll regret. My granddaughter was telling me how she met you, and correcting my assumption that you were on one of her tours. That is all. Nothing to get in a snit about."

They were crossing the farm now, where the furrows in the dirt were deep and often filled with mud. The man had no difficulty in his boots, but Sophia contemplated each step, her nose wrinkling in disgust. The man glanced at her and laughed. "I have a hard time picturing you as a tour guide. Where do you give tours, Prada?"

"You still don't understand, do you?" Maria tilted her head as she considered him, a shrewd look on her face that Lily didn't much care for. "My granddaughter's tours come here, to Poveglia. How else do you think she's able to bring me so much…company?"

"I think we should stop shielding him, Grandmamma. The idiot probably thinks he's a dinner guest."

Maria grinned wide enough to split her face. "Oh, he's invited to dinner for sure. He's the main attraction, you might say."

The man stopped walking. "Wait a minute—just wait one minute. Are you chicks telling me you brought me here so Grandma could *eat* me? Is that seriously what you're saying?"

A silent exchange passed between Maria and Sophia. Lily held her breath.

"That's about the size of it, young man. I'm especially going to enjoy that smart tongue of yours. And after I'm finished with you, my friends will eat your soul. By the time we're done, not a morsel of you will remain. Not a single remnant, in this life or the other."

The man's eyes widened. The silence grew heavy as everyone waited for someone to speak. Then Jackson started to laugh. Tears ran down his cheeks as he clutched his side, laughing until his breath escaped in little squeaks.

What the hell was he doing?

Lily kept an uneasy watch on Maria, but the child only stood there, her Cupid's-bow mouth frozen in a perfect O. Sophia appeared very much the same. Lily guessed they'd never had this reaction to their threats before. Had the man lost his mind?

Finally his laughter subsided and he straightened, wiping the tears from his eyes. "Sorry about that, ladies. That's just about the funniest thing I've ever heard."

"Maybe I should kneecap him," Sophia said. The chill in her voice made Lily shiver. "Then he'd stop laughing pretty damn fast."

"Oh, you don't want to do that, honey. I'm sure *Grandmamma* doesn't want nasty ol' bullets in her sweetmeats." The man chuckled, clearly on the verge of losing it again.

"You *idiot*. You never know when to shut up." Sophia trained the gun on his head. To Lily's horror, Maria nodded.

"Go ahead, dear. I've grown tired of these theatrics. They were amusing for a time, but they've gotten older than me. Don't aim for the brain, though. You know what a treat that is for me."

Sophia exhaled in a huff, but she obediently lowered the gun.

"Not the heart, either! Valuable nutrients."

"Well, Christ, Grandmamma—how would you like me to kill him? We don't want to have to listen to his death throes for hours. That's just fucking annoying."

Seizing the opportunity, Lily ran to stand in front of the man, stretching her arms wide. "Don't shoot!"

Everything slowed to a crawl as she watched Sophia aim the gun at her abdomen. Her pulse thundered in her ears, and for a moment she deeply regretted her impulsive act. She closed her eyes and waited for the searing pain that would mark her death.

"Wait! You can't shoot. Lily is blocking him." In her panic, Maria had slipped back into Italian, but this time, thankfully, the man kept his mouth shut. If he provoked the women too much more, Sophia would kill them both.

"So what? I can't see her. She's a ghost, Grandmamma. A bullet will pass right through her." The derision in Sophia's voice was obvious, and it wasn't lost on Maria.

"She is *not,* and don't you dare talk to me like I'm senile or I'll have you for dessert. She's a living soul, and if you shoot her, she will die. I won't let you kill my only friend."

"I'll get you another."

"You'll find another *child*? On a haunted tour? Doubtful."

Lily knew Jackson couldn't see her, probably couldn't even feel her presence, but at least he was staying put. Her arms trembled from the effort of holding them aloft.

Sophia shrugged. "So I'll kidnap one. Children are a dime a dozen. They're everywhere."

"Yes, that worked out so well the last time. Where are

you going to find another child who *wants* to be my friend, who will willingly play with me? Most of them spend the whole time crying for their parents, which is hardly fun. Lily is a real friend."

"Sure she is. I'm sure she's been acting her little ass off the whole time she's been here. Let me get rid of them both, Grandmamma. I'll find you another friend who is just as good, I promise. I'll hang around children's acting classes if I have to." She clicked her tongue. "Or perhaps a nice mentally challenged girl would do. I bet she'd believe anything you told her."

Maria's voice thundered through the village, making Lily flinch. The man's hands settled on her shoulders, steadying her. *"ARE YOU SAYING I'M NOT WORTHY OF LOVE?"*

"Of course not, Grandmamma." In spite of the weapon in her hands, Sophia shrank in the face of Maria's wrath, leaving no doubt in Lily's mind who was in charge. "I'm saying this Lily is not worthy of you, that's all. Why is she protecting *him* if she's *your* friend?"

Uh-oh.

"Because she's sensitive. Lily's a good person. Not everyone is comfortable killing people, you know."

Lily sagged with relief. Thank God all the time and effort she'd put into being friends with the girl had paid off, for both her and Jackson. Maybe there was some way she could convince Maria not to hurt him. It was worth a try.

"What's happening here? What on earth are you doing?"

Oh no. Any hope Lily had left melted into a puddle at her feet as Alessandra approached them, her face crimson with fury.

Maria's eyes flicked to Sophia. "Mother's spirit is here,"

she said, and Sophia went pale, lowering the gun to her side. Lily clutched the man's arms, hoping he would feel her and understand this was not the time to make a break for it.

Mother's spirit? Lily was tempted to rub her one good eye, but she didn't dare let go of Jackson. Alessandra looked so real to her. How could she be a ghost?

"Will someone please answer my question? You've disrupted the entire village. I'd like to know the meaning of this."

"Sorry, Mama. Sophia came to visit, and she brought us a guest." The contrite child had returned, down to the foot Maria wagged in the dirt and the hands clasped demurely behind her back.

"That much I can see for myself, Maria; thank you. What I don't understand is why Sophia is waving that silly gun around and why Lily is standing in front of that man like a human shield. This isn't the way we do things. You know better than this."

"Sorry, Mama," Maria said again, lowering her eyes. "We were having some fun and I guess we got carried away."

"Well, your fun ends now. Put them both in the barn with the rest of the livestock."

Maria's face crumpled. "But what about Lily? You can't hurt her. She's my friend."

Alessandra barely spared Lily a glance. "Your friend appears to be consorting with the enemy, something friends do not do." Her voice softened as she crouched down to Maria's height. "I'm sorry, sweetheart. I know how much it's meant to you to have a friend, but I promise you I'll find someone else. Someone better. We can't trust this girl."

"S-she's not con-SORT-ting! She just doesn't want him to die." Maria wailed, wiping her nose on her arm. "You can't take my friend away from me. You can't! I won't let you."

Straightening, Alessandra shrugged. "Fine. Then put them both in Lily's room for now. But the man has to go, Maria. He's alive—you know he can't stay here, and we can't let him leave. Either you convince Lily to stand aside and let us do what needs to be done, or I will."

"Okay, Mama." Maria sniffled and then gestured to Lily. "Let's go. No one's going to hurt him for now, I promise." As Alessandra left them, Maria turned to Sophia. "Mother says we have to wait. I'm supposed to bring them both to Lily's room. *Don't* shoot anyone. I'm warning you, Sophia. You don't want to make Mother angry again."

Sophia shrank into her coat at the thought, a much different woman than she'd been when she'd arrived. *She's terrified of Alessandra, but why? What did Alessandra do to her?* Sophia still pointed the gun in Jackson's direction, but Lily could see her heart wasn't in it. The woman's hand trembled, but whether from the effort or fear, Lily wasn't sure.

Maria scowled at Jackson. "Lily has saved your life, young man, at least for now. I personally think you'd look much better on a platter, but she has a soft spot for you, for whatever reason. Any more trouble, though, and I'll get my granddaughter to shoot you in a most agonizing spot. So I'd advise you to come along and keep that considerable mouth of yours closed."

To Lily's great relief, the man nodded. "Understood." He squeezed her hand.

"Good. It's this way."

Maria led the group to the familiar shack Lily had come to hate. The only good thing about it was that Alessandra tended to avoid it as much as possible. When Maria pulled the door open, it groaned as if it had been holding the weight of the world on its frame. She waved her hand at them. "In you go."

For all Maria's crying about their friendship, Lily could see the girl was not happy with her. Playing her part as best she could, Lily threw her arms around her, drawing Maria close in an embrace. "Thank you for saving him. I couldn't bear to see him die."

Maria shoved her away, pouting. "It's not forever, you know. You heard Mama. He can't stay."

Lily forced herself to remain quiet and calm, though on the inside she was screaming. She couldn't let them murder the man, but what could she do to stop them? The villagers outnumbered her twenty or thirty or forty to one. (She'd lost count that one night at dinner.) And Sophia had a gun. If either of them tried to leave now, they'd be shot. "Please buy him time, Maria. As much as you can. Why don't you come in and play a game with us?"

Maria's lower lip still protruded, but Lily caught a glint of interest. "Not now. Maybe later. I have to talk to Sophia."

She gestured again at the cabin, and Lily was about to head inside when the man protested. "You can't seriously expect us to go in there."

Oh no, not again. Didn't he get it? Maria and Alessandra weren't kidding around. They really would have him killed.

"That's where Lily has been staying. Is it not up to your standards?"

Lily was relieved to see Maria didn't look angry—not yet, anyway, but this man was playing a dangerous game.

"Come on," she said, hoping he would hear her, but he didn't react. She tugged on his hand, but he held her fast.

"That thing could collapse on us at any time. I'm surprised it's still standing." He sniffed in the direction of the doorway and recoiled. "And it *reeks*. Look at all these flies." He waved his hand in front of his face, but Lily couldn't see anything. She did remember hearing the insects on her first night, though, and smelling something foul. Why couldn't she see the flies anymore? "I'm not going in there."

"My, you're picky for a man who's lucky to be alive. You *are* going in there. That's where Lily has been staying, and she likes it just fine. Don't you, Lily?"

Lily nodded, but the man's reaction was creating an uncomfortable lump in her stomach. If Maria loved her, why would she be okay with keeping her in such a place? The man was a prisoner, but *she* wasn't supposed to be. So much for friendship.

"Maybe she's trying to spare your feelings. Maybe she's too polite to tell it like it is, I don't know. But this place is a dump. It's falling apart—it's not safe. And it smells like a charnel house. I am not going in there."

"Did you know there's a portion of your spine that controls movement?" Maria's voice lowered into the purr of a mature woman. It made Lily shudder to hear it emanating from the little girl. "If Sophia shot you there, you'd be helpless. We could eat your flesh while you were still alive, still conscious, and you'd be unable to lift a finger to stop us. But you'd feel the pain. Oh yes, you'd definitely feel the pain." She reached out to touch the man's lower back, presumably to demonstrate where the bullet would go, but he reacted like she'd burned him.

"Don't touch me, you crone!" His elbow came up, clipping Maria in the chest while Lily stood frozen to the spot, horrified. Maria staggered, falling into Sophia and nearly toppling her. Her hair bow hung askew.

The man rushed to help her, catching her by the arms and steadying her. "I'm so sorry. I didn't mean to hit you. You just…startled me. I'm sorry. Are you all right?"

"I'm fine, thank you." Brushing off her dress, Maria disentangled herself from Sophia. "But if you don't go into the cabin right now, I'll have Sophia shoot you on the spot. I'm done playing games with you."

He straightened his shoulders. "All right. If it's good enough for Lily, I guess it's good enough for me. Just don't blame us if the damn thing falls down around our heads."

"We'll be right outside, so don't get any funny ideas. If your head so much as pokes through this door, I'll have Sophia blow it off."

Lily yanked on his hand as hard as she could so he'd get the message. She was relieved Sophia hadn't shot him the second he'd struck Maria. Maybe the woman wasn't as tough as she'd been acting. Jackson ducked his head to get inside, and the door slammed shut behind them with a *whoof*, sending clouds of dust into the air. The particles glimmered in the afternoon sunlight streaming in from the little window.

Once they were alone, the man let go of her hand to hold his nose. "Ugh. How can you stand it in here? It smells awful." He scanned the interior, blinking in the light, and then jumped back. "What the hell is *that*?"

Lily looked at where he was pointing, his hand covering his mouth now as if he wanted to throw up. *How did that get there again? It was supposed to be hidden.* "It's a doll of

Maria's. She gave it to me to play with."

"Whatever that thing is, can you put it somewhere I don't have to see it? It's creeping me out."

She threw a blanket over it, still loath to touch the thing, and hid it behind her cot, hoping Maria would leave it there this time. "Are you going to be sick? I was sick the first day here. If you need me to yell for the bucket, let me know."

After she'd hidden the doll, the man took his hand away from his mouth. "I guess you can hear me. You can, right?"

"Yes."

"Problem is, I can't hear *you*. So here's what we're gonna do." Reaching into his inside jacket pocket, the man withdrew a small notepad and a pen. "Good thing I'm a writer now, and writers come prepared. We're going to try writing to each other. It's better than talking anyway because no one will be able to hear us."

Taking the pen's cap off with his teeth, he scribbled on the page while Lily waited with interest. Who was this man, and why was he here? She had so many questions. Within a short while, he held out the pad.

She tried to take it and found she couldn't. Lily bit back a yelp when her fingers went right through it. Remembering how she'd concentrated her energy and strength to squeeze the man's hand, she closed her eyes and focused. After a few seconds of concentrating, she tried again. This time she could feel the edges of the pad in her hand and was able to pull it toward her. Gasping from the effort, she looked at what he'd written.

Great to meet you, Lily. My name is Jackson, and I'm a friend of Kate's, the red-haired woman. You may have seen her. Your mother hired her to bring you home, and I'm trying to help her.

Are you okay?

Writing her response was an exercise in frustration. It was like learning to write all over again. Lily had to concentrate hard on holding the pen and forming each letter. If she let her focus slip for even a second, her fingers opened and the pen fell to the floor. Retrieving it was extremely tedious, so Lily lowered herself to the floor as well, lying on her stomach. At least she didn't have so far to go if she dropped the pen.

Jackson stared at the pen, and then the notepad. To him, it must have seemed like the objects were floating, since he couldn't see her.

I'm fine. Except for my eye. But I'm scared and I miss my family. I really want to go home. Pausing, she bit her lip, not sure she could tell him what had happened on her first night. She was so ashamed. Finally she settled for: *I'm too scared to eat anything here. I'm starving.*

With an effort, she pushed the pad toward him along the floor. It was much easier than carrying it, but still challenging. Strange. She could easily pick up and move any other object in the room, including Maria's doll. Why was writing so difficult?

Jackson grinned when he read what she'd written. His reply came much faster than hers. *I don't blame you. I wouldn't eat anything either. Does your eye hurt?*

Not anymore. There's a lot of pressure, but that might be from the blindfold. They tied it pretty tight.

This time she used momentum to slide the pad across to him along the floor. It worked a lot better, but she still felt like she'd lifted a heavy weight. So odd.

Can you feel anything under it? Where your eye should be?

As she read his reply, her stomach lurched. The idea of

living the rest of her life one-eyed was more than she could handle. It was almost enough to make her want to stay on the island. *Almost.*

"Don't be scared, Lily. Just try it," he whispered. "I'm right here with you."

Slowly she lifted her hand to the blindfold. She sucked in her breath as she gently ran her fingers across her eyelid. It didn't hurt.

"Does it feel like there's something in the socket? Or does it feel empty?"

It took her several tries before she could focus enough on the pen to scrawl one word on the paper. *Full.*

He smiled. "That's what I thought. Your eye's still there, Lily. They just blindfolded you so you can't use it. It's a mind game."

They sewed my eyelid shut!

Jackson's nose wrinkled. *That's messed up. But don't worry. We'll have you seeing again in no time, out of both eyes. Kate will be able to help you.*

Why can't you see me? Am I dead?

She caught her lower lip between her teeth as she waited for his answer. She didn't think she was dead. She certainly didn't *feel* dead. But maybe no one ever did, just like how her mom said no one feels older.

You're not dead. I can't say I understand it, but you're a soul. That's why I can't see you, but Kate can. She's a medium. The rest of you is fine, though. Your parents are taking care of you.

Her poor parents! Her mother must be freaking out. Guilt hung heavy on Lily's shoulders, constricting her throat and threatening to suffocate her. She'd already caused her mom enough pain. Before she could respond, Jackson wrote something else.

We have to get your soul out of here before they do something ~~irev irrevoke~~ *bad to it.*

Kate will help you. Only problem is, she can't come here. We have to go to her. We have to get out of here somehow. We have to cross the bridge.

Lily's eyes filled with tears. *Maria will never let me go. There are too many villagers, and they all listen to Alessandra, Maria's mother. They'll kill me before they let me leave.*

Jackson sighed, tilting his head back. "Let me think for a minute." While she waited, Lily looked out the window, but she couldn't see anyone. The village was oddly quiet, which scared her. Where was everyone, and what were they doing? She hoped they weren't preparing for a feast.

He passed her the pad.

The villagers and Maria's mother can't touch me. I'm not afraid of that old prune or Sophia, either. Only problem is the gun. If I can get it away from her, can I protect you from them long enough for us to cross the bridge, do you think?

Lily considered for a moment. *I don't think so. I stopped Sophia from shooting you because the bullet might have killed me too, and Maria didn't want to lose me. But she'd kill us both rather than let me escape. You could maybe stop Maria from hurting me, but I don't think you could stop her mother. Can you see her?*

His shoulders slumped, and she was sad to see some of the light leave his eyes. "No, I can't. I can only see Sophia and her granny. And that's enough, believe me."

Why can't Kate come to us?

It's a long story, but basically too many bad things have happened here. She'll feel like they're happening to her. It will kill her.

It was difficult to wrap her head around. Before she'd started fooling around with the spirit board, she hadn't believed her own grandmother's stories about the other realm and the ghosts who walked among them. And now she was here, on an island she'd never heard of. She had no idea how she'd gotten here...or how to leave.

"I could strangle that stupid doctor for getting us into this mess. I swear, if he wasn't already dead, I'd kill him."

What? Lily's eyes widened as she grabbed the paper. It was getting a bit easier. Practice makes perfect, she guessed. *Why the doctor? He didn't do anything.*

Jackson's reply came fast and furious. *He brought you here, didn't he?*

So did hers. *Only because my Nonna asked him to. She was trying to help me.*

But the more she thought about it, the more it troubled her. Why would her grandmother want her on this island? How would her grandmother even *know* about this island? A chill came over her. What if it hadn't been Nonna at all? *Who* had she been talking to?

She'd never forget how terrified she'd been when the planchette first moved under her fingers. Her scream had been so loud her father had banged on her bedroom door, demanding to know what she was doing. She'd lied, of course, and claimed she was watching a horror movie. Her dad didn't believe in supernatural stuff, but that didn't mean he'd be okay with her fooling around with it. If he'd seen the board, he would have taken it away from her. He might have even grounded her.

She'd hidden the board under her bed, swearing never to touch it again. Maybe her grandma's warnings had been right; spirit boards were too dangerous to mess with. But her own curiosity had lured her back, and before she knew what was happening, she was using the board every day, for several hours at a time, talking to Nonna and the doctor.

If Jackson could see Maria, that meant Maria was still alive. And that meant—

Are Alessandra and the others ghosts? she wrote.

I think so, but don't freak out. I won't let them hurt you.

Jackson meant well, but his reply didn't exactly fill her with confidence. If he couldn't see them, what could he do? If they *were* ghosts, he couldn't hurt them, couldn't even touch them. When she'd squeezed his hand with all her strength, he could barely feel it, and if what he was saying was true, *she* was alive. If ghosts couldn't hurt him, he couldn't hurt them either.

He bent over the notepad again. *I think our best bet is to make a break for it when they come to get us. They have to get us for "dinner," right? If I were to run for the bridge, could you keep up with me?*

At home she'd been a great runner. Before things had gotten so screwed up. But was her soul in good shape? Whoever had to consider such a thing? *I think so. At least for a little while. I don't know how strong I am anymore.*

His reply made her happier than she'd been in a long time. For once, she didn't feel so alone.

You're stronger than you think. Rest now, save your strength. We have a big night ahead of us.

~ CHAPTER TWENTY-TWO ~

THE WORLD WAVERED IN FRONT of me. I went to rub my eyes and found I couldn't. My arm wouldn't move, remaining stubbornly at my side. Panicked, I fought against the paralysis, struggling and straining.

A gruff curse issued from my own mouth, making my entire body tingle with fear. It was an Italian word, but inexplicably I could understand it—a not-very-nice word for a woman.

There is no need to rub your eyes. You are seeing things as I see them.

Filling my lungs with the damp air, I willed myself to relax. I opened my eyes again, trying to view this exercise as a wonderful adventure instead of the invasion it was. Every part of me wanted to reject the doctor's spirit, send him out of my body. It took a tremendous amount of willpower to resist. My shoulders and arms trembled with the effort.

You will be fine, Miss Carlsson. We both want the same thing: to save the girl. I will not fail you.

But did we really want the same thing? Even now, I had my doubts. What if I'd made a terrible mistake?

You did not make a mistake. I promise you.

I was sitting in an office, on a straight-backed wooden chair. While clinical in its cleanliness and choice of non-colors, the room wasn't uninviting. A window overlooked the water, which had darkened to navy, and a structure that resembled a little stone fort. When a ray of light from the setting sun struck my eyes, making them tear, I leapt to my feet.

Except I didn't move. I fought the urge to scream in frustration, assuming I would have been able to.

We have to go, Doctor. The sun's going down. We don't have much time.

I want to ensure our deal still stands. If you change your mind at the critical time, you will destroy me.

Do you really think I'd put myself in this situation to destroy you? You're in control of my body, for Chrissake. All I care about right now is Jackson and Lily. As long as you stick to your end of the bargain, you'll be fine.

All right. I had to be certain, you understand.

The muscles in my thighs tensed, pulling me into a standing position. It was the strangest sensation to be moved about in my own body without having control, like being carried on someone else's shoulders. I walked awkwardly at first, a stumbling Frankenstein's monster, and then sped up until I was sprinting to the staircase. It was gleaming and free of graffiti now, but I remembered how it really was—the broken steps like jagged teeth, the pile of rubble below.

Wait! You're going to get us killed. The stairs are broken. You have to be careful.

To my relief, my legs stopped. I could feel adrenaline coursing through my body at the near miss.

I am sorry. I forgot I have certain…freedoms you do not. It is unfortunate I cannot see with your eyes instead of mine. Where are the broken stairs?

Working from memory, I guided us down to the main floor inch by inch, my hands sliding along the wall for balance, my toes tapping on each step before allowing my weight to rest on it. Through the doctor's eyes, this seemed a ludicrous precaution, as the stairs appeared as sturdy as the ground itself under us. Thankfully, I'd remembered the truth in time, but what other hazards awaited us? Would I recall all of them? What if I forgot—

You must cease this incessant worrying. It is not helping us. We will be fine. Have faith.

If I'd been able to, I would have snorted with laughter. *Have faith?* That was rich. With everything he'd experienced, you'd think he'd know better by now.

I am still an optimist, despite everything. Enough of the world is darkness and despair. I see no point in adding to it.

Okay, fine, I thought, refusing to acknowledge how much his simple statement had moved me, though of course he would already know. There was no hiding anything from him now. *Lift my feet when you walk, and be careful. Stay by the outside wall. There's a lot of rubble on the floor.*

The doctor obeyed without complaint, and I did an awkward goosestep toward the door, stubbing my toe twice. The voice that cried out in pain was much deeper than usual, with the hint of an accent.

When I saw the door directly ahead, I exhaled deeply, unaware that I'd been holding my breath. A lot of the tension left my shoulders and back. Unlike the abandoned ruins I'd explored earlier, this version of the asylum had glossy white tiles with a vivid blue design that resembled a Greek key. The ceiling soared above us, majestic and ornate.

As we lurched into the foyer, ghostly nurses surrounded us, scurrying back and forth. The breeze created by their movements blew tendrils of my hair across my cheeks.

One of the women intercepted us. "Going for your evening walk, Doctor?" Since the doctor's mind had fused with mine, Italian was no longer a foreign language.

My head inclined as if pulled by a puppet master. "Indeed, Grace. It is a fine evening for a stroll, is it not?"

The nurse clicked her tongue and shook her head to indicate her disappointment, but the corners of her mouth twitched. "I can't believe you'd forget this." She held out the beaked mask, its surface as white and gleaming as the floors. I recoiled in horror as my own hand reached out to retrieve it.

No!

The doctor ignored me, turning the mask over in his hands almost lovingly. "Thank you, Grace. I'll return before dark."

She nodded, already edging away from us as if this brief exchange was stealing too much of her valuable time. "Enjoy yourself. I must check on the patients."

The patients. They were still here, then? I listened hard, but could hear nothing over the swish-swish-swish of the nurses and the squeak of their rubber-soled shoes on the tiles, the hum of their conversation.

I am not a fool, Miss Carlsson. I realize I am dead and gone, nothing more than a heap of ancient bones crumbled into dust. But if some form of me must remain, then I choose to remember the island this way, before those hateful creatures arrived and destroyed everything I'd worked so hard to build. So yes, my patients are still here.

As if summoned, a young girl glimmered in the late

evening sun pouring in the door. The orange light caught her blonde hair, making it seem like she had a halo. "Hello, Doctor!" She beamed, showing off several missing teeth. "Guess what I did today?"

"What would that be, Carina?" My hand ruffled the girl's hair, making her giggle.

Stretching her arms wide, she spun in a circle, faster and faster. I saw it happening as if in a dream, the child staggering, falling, the stone steps of the asylum rushing up to meet that vulnerable skull at a frightening speed.

My hands were quicker. They reached out and caught her under the arms, steadying her tiny form. Not recognizing the danger she'd been in, she only laughed.

"Did you see me? Did you see how funny I walked? Francesco taught me. It makes the sky spin."

I patted her on the back. "It's a neat trick, but make sure you stay on the grass. I don't want you to get hurt."

"Yes, Doctor!" None the worse for wear, she skipped inside the asylum. The nurses gathered around her, no doubt scolding her, warning her to be more careful. I understood then that the doctor had been telling the truth. The little girl had greeted him with affection and joy, not fear.

Hospital. The stern voice jolted me out of my own thoughts.

Sorry?

It is a hospital, not an asylum. Perhaps my patients have difficulties, but they are not insane.

I'm sorry I misjudged you. I had it wrong.

You are forgiven. Let us work together now to put things right.

Our progress was painfully slow. The hospital grounds were filled with children, and every single one had something they just had to show the doctor. Finally we were able to escape. Nurses waved from the doorway of the broken-down building Jackson and I had once huddled in, seeking shelter from the storm. That seemed so long ago.

We rounded the building, following a path flanked by flowering hedges. *This area is overgrown with thorns now,* I warned him. *Stay low.* My head lowered as the doctor duck-walked us into the woods, waving my arms in front to protect my face from dangers he couldn't see. He was hurrying now, our mutual sense of dread intensifying, and soon we reached the edge of the forest.

Across the clearing were the canal and its bridge, looking as unwelcoming and dilapidated as they did in my time.

I have no good memories of this place. No need to pretty it up. Waves of resentment and bitterness threatened to overwhelm me, roiling in my stomach.

Understandable. Are you sure this is going to work?

No. How could I be? This is an untested hypothesis.

Yeah, well, we're gambling with my life, so take it easy and stay calm. The thought was as much for me as it was for him. Taking another deep breath to steel myself, I was thrilled at the unfamiliar sensation of my lungs filling. My asthma had disappeared! At least there was one bright aspect to this situation.

Your breathing issues are mostly psychosomatic, brought on by nerves. Control the nerves, control the symptoms.

Hey, when I want a diagnosis, I'll ask for it, all right?

I apologize. Force of habit.

You're forgiven. Let's go.

The halting steps the doctor had managed earlier were gone as he grew more comfortable in my body. Once again I had the sensation of being carried, my fear increasing as we approached the bridge. Every part of me longed to run in the other direction, and if it had been up to me, I probably would have.

If the doctor was aware of my fear, he ignored it. He slowed as he moved closer, finally pausing when we were only a foot or two away.

Are you well? How do you feel?

Unable to run, I'd squeezed my eyes shut once I discovered the doctor didn't need them to see. Summoning all my courage, I opened them, shocked at how close we were to the canal. I waited for the stabbing agony of so many deaths to hit me all at once, but there was nothing.

I can't believe this, but…fine. I don't feel a thing.

Neither do I. I have never been able to get this close before. I am going to approach the bridge.

Okay. Watch out for Sophia and the gun.

Of course. No one knows better than I how treacherous these people can be.

My body flinched as one foot stepped tentatively onto a rotting wooden plank. I knew then that the doctor was every bit as afraid—he was just better at hiding it than I was. Whatever they'd conjured up to keep him on this side of the island must have caused him tremendous pain.

Unimaginable.

The doctor raised my hand in spite of my protests, slipping the beaked plague mask over my face. It was surprisingly heavy. My vision narrowed, and it immediately became more difficult to get air. The sound of my breathing amplified in my ears like an astronaut's.

There was a musty, unpleasant smell from the old herbs that still clung to the inside of the mask. I switched to breathing through my mouth. *Do we have to? This thing is beyond creepy.*

That is the point. Trust me.

Squaring my shoulders, the doctor pushed on, taking me with him.

~ CHAPTER TWENTY-THREE ~

LILY WOKE WITH A START, squinting at the vibrant orange glow from the windows. She tugged at her blindfold before remembering where she was. Once the room swam into focus, she was surprised to see the bowed head of the man right above hers. She'd fallen asleep on him, using his legs as a pillow. She pushed herself upright, cheeks burning.

"Hey, kid," Jackson whispered, his voice hoarse. "You awake?"

"Yeah," she answered before she remembered he couldn't hear her. She grabbed his notepad and wrote the same, even though it was getting harder to read in the fading light. He chuckled.

"Why don't we try one knock for yes and two for no for the simple stuff? Save us both some time."

Why hadn't she thought of that? She knocked once on the leg of her bed.

"Good."

Taking up the pad again, she wrote: *How long did I sleep? What time is it? I'm surprised they haven't come to get us by now.*

Pulling his phone out of his pocket, he held it up with a

wry smile. "My clock died, I'm afraid. I couldn't tell you."

As if she'd willed it, Lily heard the murmur of voices moving toward the cabin. Maria. Sounding like a young child one moment and an old lady the next, her vocal cords cracking like worn leather.

"That woman has a serious case of multiple personality disorder," Jackson stage-whispered. She nudged him a warning to stay quiet, but he didn't seem to feel it this time.

The door creaked open, bringing more light with it and casting Maria in shadow. Shielding her eye with her hand, Lily was relieved to find she was still a child in a slightly grubby lace-trimmed dress. She didn't think she'd be able to handle the authentic version of Maria—*that* woman sounded terrifying.

"You're awake! You've been sleeping a long time," the child said in a chirping, somewhat self-righteous voice, which gave Lily the creeps. *Has she been watching us?*

She slipped into her best-friend mode. "Good evening, Maria. You should have come to play with us. Jackson is a lot of fun; you'd like him."

Maria shook her head so the curls bounced, her hair bow wilting like a dead flower. "Mother wouldn't let me. She doesn't trust strangers."

"But he's not a stranger. He's a friend. He's come to help us."

The girl squinted at Jackson before shaking her head again and twirling in a circle. Lily's hands balled into fists. Sometimes Maria was so frustrating. As much as she didn't want to see the other version of her, it would be a relief if she'd grow up a *little*. "I don't know what he's been telling you, but he's lying. Mamma says he's a bad man."

Jackson laughed. "*I'm* the bad guy now? She's one to talk."

Lily tugged his sleeve. *Stop baiting her!* "If he's a bad man, why did you leave me alone with him, Maria? I thought we were friends. That's not what you do to your friends."

"I don't think we can *be* friends anymore." At least Maria had the decency to stop spinning around the cabin as she relayed this news. "Mamma says it's best if I find a new friend."

Lily stiffened in fear. "Your mother doesn't know me. Not the way you do. What you said before is true; you'll never find another girl who *wants* to stay. I was planning on staying with you forever."

Maria shrugged her thin shoulders, but her lower lip trembled. "Mamma says you're lying, that you've wanted to escape from the start."

"Can you blame her? This place is a dump." Jackson grimaced, kicking at the dirt floor. Lily aimed her own foot at his ankle.

Jackson, shut up!

"I'm sorry it's not fancy enough for you, but we do what we can with what we have." Lifting her chin, Maria attempted to stare down her nose at him, but it was no use. He was too tall. "You won't have to put up with it much longer, in any case."

Lily seized the girl's hand in both of hers. "Please, Maria. If you no longer want me here, please let me go home. I miss my family, and they must be going out of their minds with worry. You have your mother; please let me have mine."

"I thought you hated your family. You wanted to be anywhere but there, remember? You begged us to take you away from that place." Maria snorted. "You wanted to live here on the island with me."

Tears stung Lily's eyes at the idea of never seeing her mother again. "I didn't mean it! I was stupid. Haven't you ever had a fight with your mother where you've said mean things? I was just angry."

"Well, you should be careful what you wish for, shouldn't you? Now you're here, and you can't go home. And I've never said things like that about my mother, ever. Maybe if you'd watched *your* mother get sick, you'd appreciate her more, but it's too late now."

Lily felt like she'd been hit in the stomach. She sobbed, curling in on herself while Jackson lunged at the tiny figure in the doorway.

"You need to watch your mouth."

Maria gazed up at him, a smirk playing around the corners of her lips. "Go ahead and try it, smart man. You'll only be hastening your own death."

"Maria?"

Lily cringed at the sound of Alessandra just beyond the door.

"Enough playing now, sweetheart. It's time for dinner."

"Yes, Mamma," Maria called. She turned to Lily and extended her hand palm up, an expectant look on her face. "Where's Mary? I want her back."

For a moment, Lily couldn't move. Stunned, she slowly made her way to where she'd hidden the doll in a blanket and brought it over to Maria, who cradled it close.

"Jesus Christ! You know what that thing is, right?" Jackson's face contorted with revulsion. "That's not a doll. It's a—"

"That's enough. We've wasted too much time as it is.

Let's go." Standing to the side, Maria gestured for them to pass. Villagers clustered on the other side of the door, their expressions disturbingly blank. Lily's hand shook as she held onto Jackson's arm, but he didn't appear to be afraid. She wondered if he could see them.

Sophia brandished the gun at Jackson. "Move it, you. Let's get this over with. I have to get back to the mainland, and Grandmamma is hungry. We've waited long enough."

"I'm pretty tough, you know. Wiry. Stringy. I'm sure I'll be a disappointment."

"Not to worry. Grandmamma will find something that's tender." The lasciviousness in her voice was clear enough, but Sophia still looked pointedly at Jackson's crotch just in case he'd missed her meaning. Lily's face burned with embarrassment and she turned away, catching a glimpse of something in the bushes nearby. Something white. Her hand tightened on Jackson's arm.

"That old bitch can suck my—"

A voice thundered over the village, cutting him off. "This monstrous practice has gone on for far too long. Release them. *Now.*"

"What the fu—" Sophia spun in the direction of the voice, looking confused. At that moment Jackson leapt forward, bringing his arm down hard against her wrist. Screaming in pain, she dropped the gun and clutched her injured arm. "You broke my wrist, you asshole! You fucking prick."

"Sophia, mind yourself." Maria scrambled for the gun as Lily crept toward the bridge, wondering if she should make a break for it. Jackson had told her to run, but she didn't want to leave him here. What if Maria killed him? She'd never forgive herself.

A foot tromped down on the firearm, pinning the barrel to the ground. "I do not think so, old woman. In case you are slow to comprehend, your reign of terror is over."

Maria glared at the person looming over her. "You! How are you here? The barrier is supposed to keep you out."

"Kate? Kate, what are you doing here?" Jackson reached out as if to touch the strange creature in the mask, but then hesitated, his hand hovering awkwardly in the air.

"I will explain later. But first I have to do something." Shoving Maria so the child fell backward with a shriek, the unexpected guest bent to retrieve the gun. Sophia ran to help Maria, but scrambled away when the visitor pointed the firearm at her forehead. She raised her arms in surrender.

"Please don't shoot. It was only a game. We just wanted to scare him. We weren't actually going to hurt him."

"Stop with your lies. I know *exactly* what you were going to do. I have been watching you for years. I am well aware of how many people you have lured here to be slaughtered and consumed by this"—the visitor pointed the gun at Maria—"*monster.*"

The strange creature appeared to be a woman, going by the long hair that billowed out from behind the frightening mask, but the voice was that of a man.

"Please don't shoot her," Sophia said, wrapping her arms around Maria. "She's almost a hundred years old. What harm could she do?"

"With your help, plenty. That is why you both must go." The visitor leveled the gun at Maria's forehead.

"Kate, what are you doing? Kate? Let's calm down and let the police deal with this, okay? Let's just get out of here."

"Leave me alone, Jackson. I know what I am doing," the one he called Kate said in a decidedly unfeminine voice.

"Don't you dare touch her!" Alessandra stepped between Maria and the visitor. "I'll kill you first."

The figure laughed. "You already did, Alessandra. Your threats mean nothing to me now and you know it. It is about time you paid for all the suffering you and your daughter have caused."

"Jesus, Kate. What the hell did you do?" Jackson muttered under his breath, but only Lily was close enough to hear. She squeezed her eyes shut, expecting to hear the gun go off at any moment. Whoever this person was, they wanted Maria dead.

"*No!*" the person screamed, this time sounding more feminine. "I will *not* kill anyone. That's not what we agreed."

"I agreed to nothing. This is the only reasonable course of action. It must be done!" the strange visitor replied. She appeared to be fighting with herself, a hand clamped around the one with the gun.

Jackson muttered over his shoulder. "Girl, you still with me?"

Lily took his hand in both of hers and pressed down.

"Good. Remember our plan? I think we should use this opportunity to skedaddle. Let's go."

Jackson walked backward toward the bridge. Lily kept a tight hold on his hand, matching her steps to his. Closer, closer…almost there…

"They're leaving!" Maria said in a high, wavering voice. "Someone stop them."

"Time to run, girl," Jackson said. "Let's get the hell out of here." He sprinted for the bridge, head down, arms pumping like an Olympian. Lily was thrilled to discover she could keep up with him easily, her feet floating over the ground as she gained speed. Crossing the bridge, she threw her arms in the air and cheered. Now she was one step closer to going home.

Jackson jogged to a stop. "Are you still there? Are you with me, Lily?"

She was looking for something to knock on when they heard the sound. A single shot ripped the sky apart.

Her new friend turned toward the village, his eyes widening. "Oh, shit. Kate, what have you done?"

~ CHAPTER TWENTY-FOUR ~

BY THE TIME I REALIZED what a horrible mistake I'd made, it was too late. I never should have trusted him. He didn't care about Lily at all. The only thing he wanted was revenge.

You are wrong. I do care about Lily. I also care about the multitude of Lilys these women will continue to destroy if we let them.

The doctor's spirit was more powerful than I'd thought. With an incredible effort, I managed to gain control over one of my hands enough to grapple for the gun. I wasn't able to wrest it away from him, but at least he couldn't aim.

You fool! What are you doing? You're going to get us killed.

I'd rather die than take the life of someone else. No matter what they did to you.

This is not about me. This is about—

Oh, spare me, Doctor. I have access to your mind too, remember? This is all about you.

The earth spun at a dizzying speed as I fought for control of the gun. Alessandra threw herself in front of the old woman as if she could protect her, while Sophia cowered nearby, covering her head with her hands. No matter how evil their actions, I would not shoot these women in cold blood.

But in the second I'd been distracted by Alessandra, the doctor had regained control. I could feel my finger tightening on the trigger.

"No!"

With everything I had, I tried to expel the doctor's spirit from my body. The pressure on the trigger eased.

What are you doing? We will both die. Stop, I beg of you!

No, only I will. You're already dead. And you're past the bridge—well done. You can have your revenge. I just won't be a part of it.

I pushed harder. There was a popping sensation, as if a suction cup had adhered to my skin and was now being removed.

Wait! Consider the repercussions of your actions. Lily cannot return to her home without you. They will destroy her soul. They will kill her.

Shit. The doctor was right. In my rush to save the two women, I'd forgotten about Lily. Jackson had gotten her safely away from the village, but I doubted he could even see her, much less help her soul reunite with her body. He'd have no idea what to do.

Sensing my hesitation, the doctor made another bid for the gun. The power of the shot traveled up my arm to my shoulder in a shockwave, throwing me back. Sophia slumped to the side, her eyes glazed, as Maria screamed.

"You killed her! My granddaughter! My beautiful, beautiful granddaughter." She sobbed piteously, attempting to pull Sophia to her, but the younger woman was too heavy.

Strong hands grabbed me around the upper arms and began to haul me away from them. "Kate, what in the hell

Once safely on the other side, Jacks yanked the horrible mask off my face. "What the fuck? Your eyes are *brown*."

This time there was no indecision. Forcing the doctor out of my body, I felt his spirit tear from mine. It took the rest of my strength and I collapsed to my knees, gasping for air. Jackson pressed an inhaler into my hand, and I sucked the medicine down my throat, grateful for the relief.

Kneeling beside me, he rubbed my back. "Are you all right? Please say something."

I met his eyes, relieved to see he no longer looked repulsed. "I'm okay, no thanks to our doctor friend." The man in question sat a short distance away, his shoulders slumped forward, his beloved mask in his hands. "I can't believe I was stupid enough to trust you."

His face was etched with lines of pain, but I refused to be moved. "They have hurt so many, stolen so many souls," he protested. "Caused the suffering and death of countless people—"

"That doesn't make it right to murder them! I don't care what they did. Nothing justifies that."

The doctor hung his head again. "I am sorry."

Jackson rested his hand on my shoulder. "Hey, no one was murdered. He shot Sophia in the arm. As long as I can figure out how to drive Vincenzo's boat, she'll survive. But we should go. How long will it take you to send Lily back?"

Lily. Pulling away, I searched the clearing, sagging with relief when I spied the girl. Her blindfold was pushed to one side, and I caught a glimpse of the ugly black stitches holding her eye shut.

"Doctor? Stop moping around. I have a job for you."

❦

Lily's hand clutched mine as the scissors drew closer to her eye. She flinched when the cold metal touched her skin. The doctor glanced at me. "I'm going to need her to hold still."

Placing a hand on her forehead, I told her to close her other eye. "It'll be over in a few minutes, Lily. You'll be fine, I promise."

I hoped I hadn't misjudged him again, but I trusted that, in his own warped way, the doctor still viewed Lily as his patient. Jackson hovered behind me, anxiety radiating from him. "Is this really necessary? Can't it wait until we get back?"

"I can't return her soul damaged." I imagined the ugly stitches suddenly appearing on Lily's face in the hospital while her parents screamed. "It might stay this way."

He clung to my free hand with a grip that belied his nerves. "I don't trust this guy."

"Your faith in me is overwhelming," the doctor grumbled, but he didn't waver. Bending over Lily, he gently guided the scissors to the thick black thread. *Snip snip snip snip.* Pulling the threads from her skin was worse. She shivered under my hand.

"I know it hurts, but you're almost done." It made me queasy to watch, but I couldn't look away. I would never relax my guard around him again.

"I am finished. She should be able to see normally." Leaning forward, he dabbed tiny dots of blood from Lily's eyelid.

"Thank you." The man's face twisted in anguish. In spite of everything, I couldn't help but feel sorry for him. "Lily will be able to see everything as it truly is now."

He nodded, staring at the ground, waiting for the inevitable rejection, the exclamation of terror. Would Lily see the crushed skull he'd suffered as the ground rushed up to meet him almost a century before? Would she see a floating skeleton, or worse? I wouldn't do that to her, and I didn't want to do it to him, either.

I couldn't allow him his vengeance, but at least I could let him have his dignity. "You should go."

He raised his head to meet my eyes. "And what of the others?"

"Sophia needs medical help. We'll take her with us, and send the police back for Maria." Though I wasn't sure that would be necessary. The trauma of seeing her granddaughter shot was probably enough to do the ancient woman in. "It was Maria who held Alessandra and the other villagers here. Once she's gone, I suspect you'll have a lot more peace and quiet."

"That will be nice."

I extended my hand. "I don't expect I'll see you again, Doctor."

"You stay on your side of the world, and I'll stay on mine. Good day, Miss Carlsson. It's been a pleasure."

He slipped on his mask and was gone.

I helped Lily sit up. "It's okay. You can open your eyes now."

Squinting, she peered through half-shut lids until she gained the courage to open both eyes. "Why does everything look so strange?"

"Because you have one foot in the spirit world and the other foot in the living one. One of your eyes sees the past, while the other sees things as they really are. Maria and her mother didn't want you to know the truth, so they had that eye sewn shut. Once you're home, everything will go back to normal, I promise."

Her expression brightened. "I can go home?"

I nodded. "In a few minutes. We just need to get Sophia. Are you comfortable coming to the bridge with us? You can wait here, if you'd like."

"I'll come with you." She slipped her hand into mine and slid off the gurney.

"All good?" Jackson asked.

"It's all good. The doctor removed the stitches and Lily's eye is just fine. We can go now."

His shoulders twitched like something was crawling on him. "Where is that guy?"

"He's gone. He gave us his word we won't see any more of him."

"Yeah, well, we found out what his word is worth. Let's hope he keeps it this time."

Even with her hand clinging to mine, Lily stumbled. Her uneven vision made it difficult to walk, and finally she pulled some of her hair over her face to cover her left eye. "What I'm seeing—the buildings boarded up, the junk everywhere—that's how it is for real?"

"Yes. You're seeing true now."

Jackson and I bent low to navigate the tangled forest, using our elbows to push the clinging thorns aside. As a soul, Lily had no such issues, and floated calmly along beside us. Every few minutes, she would hold up one of her hands, marveling at its transparency. Once we got to the clearing, I hesitated.

"If you come any farther, you're going to see Maria as she really is. Are you sure that's what you want?"

"Yeah, it's okay. She can't hurt me, right?"

"No, she can't hurt you. We'll stay on this side of the bridge."

Without the doctor's help, I couldn't even put my hand on it. My skin burned as if thousands of unseen mouths were biting me.

"You okay, Kate?" Jackson asked.

I had to retreat a few steps before I regained the strength to speak. "I'll be fine. But please hurry."

Nodding, he dashed over the bridge, and for a moment I envied him, envied his freedom from the agony of tortured souls, from the never-ending pain. Lily's hand let go of mine, distracting me from my thoughts.

I was about to ask her what she was looking forward to the most when she took off at a run, following Jackson.

"Lily, wait! It's too dangerous."

She paused when she reached the bridge. "I'll be fine! Don't worry. I'll come right back."

Sinking to the ground, it was all I could do not to pull my hair out.

Lily might have just signed her death warrant.

~ CHAPTER TWENTY-FIVE ~

SHE FELT BAD ABOUT TAKING off on Kate, but she had to know. She had to talk to Maria one last time, to see her for who she really was.

Lily flew over the bridge but then stopped as abruptly as if she'd run into a wall. She gasped. Jackson looked the same, but he was the only thing that did. The neatly plowed farmland was gone. In its place was a field of weeds.

Something tugged her hospital gown, and Lily bit back a cry. A withered hand spotted with age clung to the hem.

"You came back." The woman's eyes glittered with unshed tears. "I knew you wouldn't leave without saying goodbye."

Her spine was hunched, her gray hair tangled. A child's dress, tattered and filthy, clung to her wasted body. Fresh blood speckled the dress's skirt, but Lily saw plenty of older stains underneath.

"You tricked me, Maria." She could hardly believe this was the same person, but when she covered her right eye and pulled the hair away from her left, she saw it was true.

"Forgive me, child. I've been so lonely out here, with only some spirits and that dreadful doctor to keep me company. Sophia's visits are so short these days." Her voice broke and she pressed her hand to her chest as if it hurt her. "It was Mother who first found you through the board, Mother who thought you'd be happy here with me. You *were* happy, weren't you?"

The hope in the ancient lady's eyes was palpable. Lily found she couldn't hate her anymore. Maybe she'd done some evil things, but she wasn't to blame for what had happened. That rested squarely on Alessandra's shoulders— Alessandra, who had pretended to be Lily's nonna to lure her here.

Still, the terror she'd experienced in the village had left scars that wouldn't soon heal. Lily shuddered as she remembered Alessandra's plans for her. "Goodbye, Maria. Tell your mother I never want to hear from her ever again."

Jackson carried Sophia in his arms. She was unconscious, her head lolling against his shoulder. He paused beside them, looking down at Maria. Though Lily could see the disgust in his eyes, his voice was kind. "She's going to be fine. I'm taking her to the hospital. Would you—would you like to come with us?"

The tears spilled over Maria's eyes now, running freely down her face. "Thank you, young man, but this is my home. This is where I belong." She pressed her hands to her chest again. "I suspect I won't be long for this world, in any case."

"If you're sure. We're going to have to tell the police about this, you understand."

Maria smiled through her tears, and Lily winced to see she was missing several teeth. Those that remained were either worn to nubs or badly stained. "It's for the best. I'm sure there are many families who would like to receive the answers they've been seeking."

Shaking his head, Jackson walked toward the bridge. Lily was about to follow him when Maria called out.

"Lily, take Mary with you. I want you to have her."

The idea of seeing that disgusting plaything again, let alone touching it, made her ill. But her mother had raised her to be polite. Maria might have done some evil stuff (okay, a *lot* of evil stuff), but she was still an old lady stuck on this island by herself. And she was probably dying. What would be the harm in taking the doll? She could throw it out later.

Bracing herself, she turned, surprised to see that Maria had a delighted grin on her face. She held something out to Lily, but now Lily could see it wasn't a doll at all.

Leathery skin with strands of hair still clung to the infant's skull, but some of the bone was exposed, the eye sockets empty. Maggots squirmed around its collar. As Lily recoiled from the child's corpse, it slowly dawned on her that *this* was the thing she'd been sharing a room with. *This* was the thing Maria had tucked into her arms when she was sleeping. It made sense now—the flies, the stench, Jackson's revulsion.

She screamed.

☾

"Can you really send me home?"

Lily wanted to believe it, but after witnessing that strange struggle over the gun, she didn't feel entirely comfortable around the redheaded woman. Jackson had explained that Kate had been possessed by the doctor's soul when all that stuff was happening, but still—she didn't quite trust her. She wished Jackson could send her home, but Jackson wasn't a medium.

"Not quite," Kate said, and Lily felt so miserable she nearly burst into tears. She'd *known* it couldn't be that easy. She would never sleep in her own bed again, or taste her mom's gnocchi. She'd be forever stuck on Poveglia with the rest of the ghouls. Maybe the doctor could teach her how to be a nurse, and she could teach him not to be so damn creepy.

"Hey, take it easy. Just because I can't send you doesn't mean you're not going home."

Sniffling, Lily wiped her nose with the tissue Kate handed her. "What do you mean?"

"Well, no one's holding you here anymore, right?"

She wiggled her arms and legs like she'd been taught to do in gym class to get the blood flowing. Except there was no blood to flow—not anymore. She was a soul. It was still difficult to believe. "I don't think so. I can't feel anything."

Kate smiled. "Good. And I'll be here to make sure no one interferes. Remember how I taught you to slip out of those restraints?"

Your arm is water. "Yeah."

"Well, it's very similar. Close your eyes, and imagine you're home. Picture your body. Pretend you're moving toward it."

Maybe she didn't completely trust the redhead, but Lily wanted to go home so badly. She closed her eyes and pictured her bedroom, her bed, the posters on her wall. "Nothing's happening."

"Are you thinking about your home? Don't visualize your home; visualize *you*. Where are you, Lily? Can you find yourself?"

Lily tried again. It seemed to take forever. She was in a black, empty space, whirling around, searching for something that wasn't there. Then she felt a sharp tug on her chest that led her forward. "I can feel something, Kate. Something's pulling me!"

"Can you see anything, though? Don't follow it too far until you know what it is." The woman's voice sounded far away, faint, but Lily could tell she was worried.

Keeping in mind what had happened the last time she'd fallen down a rabbit hole, Lily crept along, peering into the darkness. Then she saw a pinprick of light winking at her. As she moved toward it, it grew bigger. "I see light. It's getting really bright. It's hurting my eyes."

"You're in the right place, Lily. Keep walking toward it. You'll be home soon." The woman's voice floated back to her, so far away now, almost gone.

Lily raised an arm to shield herself from the light. It was blinding, more powerful than the sun. She could hear people talking, but it didn't scare her. The slight tug she'd felt before became an irresistible urge to run. She didn't belong in Poveglia—her place was on the other side of that white light. Taking a deep breath, Lily leapt through it.

"Honey? Honey, can you hear me? Squeeze my hand. Dennis, call the nurse. I think she's coming around."

A shape wavered in front of her. Blinking, Lily willed it into focus. When she saw it was her mother's face, she sobbed. Her mother stroked her hair, the familiar scent of her flowery perfume the best thing Lily had ever smelled. She wanted to hug her, to crawl into her lap, but there were tubes everywhere. She could barely move.

"Calm down, Lil. It's okay; you're home. You're safe now." Her mother bent close to her ear. "Kate brought you back, didn't she?"

"Yes," Lily said, her voice raspy, although the truth was a little more complicated.

~ CHAPTER TWENTY-SIX ~

THE DAY I WALKED TO the hospital to visit Lily was a windy one, stirring up the leaves on the sidewalk and reminding me of the day I'd first met her mother. This time, though, the leaves held no message for me. And this time, I wasn't alone.

"I hope she's okay. I hate hospitals."

I squeezed Jackson's hand. "She'll be fine."

"So, after all the crap we went through, Lily could have gotten home on her own?"

Jackson hadn't stopped harping about that. I never should have told him, because the concept was impossible for a mainstreamer to understand. But I got where he was coming from. To say the police had given us a hard time would be the understatement of the year. The last we'd heard, they'd rescued Maria, who'd suffered a stroke and was struggling to recover in a Venetian hospital. She'd been clutching the remains of a murdered child when they'd found her. If that hadn't convinced the cops we were telling the truth, nothing would.

"Technically, yes, but she didn't know how. And Alessandra's power over her, not to mention the doctor's agenda, made it more challenging. If it were to happen again, though, she wouldn't need us."

I sounded more confident than I felt. From what Abbandonato had told me and from what I'd seen, Lily was going to need a lot of help in the coming years.

Pushing the thought away, I smiled for Jackson's benefit. "Looking forward to seeing her for the first time?"

"You know I am, girl. Let's do this."

He held the door for me, and I waited for him once I'd walked through so I could tuck my arm in his. "What is it?" he asked. "What's wrong?"

"It's nothing." I closed my eyes for a second, willing away the spirits who reached for me, pleading for help, desperate to connect with their grieving loved ones. *Not now, not now*, I told them. *I'll try to help you later, but today I'm here for the living.*

Lily threw open her arms when she saw us, jangling her IV against its pole. "Jackson! You came to see me."

"Of course I came. How are you feeling, girl?"

A middle-aged man looked stunned as Jackson enveloped his daughter in a hug. The man rose from his chair, but Vittoria held out her hand. "It's okay, Dennis. These are friends of mine."

"Good. I'm good," Lily said. Now that they'd hugged, I saw she was blushing. Jackson tended to have that effect on women.

There were dark shadows under Lily's eyes, but other than that, she looked better than I'd ever seen her. There was no trace of the ugly black stitches that had marred her face on Poveglia.

"Hi, Kate." She waved at me. "Thank you so much for everything."

"No problem." I glanced at her father, wondering what

Vittoria had told him about us, if anything. There was something odd about Dennis, or rather, about the spirit that shadowed him, but I shrugged it off, chalking my nervousness up to fatigue. I supposed it was normal to see monsters everywhere after what I'd just been through.

Extending my hand, I introduced myself to him, and Jackson did the same. The man moved as if he were in a dream, and he probably thought he was. Poor guy. To suddenly lose your daughter and then get her back again in less than a week. It couldn't have been easy.

Jackson turned on the charm, and once everyone was talking and laughing together, I touched Vittoria on the arm.

"Can I talk to you for a minute? Out in the hall?"

Worry lines creased her forehead, but she nodded. "Sure. Dennis, I'll be back shortly."

Once we were out of the room, Vittoria threw her arms around me, holding me so tightly I squeaked. "Thank you, Kate. Thank you so much. I'll never forget what you did for me, for my family." Her eyes shone.

"You're welcome. I was happy to help." I took a deep breath. Sometimes I really hated this job. I wished I could just congratulate her, give her daughter a teddy bear, and call it good. But it wasn't that simple. *Life* wasn't that simple. "But it's not over, Vittoria."

The worry lines returned. "What do you mean? She's going to be all right, isn't she?"

"A lot of that depends on you—on us. Vittoria, did you know Lily hurts herself?"

Vittoria lowered her eyes, unwilling or unable to meet mine. "Yes, I knew. Both Dennis and I were aware of Lily's…problem. We got her some help, a counselor, and he talked to her for a time, and then Lily told us she didn't need to see him anymore. She said she was fine, and we believed her. But what does this have to do with what happened?"

I sighed. "This is going to be difficult for you to hear, but it's important that you're aware of it. Lily's self-loathing made her a target."

Tears welled in Vittoria's eyes, but not happy ones this time. "I don't understand. What am I supposed to do? How can I help her?"

"Lily has a gift, Vittoria. It's a powerful one, probably one of the most powerful I've ever experienced. I could be wrong, but I think a lot of her self-image problems are stemming from that. She's about to be a teenager, and teenagers aren't supposed to be different. This gift makes her different." I gave her a rueful smile. "Trust me, I'm well aware of what that feels like."

"What are you talking about? What kind of gift?"

"Your daughter is a medium, and I think in time she'll be a formidable one. But until she learns how to control her abilities, she'll always be at risk from spirits who may want to do her harm. What happened to her last week could happen again. Unless someone teaches her to protect herself."

Vittoria sagged against the wall. "I was worried you were going to say something like that. My mother, she was the same way. People used to think she was crazy."

"She wasn't, and neither is Lily. But you know that."

She nodded. "So what can I do? I don't have this ability. I can't teach my daughter to use something I don't understand."

"I know. But I can. And with your permission, I would

like to." I had a last moment of soul-searching. *Was I doing the right thing?* I'd never been driven to offer anything like this before. But then again, I'd never met anyone like Lily before. "I'd love for Lily to start working on this with me when she's ready."

"What will I tell her father? He'll never understand. He doesn't believe in any of this stuff."

Remembering what I'd seen near her husband, I knew the perfect solution. "Well, I could have a little chat with him about his brother. Do you think that would help?"

Vittoria sucked in her breath. "He's never gotten over Bill's death."

"I know. That's why Bill's still here. Would that work?"

"I don't think he's ready for that. What happened to Lily has been shock enough. I don't want to have to visit two members of my family here."

I patted her on the arm. "I understand. Why not call me a mentor for now? We can talk to him about it more when he's ready. Once he's recovered."

Vittoria continued to lean against the wall as if too exhausted to stand. "That's perfect. And it wouldn't be a lie, would it?"

"No. As long as Lily is agreeable, it wouldn't be a lie at all."

❧

It took some doing, but Vittoria finally convinced Dennis and Garrett to get everyone some sodas from the cafeteria. Jackson went with them, knowing I needed time alone with Lily.

"How are you feeling?" I could see the wariness on her face. I understood why she didn't trust me, but that didn't make it easier.

"I'm great."

"You can be honest with me, Lily. I'm not your mother."

The girl slumped against the pillows. "I'm so happy to be home, really, but I'm—"

"Overwhelmed? Exhausted? Having nightmares?"

Her expression cleared. "How did you know? I keep dreaming I'm back there. It's horrible."

"A soul's memory is a powerful thing. And Dr. Abbandonato cares about you. He'll probably always think of you as his patient."

She blew out a breath that lifted her bangs from her forehead. "He wasn't a bad guy. He was scary, but I think he meant well."

"He has his own issues, though, believe me. It's best you stay away from him."

"I will, but how do I keep him away from *me*?" The fear in her eyes hurt my heart.

"Don't engage with him. If you see him again, tell him you don't want to talk to him anymore. You don't have to be cruel, but be firm. And the same goes double for Alessandra."

Lily stuck out her tongue. "Don't worry. I want nothing to do with *her*."

"Good. Remember that; remember how much you dislike her. That will help."

"Dislike her? I *hate* her. She took me away from my family."

No, *you* did, I thought, but didn't say. That would come later. The poor kid had been through enough.

There was an awkward silence as I tried to come up with the best way to broach the subject. "You have a gift," sounded unbearably cheesy. How had my grandmother told me? I struggled to remember.

It was Lily who broke the silence. "Will you help me?"

"Of course I will. I'd be happy to. You're not alone, you know. I get that it seems scary right now, but there are lots of people who are just like us. You'll see."

Her face brightened. "Us?"

"Us. Lily, I've asked your mom if I can show you how to use your abilities, how to protect yourself. You can even work on cases with me later if you want, when you're older. Your mom's okay with it, but it's totally up to you."

She straightened in bed, one of her many pillows toppling to the floor. "Really? You mean it? But what kind of work do you do? You help people like me, right?"

I retrieved the cushion and she leaned forward so I could smoosh it into place with the others. "People like you, and people like your mom, yes. But also people who have lost someone and who are really sad about it. Sometimes talking to the spirit of the person they've lost helps them let go, and that helps the spirit too. Once the living let go, the spirit can usually move on."

"Where do they go? When they move on, I mean?"

"I've been doing this most of my life, and I still couldn't tell you. I don't think we're supposed to know until it's our time."

"Hmm…" The room was quiet for a moment—that is, as quiet as a hospital room could be. "You'd really want me?"

"I'd be thrilled to have you. You have a very powerful gift, Lily. If you learn how to use it properly, you'll be unstoppable."

"You think so?"

"I know so. But it starts with taking care of yourself here."
I touched my heart. "And here." I touched my temple. "So
you'd need to start going to that counselor again, okay?
Are you willing to do that?"

She bit her lip. "Yeah. I was thinking that would be a
good idea anyway."

"Great. The most important thing right now is your
health. Once you're out of the hospital and caught up with
school, we can talk about this other stuff. It's important
you learn how to protect yourself, but there will be plenty
of time for that later. In the meantime, though…"

Reaching into my bag, I pulled out a corner of her spirit
board just enough so she could see it. "I think this should
stay with me, if that's all right with you."

She flattened her back against the pillows, holding out
her hands in a warding-off gesture. "You can keep it. I
never want to see that thing again."

Satisfied she now understood the dangers, I pushed the
board deeper in my purse again. "You will. It's your board,
and it will always be your board. Once you learn how to
use it, you'll find it can be very helpful. But until then, I'll
look after it for you. It needs a good cleansing."

"Okay. I guess I'll take your word for it."

"I'll go now, let you rest." I'd noticed how heavy the
girl's eyelids were getting. "We'll talk later, but I'm always
here if you need me—for anything."

"Okay. Kate?"

"Yes?"

"Thank you for bringing me home."

"You brought yourself home, Lily. I just showed you
how."

~ CHAPTER TWENTY-SEVEN ~

JACKSON'S MOOD WAS INFECTIOUS AS we left the hospital. He began to whistle, and I smiled when I recognized the tune. *What a Wonderful World.* Even the cold breeze, carrying with it the promise of winter, didn't seem quite so biting. At least it wasn't raining.

"So what's next?" he asked.

"I was thinking lunch."

"God, *yes.* That would be good. I don't know what they think they serve in that cafeteria, but it isn't food."

"There are a few nice places up ahead. Italian?" He looked at me sideways. "Sushi it is, then."

"Now you're talking. Good we got that figured out, but it wasn't really what I meant when I asked what's next."

I hesitated. "What did you mean?"

"Well, Lily's back and she's fine, right? She's gonna be okay."

I nodded.

"So I'm wondering what's next—for *us.*"

"Well, I'll be waiting until someone else needs my help. That never takes long. And I suppose you'll want to go home." I couldn't imagine not having him around to banter with. I'd be fine, of course. Noddy and I had lived on our own for a long time. We didn't *need* Jackson. But I knew my life would feel a lot emptier without him in it.

"Do you want me to go home, Kate?"

I shrugged, trying my best to appear casual. "It doesn't really matter what I want, does it? You're a city guy, and I'm small town/country. We've been over this a million times."

Jackson gestured at the street around us. Aside from an elderly man sweeping the sidewalk in front of his shop, we might have been the only two people in the world. "Are you kidding? Compared to Poveglia, Nightridge is a bustling metropolis."

"It is that."

"And besides, it kind of grows on you." He wrapped his arms around my waist and pulled me close.

"Kind of?"

"Definitely."

"Hmm…I guess it could be useful to have a guy like you around."

"And I'm a guy who likes to be useful."

I raised an eyebrow at him. "Since when?"

Jackson grinned. "I don't know. It just sounded good."

"Well, you *do* have that book to write."

"Of course! The trip wouldn't be a write-off without it. I'll want to know everything about how you first met Lily and Vittoria, and I'll need to interview Lily too, if she's agreeable."

"There you go. There's lots to keep you busy." My heart felt like it was going to burst out of my chest. I hadn't dared hope he'd want to stay.

"You know, it doesn't have to be a thing. I can get my own place and just help out when you need me."

"Is that what you want? For this not to be a thing?"

He touched his forehead to mine. "I very much want this to be a thing. But what do *you* want?"

"I want—" I sucked in my breath as a series of horrifying images invaded my brain. Something had been bothering me ever since we'd left the hospital, niggling at the edges of my mind. I'd been pushing it aside, trying my best to focus on Jackson and enjoy his company, but now it hit me like a punch to the gut. "Oh no. Shit!"

Jacks pulled away, searching my face for answers. "What? What is it?"

"It's Bill, Dennis's brother—the one who died overseas." Seeing the confusion on Jackson's face, I shook my head. "It doesn't matter. Anyway, I saw him at the hospital in Lily's room, but he isn't who he seems. It's not Bill. The spirit is not Bill! Do you know what this means?"

"I'm sorry, but I have no clue what it means."

"It means Lily is still in trouble. I'm sorry, but we have to go back."

To my surprise, he didn't argue, didn't demand an explanation. Picking up his pace to match mine, he said, "If whatever it is touches her, I'll kick its transparent ass."

Holding hands, we ran to the hospital.

Together.

☙

THANKS SO MUCH FOR READING! If you enjoyed this book, please take a minute to leave a review on Amazon.com and Goodreads. Reviews make a huge difference to an author's sales and rankings—the more reviews, the more books I'll be able to write.

My readers mean the world to me, and I'd love to stay in touch. You can keep up with me on Facebook, Twitter, Pinterest, or sign up for my newsletter at **bit.ly/ MoncrieffLibrary** to receive a new spooky story every week, along with access to an exclusive Hidden Library bursting with FREE books!

J.H.

ACKNOWLEDGMENTS

SPECIAL THANKS FOR THIS BOOK go to Michele Olivo, the best hotel manager in the world, for helping me with the Italian translation and convincing a water taxi to take me to Poveglia. This book would not exist without your assistance.

When my first novel was published, I was very much a minnow in a gigantic pond, and I will never forget those who encouraged my early efforts, especially Chris Brogden, Jeff Ryzner, Christine Brandt, Frank Errington, Erik Smith, Rodney Merana, Ev Bishop, Lisa Saunders, Jan Murphy, Rick Caslake, Crystal Bourque, Lisa Case, Dean Cooper, James Rewucki, Wai Chan, Nicole Chia, Brenda Furst, Maxine and Mike McQuarrie, and the Barracloughs, who never stop asking when "that bat book" will be published. To all those who gave me valuable advice, came to my readings and panels, bought my books, commented on my blog, or simply hugged me when I needed it—thank you.

Thanks to Dee-Dee Gould and Drew Kozub from my writing group, my personal cheerleaders Anita Siraki, Nikki Burch, Henry Harner, Brett Lashuay, Spencer Richard, Garrett Davis, Jared Synn, Louise Gibson, my peeps at the Insecure Writers' Support Group, my parents Gary and Shirley Moncrieff, blog readers, and friends. Nikki and Henry also proofread this book, and deserve tons of kudos for sheer awesomeness.

Dark fiction writers are the nicest people you'll ever meet, and I can't thank Chuck Wendig, Russell R. James, Somer Canon, Catherine Cavendish, and JG Faherty enough for being so damn supportive. You rock!

More tales of spine-tingling supernatural suspense from
J.H. Moncrieff and DeathZone Books!

Enjoy this excerpt from
THE BEAR WHO WOULDN'T LEAVE,
available now.

Book Three of the GhostWriters series will be released in
October 2017.

THE BEAR WHO WOULDN'T LEAVE

Sometimes evil looks like a fuzzy teddy bear.

STILL GRIEVING THE UNTIMELY DEATH of his dad, ten-year-old Josh Leary is reluctant to accept a well-worn stuffed teddy bear from his new stepfather. He soon learns he was right to be wary. Edgar is no ordinary toy… and he doesn't like being rejected. When Josh banishes him to the closet, terrible things begin to happen.

Desperate to be rid of the bear, Josh engages the help of a friend. As the boys' efforts rebound on them with horrifying results, they're forced to accept the terrifying truth—Edgar will always get even. Can Josh find a way to put an end to this nightmare before he loses everything?

☾

CHAPTER ONE

IT WAS THE UGLIEST THING I'd ever seen. "I don't want it," I said, pushing it back at my mother. "Now, Josh—be nice. This was your father's when he was a child, and he really wanted you to have it." I folded my arms across my chest as she continued to shove the toy at me. "He's *not* my father."

My father had died two years ago, when I was only eight. Mom said his heart stopped, which was terrifying. How did a person's heart just...stop? Dad's heart quit working while he was sleeping, so for a year I didn't want to go to bed. I was afraid the same thing would happen to me.

The only thing I liked less than the ugly toy was Michael, my new stepfather. Oh, he seemed nice enough, I guess, but there was something about him that gave me the creeps. Maybe it was the way his smile never reached his eyes. Or the times I'd caught him staring at me when he thought I wasn't looking. I couldn't understand how Mom could love someone like that. My real dad had been so nice. His eyes had crinkled at the corners when he laughed, and he laughed *a lot*. Michael hardly ever laughed, and when he did, it made me shiver.

Mom sighed. She tried to hide it, but I noticed her lower lip was trembling. Again. She cried at anything these days, even those sappy commercials about starving kids in the Sudan, wherever that was. "He's trying, Josh. Can't you be a little nicer to him? It would mean a lot to me."

I didn't want to see her cry again, so I said sure, I would be nicer. She looked relieved as she pressed the toy into my arms and thanked me. Then she asked me what I would like for dinner, which was a treat. Lately we'd only had Michael's requests, and Michael wanted weird things like steamed spinach and broccoli soup. What kind of person actually likes broccoli?

She seemed a bit troubled when I requested macaroni and cheese—she was probably worried Michael wouldn't like it. She hurried to the kitchen, leaving me alone with the bear. A teddy bear. Who gives a ten-year-old boy a teddy bear? I was into The Incredible Hulk and riding my bike. A teddy bear was a little kid's toy. I turned the bear over in my hands. Even its fur felt nasty, matted and a bit greasy. I guess it was supposed to be a panda, even though it wasn't like any panda I'd ever seen. Its body was mostly black, and it had black patches over both eyes. Around its neck was a tattered yellow ribbon.

Its eyes were beady, the kind of eyes you see in scary cartoon paintings—the type that seem to follow you around. But the worst was its mouth. It was curled into a vicious snarl so you could see its teeth, and it had huge fangs. What kind of teddy bear has fangs? Nothing about it was soft or cuddly. It was so stiff it was like a piece of wood in my arms.

The longer I held the bear, the spookier it was. I could swear it was staring back at me, but that was crazy—it was only a toy. It was my imagination playing tricks on me, just like how I was always sure someone was chasing me whenever I ran upstairs from the basement.

All I knew was that I wanted to put as much space between it and me as possible. I threw it in my closet, under a pile of dirty clothes that smelled so bad even Mom wouldn't go near them.

She might be able to make me take the bear, but she couldn't force me to play with it.

I went outside to join my friends and forgot all about the bear—until it was time for bed.

☾

THE BEAR WHO WOULDN'T LEAVE is available through most online retailers. Ask for it at your local library and bookstores.

ABOUT THE AUTHOR

J.H. MONCRIEFF'S work has been described as early Gillian Flynn with a little Ray Bradbury and Stephen King thrown in for good measure.

She won Harlequin's search for the next Gillian Flynn in 2016.

Her first published novella, The Bear Who Wouldn't Leave, was featured in Samhain's Childhood Fears collection and stayed on its horror bestsellers list for over a year.

When not writing, she loves exploring the world's most haunted places, advocating for animal rights, and summoning her inner ninja in muay thai class.

To get free eBooks and a new spooky story every week, go to **bit.ly/MoncrieffLibrary.**

Made in the USA
Middletown, DE
16 May 2017